ONE WOMAN WITH
A SHOCKING SECRET...

FAY COLBY. Beautiful, elusive, unsatisfied. Something in her past drives her to acts that would shame some women...and inflame most men.

...AND THE MEN IN HER LIFE.

JOE. In his own eyes, just an average guy. In the arms of Fay, he finds a power in himself he has never known before.

SAM. Blessed with the understanding only an older man can have, he finds his deepest satisfaction in granting Fay her freedom.

KEVIN. Aggressive and irresistibly virile, he goes one step too far with Fay...and pays a heavy price.

EARL. The detective with a haunted memory, he must pit his duty to justice against his desire for Fay.

TOO LATE TO BE GOOD

Craig Jones

BALLANTINE BOOKS • NEW YORK

Library of Congress Catalog Card Number: 85-91157

ISBN 0-345-32130-8

Manufactured in the United States of America

First Edition: February 1986

*For
Harriet and Patricia*

The heart asks pleasure first,
And then, excuse from pain;
And then, those little anodynes
That deaden suffering.

Emily Dickinson
The Heart Asks Pleasure First

BOOK ONE

The Stable

1

FAY COLBY'S EYES BRIMMED WITH TEARS THAT MADE the ceiling look like the rippling surface of a lake, and she felt she was being dragged to the bottom by the weight in her throat. The voice, raw and quivering, did not sound like her own: "I pushed him, he fell over, and he was dead. I didn't run, I wasn't afraid, I don't know if I was sorry or not. I just walked away."

Dr. Olivia Maxson, sitting in the chair three feet behind the patient couch, didn't respond at once. Perhaps, thought Fay, she was waiting to hear more, or perhaps she was aligning this information with what she had heard in a previous session. Finally, Maxson asked, "Did this dream wake you?"

"No."

"Was it exactly like the other one?"

"Yes."

"Nothing different at all?"

"Not that I remember."

3

Fay reached for her purse on the floor to find a tissue, but before her fingers could open the snap, Dr. Maxson said, "Don't. That can wait. The last time, you said 'fell down,' and this time you say he 'fell over.' Was there a difference in the way he fell?"

Remarkable, thought Fay, how this woman remembers such details. "No difference. I don't know if he fell forward, backward, or sideways. I just know he fell."

"And you knew he was dead?"

"I—sensed it."

"He didn't come at you? You weren't defending yourself against a threat of physical violence?"

"No. We were face to face, just like the other dream, his eyes were large and . . . condemning. I wanted to get away, but I knew I couldn't unless I pushed him. And after I did I just walked out of the room."

"And the room itself?"

"I don't remember anything in particular. Except that it might have had a high ceiling—I felt space overhead."

"But you weren't outdoors?"

"No, it was a room."

Dr. Maxson waited a moment. "Is your social schedule the same as it was when you had the other dream?"

"In what way?"

"Think a minute."

And it took Fay less than a minute to see the connection. "I'm having dinner with him tonight, at his place. And I had dinner with him the night after the last dream."

Dr. Maxson proceeded with the interpretation. The dream was rooted in wish-fulfillment: Fay wanted to eliminate this man from her life once and for all; he was figuratively and literally standing in her way, blocking the path to freedom; his "hold" on her was such that he had to be pushed away; her not seeing him dead but only "sensing" him dead most likely meant that he was merely dead as a threat—hence, his inability to rise from the floor and prevent her from walking out of the room. But, of course, there was guilt in having "pushed" him.

"Our time is up," she concluded, and Fay heard the soft rustling of the silk skirt as the woman uncrossed her legs. "But I'd like you to think about why you waited so long in our session before mentioning this second dream."

The two stood up simultaneously. Fay hurriedly dabbed her eyes, cheeks, and nose so that the next patient waiting outside would not witness the evidence of turmoil. "I suppose," she said wryly, "that tears indicate progress."

Dr. Maxson's smile was crisp and brief. "That depends upon whom they come from, doesn't it?"

Fay managed a smile of her own. "See you next week."

She repaired her mascara in the lavatory off the waiting room, then took the elevator down five floors to join the lunchtime foot traffic on lower Fifth Avenue. Her anger over the tears, the loss of control—even her anger at the cause—faded as she realized to her surprise how thoroughly relaxed she was now, calm enough to tackle with vigor the required finishing touchs for the MenthaRub commercial she was working on.

And she felt fortified for tonight's dinner engagement with the man she had confronted, pushed, and somehow killed in two dreams.

At four-thirty, standing by the open bathroom window in his East Thirty-fifth Street apartment, Joe Blakis puffed twice on a joint and blew the smoke out into the windless December chill. Afterward he gargled, and sprayed the air with Lysol, then got into the shower and used a Telfa pad on the finger-and-thumb tips that held the joint. Ann— Elusive Annie, he nicknamed her privately—was due at five. She did not smoke, grass *or* cigarettes, and although she had never spoken disapproval of either, he felt nonetheless that it was there: her rigid self-containment in everything but sex made him wary of revealing to her even the smallest bad habit. Their setup was tenuous to the point of being tentative, and in no way was he going to jeopardize the twice-a-month trysts. Everything was on her terms, but he was unresentful. A plain man subservient to a beautiful woman was rather commonplace, yet that wasn't the reason he felt no shame or loss of pride; simply, acceptance of her terms was infinitely preferable to empty freedom.

He dried his hair slowly and cautiously with a towel, determined not to contribute to the thinning process that had begun in his early twenties. After a careful combing he went into the bedroom and viewed his naked self in the full-length mirror on the door. Average from head to toe, although he gave himself a C-plus on the days he jogged, a C-minus on the days he didn't. Today was a C-plus, for he always jogged before he was to see her, jogged to lessen his over-excitement. And he always smoked half a joint to slow down the passing of time with her; their customary two hours would often seem like three, the elongated moments allowing him to learn her body better (if not her thoughts) and to record it to memory until the next meeting.

Eight months ago he had happened to sit next to her at an off-Broadway play on Astor Place. Before the performance began he had had to fight the impulse to keep from turning and staring at her. Then—altogether accidentally, he had thought—he had dropped his program right next to her foot, and when he retrieved it she smiled politely, but not invitingly. She was superlatively beautiful, but New York was filled with superlatively beautiful women at whom he might gaze longingly but never with any hope. During the play's first act he thought only of the smile she had given him: cool though it was, it seemed to convey an empathy that said, Don't be embarrassed, *I've* dropped programs too. At intermission he smoked a cigarette in the lobby and counted the men—most of them with women— who kept stealing glances at her as she sat on a bench, pensive and jotting brief notes onto a small spiral pad. He thought that she could easily fulfill the role of Snow White if her hair were in a pageboy instead of a kind of French twist, and if it were cropped short and lacquered down she could pass for one of those ravenous and calculating temptresses in silent movies, someone like Louise Brooks's Lulu. Her beauty was made up of startling contrasts: white-as-paper skin, ink-black hair, azure eyes, primary-red lipstick. The luminous oval face was poised atop a long slender neck. Her very narrow body nonetheless consisted of curves instead of angles; and now, as she sat with legs crossed and shoulders huddled, her demeanor suggested serenity from the waist down and intensity from the waist up.

The lobby lights dimmed twice, and she flipped shut the spiral pad and returned it to her purse. After the audience was seated again, there was a delay in beginning the second act. Before he realized what he was doing, he turned to her and said, "Are you a critic?"

The smile this time was quizzical. "No. What gave you that idea?"

"Your writing pad." He hoped the heat in his face didn't show.

"No, it's just . . . a shopping list."

He could see a man down the row staring at them, one of those slick but subtle stud-types who have had emotional and sexual confidence since kindergarten. He imagined what the man was thinking: "Stop wasting your time, buddy. Now if I were sitting where you are . . ."

"Well," he said, "let's hope the second act is better than the first."

Her assessing eyes traveled from his receding hairline to his chin, and her definite look of approval made his palms sweat. "Exactly," she answered.

When the play was over they agreed that it had not deserved its rave reviews, and she accepted his invitation to go for a drink. Three blocks away they found a restaurant whose bar was uncrowded. Running the swizzle around in her glass, she asked him to tell her about himself. In a rush he revealed that he was a librarian in the Art and Architecture room at the Fifth Avenue branch, that he was thirty-six, originally from Iowa, and had come to New York for graduate school. Since he had no children, he thought it unnecessary to mention that his wife of eight years had left him to marry their dentist.

She herself, she confessed, *was* married, but the relationship continued only because of the children, who loved both of them and did not know about their father's rampant womanizing. Her age, she said, was twenty-eight, although he would have guessed twenty-three or -four.

She refused a second drink, checked her watch, and told him she had promised the babysitter she wouldn't be late. He gave her his phone number, and she assured him she would call so they could have another drink together sometime.

They had that drink two weeks later; afterward, there were three more meetings, over drinks, always at different places. The third time he saw her, she stated that she could not become "involved," but she was growing "fond" of him. Finally, fond enough to sleep with him.

For the first four months he was deaf and blind to everything but her: walking home from work one evening he was nearly struck by a bus on Lexington Avenue; a couple of his co-workers at the library were concerned enough about the daze he was in to ask if something was bothering him, something he might like to confide; over the telephone one Sunday his father remarked that he had been sounding "funny" the past few weeks—was that bitch of an ex-wife needling him in any way?

His answers were evasions, because there seemed to be no words to explain Elusive Annie and her effect upon him without sounding ridiculous. He was in love. She, clearly, was not. Yet, except for her time, she gave him far more

than his ex-wife or any other woman had. Constantly—
and, he thought, sincerely—she complimented him. She
liked his "quiet taste" in clothes and furnishings, the relaxed
and unrigid order of his apartment, his aquarium and his
love of beautiful fish. He, in fact, often *felt* like a fish, a
beached one, when they finished making love; her little
cries and murmurings of "yes, yes, oh Joe, yes," the move-
ments of her hips that felt like gentle gulps pulling him into
a cove where he wanted to live forever—these gave him a
stamina whose price was paid only after he kissed her neck,
softly now, and fell away from her, his toes splaying out as
if they might help his lungs bring in air. It was during one
of these recoveries—his ears ringing, his buttocks sweat-
soaked—that she gave him the prize compliment. She was
lying still, staring at the ceiling, and when she spoke her
voice was hushed, almost reverential. "Everything about
the way you love me . . . I hadn't expected to be given so
much. And you emanate such saneness, Joe. That's something anywhere, but in New York it's miraculous." Although
deeply pleased, he had wanted to answer, "Ask my father
and the people I work with just how sane I've been since
I met you."

The intercom buzzer sounded in the living room, jolting
him from his reverie and filling him with panic at being
naked still. He raced to the button, pressed it, listened to
the doorman announce that Mrs. Decker was downstairs.

"Yes, Carlos, send her up."

Hurriedly, he dressed, bypassing his underwear in favor
of a second combing of his hair. She might not disapprove
of his answering the door in a robe, but if he could not utter
his hopes for their relationship advancing beyond the bed,
then he wanted his attire to speak for him: the combination
of casual corduroys, flannel shirt, and moccasins suggested
quiet evenings at home, lingering over a simple dinner for
two.

The buzzer sounded again, and before admitting her he

paused at the bathroom and sniffed for any telltale signs of
the marijuana, then cupped his hand over his nose and mouth
and exhaled. All clear.

Her cheeks and nose were red enough to indicate that
she had walked a good distance, had not come directly to
the building in a taxi.

"Hello, Ann. Pretty raw out there, isn't it?"

Smiling, she answered, "I love it. I'm strictly a cold-
weather girl."

Yes, he thought, that must be true. Not once over the
summer had that white, white skin been touched by the sun,
perhaps because she wanted to retain the striking contrast
with the ink-black hair.

Helping her out of her coat, he said, "A little white
wine?"

"Lovely."

When he returned to the living room with two glasses,
he found her exactly where he expected to, kneeling before
the aquarium. He squatted next to her.

"Two of them look listless," she said. "They aren't sick,
are they?"

"Those two are always listless after they've been fed."

They got up, sat on the sofa, and the conversation turned,
as always, to him or the arts. She did not talk about herself,
about neither her husband nor her children. Nor about her
status as an idle housewife. All he knew of her private life
was that she lived on the West Side, had two brothers and
parents who also lived in the city, and that should she and
he ever run into each other in public they must never speak,
even if both of them were alone. After all, she might be on
her way to meet someone who could be waiting on the next
corner, within view.

As he set his wineglass, holding the remains of his second
refill, on the coffee table, he glanced surreptitiously at his
watch. Forty-five minutes gone, an hour and fifteen minutes
remaining of her usual two-hour limit. They must get to

bed soon, for he disliked her having to rush off as soon as their lovemaking was finished. "A little more wine?" he asked.

"Better not."

"You could have a cup of espresso just before you leave."

"No thanks. But you have a refill if you want."

Instead he reached out and stroked her cheek; she kissed his wrist, the palm of his hand, and they moved into an embrace. This was ritual, established the very first time she had come to the apartment. Gently, he grasped her jaw with one hand, the back of her head with the other, and seconds after the soft exchange of lips came a more intense exchange of tongues.

"Shall we go inside?" With her, he always substituted "inside" for "into the bedroom."

Ten minutes later, he was riding her, slowly and luxuriously, while her eyes stared straight into his so intensely that she seemed to be trying to look clear through to the back of his head. Then, when the eyes squinted—her brow creasing and her mouth forming a large "O"—he knew he was taking her where she wanted to be taken. Able to chart by her expression what was going on inside her, he brought her to the edge three times and slowed down, almost withdrawing, so that he could start the momentum all over again. At last, he began to thrust at full tilt. There were the familiar noises in her throat, the flaring of her nostrils, the hands traveling down his back to the tops of his buttocks.

"Dig," he rasped. "Go ahead and mark me." And her nails obeyed at once.

Afterward, he covered her with the quilt, told her to lie still, left the room, and returned with a cup of espresso. She was huddled on her side, staring at a rack of books next to the dresser. He sat down beside her, held the cup so that she could sip without moving more than her head. She drank, thanked him with a half-smile, and looked again toward the books.

"Joe, are you still sure . . . still sure that I'm not blocking you from having a relationship with someone else?"

"Positive. Absolutely positive." The evenness of his tone belied the panic within, the panic he always experienced whenever she questioned his satisfaction with their arrangement.

"It just seems you're so well-suited for marriage. And fatherhood. If you met the right woman. Am I really the only one you sleep with?"

The squeeze. If he answered with the truth, would she think him a fool, some kind of weakling? And if he gave her a lie, would she then assume she truly was blocking him from another?

Fortunately, an amendment to the truth occurred to him.

"So far, these days, yes, you're the only one."

A pause.

"And that's enough for you?"

He added a smile to lighten the topic. "So far, yes."

When she rose from the bed he got up with her. "Oh," she said, "I really *did* scratch you." She bent to kiss the widest mark, and he clenched himself against the desire to throw his arms around her and beg her for twice a week instead of twice a month.

She took her purse with her into the bathroom, where she spent fifteen minutes preparing for her departure. He dressed and combed his hair.

At the front door she gripped both his hands. "I won't see you until after the holidays, so do have a nice Christmas."

"You too, Ann."

She gave him a brief searching look, kissed his chin, and left.

The bedroom still retained the heat and humidity of their encounter, which he relished in the darkness. He moved to the bed, lay on his stomach, and turned his face into the pillow that had cradled her head. The scent of cinnamon-sweat made his throat harden and his chest constrict, opening the doors to depression; it would last three or four days. And then he would be rescued by the anticipation of seeing her again, on their next Friday together.

Fay Colby got out of the taxi at Park and Eighty-first, purposely undertipped the driver, who she was sure was drunk or stoned and who had ignored both her requests that he lighten his foot on the gas pedal. She managed to walk several paces away before he realized the slight. Then he called out: "Fuck you, bitch."

"Only in your dreams," she retorted over her shoulder.

Donald the doorman grinned his delight at her. "Good evening, Miss Colby. A rough ride, was it?"

"I've been in slower *jets*. Honest to God, how much more money can they make in an evening by driving ninety miles an hour?"

"They just like to race with themselves," observed old Donald. Here was a man who liked his work and did it well, so well that Fay's aunt once remarked that surely Donald had walked out of the womb in uniform and with perfect posture.

There was, of course, no need for her to wait while he announced her over the intercom. She strode through the large slate-floored, walnut-paneled lobby to the elevator.

Waiting for it to arrive, she appraised the Christmas decorations. Elegant and quietly cheerful, as always. Copying a tradition of Altman's department store, the management replaced the cream-colored lampshades with red ones for the winter holidays. A decorated tree stood next to the fireplace, which contained the same three unburned logs that had been there ever since she could remember. On the rosewood table under the mirror stood two ironstone pitchers filled with red and white carnations, compliments of a self-appointed beautifying committee of four tenants.

Riding up to the sixteenth floor she felt her apprehensiveness sharpen. *I pushed him, he fell over, and he was dead. . . . I'm having dinner with him tonight.*

It's only a dream, she told herself, you don't really want him dead.

To regain steadiness she summoned the happier memory of the past two hours when she was Ann Decker in Joe's apartment.

The elevator opened. Directly across from it he was waiting for her in the doorway. Her back straight and her eyes unflinchingly trained on his, she advanced and then dutifully paused to accept the perfunctory kiss on her cheek.

"Hello, Fay."

"Hello, Father."

2

THE BLACK-AND-WHITE-TILED VESTIBULE WAS NEARLY as large as some studio apartments she had been in, and the staircase behind it—access to the three bedrooms and two baths above—was certainly as wide as the corridor between the front door and the elevator. The dining room was spacious and formal, the kitchen enormous and institutionally equipped. The living room was cozier, with built-in bookshelves, a beamed ceiling, a fireplace faced in natural fieldstone. The most inviting room, however, was her father's private office, converted from former maid's quarters off the kitchen. Naturally, Fay had been to his "official" office at Dowd & Dunay Publishers, and *that* was homier and more inviting than any space he entertained and/or supposedly relaxed in.

"I've just got home," he said, helping her out of her coat. "You'll have to excuse me while I shower and shave. Sheila's in the living room. Claire should be down in a minute—she's running late too. She and Arthur"—the cook—"dis-

15

covered the pork smelled funny once it was roasting, so she raced out to the fish store. I hope you like turbot."

"I do."

He went upstairs, she to the living room, where Sheila was sitting on a sofa, watching the weather report, a tumbler of bourbon in one hand and a cigarette in the other. Unnoticed, Fay paused to observe her stepmother from behind. The tinted platinum hair was curled and just slightly teased to make it appear thicker than it was, and she wore her lavender cashmere with a white pleated skirt; her shoes were under the coffee table, her feet tucked up against the backs of her thighs. At forty-four she had a figure that women half her age might envy, given to her by chance or heredity and definitely not maintained through any strenuous effort of her own. Sheila scorned all exercise except walking, started her bourbon promptly at five and continued until bedtime, slept nine to ten hours a night, and ate three full meals a day. She also got away with something that Fay's previous two stepmothers never could have: she smoked, going through a carton a week. Fay wondered if this signaled a softening in her father, then thought, no, some bargain must have been struck, a trade-off that allowed a vice for a vice. Despite Sheila's self-possession and air of independence— and although Fay genuinely liked her—Fay surmised she was weak at the core. No woman of any real strength would attach herself to a cold three-time loser at marriage.

If she was looking forward to a rewarding widowhood, then she should be prepared for a long haul in getting to it, and the possibility of never reaching it at all. Curt Colby's granitic self-discipline was no more awesome than his constitution; like his emotions, his health was contained in an impenetrable bubble that repelled even the most virulent prevailing strains of virus. And if there'd been three wives relegated to the past, there was little ground for assuming he wouldn't make it four.

The present Mrs. Curt Colby leaned toward the coffee table to stub out her cigarette, and Fay advanced to the sofa.

"Hello, Sheila." No false kisses for them; by way of greeting, they simply gripped hands, left to right, as they usually did.

"Beautiful dress. New?"

"No, 'rarely worn.'"

"Red *is* your color," said Sheila, getting up and into her shoes. "How about a drink? There's a pitcher of martinis."

"All right, but in a—"

"Small glass, just a third full, lots of ice."

Fay sat on the opposite sofa and watched the woman switch off the television and carry off her own drink, which looked dark and full enough not to need refilling.

"I hear the pork was no good."

"Right. And the cupboard was bare. You know how your father won't allow meat to be frozen. So your aunt Claire went dashing out, and since the fish store is nearest, that's what we're having. Personally, I'd have settled for hamburger. Fish to me is warm-weather fare. And you can be sure it'll be plain-as-Jane, since Arthur isn't allowed to serve rich sauces. I'm going to help myself to plenty of potatoes." There was not complaint, not even irritation, in what she said; she might have been giving a summary of the weather, a condition that no one could help.

"Cheers," said Sheila.

"Cheers." They clicked glasses, and Sheila sat down.

"Well, how's the advertising business this merry season? Did you get your bonus?"

"Oh, yes. It went straight to my stockbroker," said Fay.

"At the rate you're going you'll be able to retire at forty. Claire told me another agency tried to lure you away with twelve thousand more a year. Why didn't you take it?"

"Because I have good friends at Mayhew and it's not an oversized outfit riddled with jealousy and back-stabbing. And that's very important to my workday."

"I'm surprised some nice young vice-president hasn't moved in on you and offered to take you away from it all."

"You mean offered to combine salaries so he can live better. No thank you."

Sheila laughed, then said softly, "Just between us, this hasn't been a good month for your father. His newest young author has sold only three thousand copies despite a fair amount of hype. He's afraid that because of this flop the powers-that-be will trim the ad budget on the new Brent Matheny novel."

"Matheny! I thought he went to jail for cocaine smuggling."

"He did, that's where he wrote the book. Ever read him?"

"I tried two of his. At fourteen ninety-five each, sleeping pills would have been cheaper."

Curt Colby had his own editorial imprint at Dowd & Dunay; at the bottom of the largest title page was his logo:

C

A CURT COLBY BOOK

Colby's literary tastes ran to two extremes: one was neo-Hemingway prose, hard and spare; the other was pyro-technical writing that, Fay believed, sacrificed plot and character for outlandish imagery, and whose story lines, if they could be deciphered at all, went nowhere slowly. But, beyond style, there was a consistency in her father's acqui-sitions that Fay had long ago come to recognize and expect. Every third or fourth author invited into his camp was obsessed with death—violent, often suicidal death—and flawed by the inability or perhaps unwillingness to create women characters who were more than matchsticks or phan-toms. And during the twenty-three years he had had his own imprint, Curt Colby never endowed it upon a woman writer.

Fay waited as Sheila lighted a cigarette, then asked, "Is he worried that they might let him go? Or drop his imprint?"

"No, no. Don't forget, he's still got Kincaid and Danner and Sendar. Kincaid and Sendar always make money, amounts that can be predicted, and Danner even hits the bottom of the bestseller list now and then. It's just that . . . well, I think he's getting tired and doesn't know it yet. And when you're tired but have never learned how to relax, you've got a problem."

Sheila stopped abruptly at the sound of Claire's descending tread on the stairs and gave Fay an unnecessary signal to switch tracks in the conversation. The harmony that existed between wife and sister-in-law depended upon a minimum of intimacy and the unspoken agreement not to discuss Curt at any serious depth.

When Claire's husband died seven years ago, Curt had proposed that she sell her co-op apartment and come to live in his; because she was childless, not working, and unused to living alone, she accepted. Curt was then in the process of divorcing Fiona, and so when Sheila came along two years later she was most certainly aware that a sister-in-law-in-residence was included in the marriage bargain. Fay supposed that for whatever sacrifices of privacy Sheila had to make, she was compensated by Claire's managing the household—smoothly, quietly, almost effortlessly. Although Claire might strike most people as cool, her disposition and manner were several degrees warmer than her brother's. And if Fay did not exactly love her aunt in any traditionally familial way, she most assuredly respected the woman, although she had lived a life Fay would have shunned. Claire's husband had not been an easy man, perhaps owing in part to the fact that it was he who could not produce children; and in addition to his refusal to adopt any was the refusal to let his wife work, even though Claire had a New York City teacher's license and could have done substitute service. Now, after so many years of no practice and given the putrid state of the school system, she would not even fleetingly consider a return to the profession. If she harbored any bitterness for having acquiesced to the bulk of her husband's wishes, she didn't show it. Claire never talked about him, just as Curt never talked about Fay's mother. In this family the dead were not discussed.

"Hello, dear." She kissed Fay much more warmly than her brother had.

"Hello, Claire." She had never been instructed to use "Aunt" and so never did.

"Did Sheila tell you about our little culinary fiasco?"

"Yes. Thanks for going out to the rescue. Arthur's talents would have been wasted on scrambled eggs."

Claire crossed to the bar, returned with a martini, and sat with Fay, facing Sheila. During the pause that followed, Fay wondered which of them would pick up the ball of conversation; in the presence of these women together she herself felt restrained from anything beyond small talk. There was her own resentment for being part of this circle: three attendants awaiting the appearance of the master, using chatter to disguise their stations of subtle subservience.

Claire, as always, appeared comfortable during lulls in conversation. She now pulled a cigarette from her leather case and snapped a flame from a slender gold lighter. In contrast, Sheila carried no case and used book matches. Fay admired the care and special touch that her aunt lent to everything, even to this habit. And the care she gave herself rendered her, at sixty, still a boldly striking woman. The hair had been allowed to take its natural course into white, but the silvery highlights at the peak of each wave suggested regular treatment to produce them. Lipstick was her only concession to makeup, a cherry red that, whenever she smiled, encouraged further notice of the even and white-as-her-hair teeth. Her clothing was always elegantly simple, and she never used scarves or turtlenecks to hide the going-to-crepe neck, with its mysterious, razor-thin scar, perhaps because she was proud of its long and slender grace. Fay always found that Claire's presence lessened Sheila's beauty.

"I suppose," Claire said to Fay, "the round of Christmas parties has already started for you."

"Yes. Whenever possible I try for only a brief appearance and an unnoticed exit. Somehow these parties get grimmer every year."

"Enforced gaiety is always grim. But what can you expect when the radio and the stores start in on the carols the day after Thanksgiving?"

"I swear," said Sheila, "if I hear 'Silver Bells' one more time I'll spit up."

Another silence. *Why*, thought Fay, is he taking so long? Is he doing this to us on purpose?

Then, as if to chastise her for ill suspicions, he came briskly down the stairs. "Sorry, but I had to lie on the heating pad for a few minutes."

Of course—his bad back, of which they were all aware. It had worsened since he had entered his fifties. Fay often thought the trouble was aggravated by his ramrod, military posture—an outer manifestation of his rigid and unyielding nature. In terms of total image, she conceded, he was thoroughly consistent.

She watched his gaze glance off Sheila's bourbon bottle, the way a wet fingertip tests a hot iron. Then he said, "The fish shouldn't take too long, should it?"

"We'll eat in fifteen minutes," answered Claire. "Arthur's making a beet-and-endive salad to jazz things up."

Colby poured himself white wine, sat next to Sheila, and said to Fay, "What are you working on now?

"MenthaRub, Snowdrift soap."

"Never heard of Snowdrift."

"It's new. We're preparing the campaign."

"With *your* skin," said Sheila, "they ought to use you in the commercial."

Fay saw her father lower his eyes at Sheila's effusiveness.

Whether he was embarrassed or grudgingly proud of her she could not tell. And neither did she know if he was resentful of the fact that her salary exceeded his. If he was, then the source would be strictly a competitiveness for prestige, not the money itself. Before Fay was born, her grandfather had left Curt and Claire sixty thousand each and a small number of stocks. Claire and her husband had not been particularly shrewd in their investments, but Curt Colby put a few thousand into IBM and took a then wild chance on South African gold stocks that now brought him an average of $200,000 a year.

"Just yesterday," continued Sheila, "Agnes and I were talking about you, and she asked if you did anything special like facials or mud-packs and I said no, it's all God-given."

Colby's eyes were lowered further, and shifted to the fireplace. Fay knew that this topic, regardless of how it was broached, was uncomfortable for him, because she had her mother's skin—her mother's eyes, her mother's mouth, her mother's body. In every photograph she had seen—and in the three-by-four-foot portrait he had stuck away in a disused closet—there was an uncanny resemblance. No, it went beyond resemblance: it approached duplication.

Claire, whose emotional antennae were always sensitively tuned, smoothly and propitiously changed the subject to soap-as-a-Christmas-gift and then to the horrors of holiday shopping. Fay contributed, and together they carried through until it was time to get up and go into the dining room.

Claire assisted Arthur in getting the food to the table, and when the cook returned to the kitchen, discussion began about Brent Matheny's release from jail, the terms of his probation, and the general subject of his new novel. Then Fay received from her father a long account about which stocks she should be buying and which selling. Claire ate slowly but with appetite; Sheila picked at the fish, had two helpings of the parsleyed potatoes, and refused wine, the better to savor her bourbon.

In the living room, over coffee, Colby asked his daughter the inevitable: "Are you seeing anyone these days?"

And the inevitable answer: "No one special."

"Even someone *un*special would be welcome here."

Fay was startled: here was something new. Her father's tone of voice and his choice of words were casual and therefore awkward, since casualness was not one of his accomplishments.

Claire rescued her. "How is Marsha?"

"Well and busy. She has to travel a lot."

"Does she like it?" said Sheila.

"Not particularly. But the money's good."

"We certainly haven't seen her in a long time," said Colby, lighting his pipe.

Fay thought quickly: he deserved no access to even the most innocent relationship in her life. "Her work schedule is unpredictable. It's hard for her to make plans."

Claire offered after-dinner liqueurs, which all refused, and Sheila told a story about two friends who had been mugged the day before. Fay forced herself to remain another half hour, but at one point, when she caught her father staring at her, she wanted to jump up and run. She felt the familiar fear, then anger at having the fear; she managed to balance herself with the realistic reminder that only ten months of analysis could not subdue a response reinforced over a lifetime.

Finally, the time came when she could unsuspiciously announce her departure. "Big day tomorrow."

At the front door her father ritualistically helped her into her coat. Turning around to say good night, she saw the urgency in his eyes, a force that first had become apparent months ago. There was something waiting to be spoken, and once again she was relieved by its being held in check.

She said good night to Donald, refusing the doorman's

offer to hail her a taxi; the walk to her apartment on Seventy-fourth Street would do her good, perhaps even help her to go to sleep. What she really wanted was to have a non-professional meeting with Dr. Maxson, a drink in a quiet café. If she could not absorb the woman's serenity, then she wanted at least to witness it, feel it surround her like some warm and luxurious fur. Right now, she was willing to have her life shortened by ten years if only the remainder of it could be serene.

While Sheila was in the bathroom, Colby told his sister that he wanted to talk to her as soon as his wife went to bed.

At ten-forty-five Claire entered his at-home office, off the kitchen, and sat in the chair next to his desk. He put aside a manuscript he was considering, rubbed his eyes and cheeks with both hands, then leaned back and looked at her.

"Something is wrong with her," he said.

"Sheila?"

He blinked languidly to indicate he wanted no false ignorance. "Don't tell me you can't sense it."

"I've sensed a lot of things over the years," she countered evenly.

"Am I to gird my loins for some oblique recrimination?"

"Mine doesn't count. It's Fay you're worried about. Suddenly."

"Either she's hiding her real life from us or she's truly leading the dullest existence imaginable. And I cannot believe the latter, not about a woman who's as bright, successful, and beautiful as she is. She's never brought a man here; she never *mentions* a man. You heard what she said tonight about not seeing anyone special. There hasn't been anyone special in six years, since she left college."

"Not that *we* know about."

"But why shouldn't we know? No matter what her . . .

her feelings are about me, it would seem only natural for her to mention her personal life to you."

"Not necessarily. She's got Marsha to confide in."

"Exactly. Maybe it's a 'special' friendship."

Claire did not reply.

"This withdrawal of hers during the past year—she's become downright odd."

"Aren't we all."

"Don't be glib."

"I'm not being glib. And you know it."

She let this settle upon him, and then continued. "You're going through a bit of déjà vu, aren't you? Fay will be twenty-nine next month. Rosemary was twenty-nine when she died, and very distant that last year of her life. Well, this is not going to be the last year of Fay's life. Her circumstances and frame of mind are totally different from her mother's."

"I would like to think so. I would like . . . her to be happy."

You should have wanted that years ago, she could have said, but bit back the words. "Maybe, Curt, in her own way she *is* happy. In any case, her happiness or lack of it is her own business. There's nothing you can do about it."

Keys in hand, Fay looked behind her before entering the small vestibule of the brownstone she lived in. She unlocked her mailbox and withdrew the contents, then unlocked the door to the inner hallway and climbed the oak-banistered staircase to her second-floor apartment. To live in such spaciousness and to have such privacy in Manhattan ordinarily cost a fortune; Fay's rent was high, yet only two-thirds of what the landlady could have got for it. Mrs. Fleming occupied the apartment below Fay's, and because she appreciated Fay's quietness, cleanliness, and lack of visitors, she had given the young woman only one rent

increase in five years. And Fay's friendliness did not hurt
her interests. On her way to the dry cleaners or the laundry
she would always stop at the first floor and ask Mrs. Fleming
if there was anything she wanted taken out; once every week
and a half she came down for a drink and listened forbear-
ingly to the landlady's stories about New York in the "old
days" when it was "still white."

Fay closed her door, locked it, and looked at the contents
in her hand. None of it was "real" mail—her utility bill
and two solicitations, one for a magazine, the other for
American Express's Gold Card. She dropped them onto the
oak chest and went to the kitchen to make a spritzer.

As she was drawing her bath, one of her two telephones
rang.

It was Marsha. "Let me turn off the water," Fay told her.
She did, and returned to the living room phone.

"Well, how did it go with Maxson?" Ever since she'd
convinced Fay to go into therapy and had introduced her to
Dr. Maxson, Marsha had assumed the concerned but irri-
tating role of monitor. Fay always volunteered as little as
possible—just enough to pretend confidence and avoid sub-
stantial revelation.

"It went fine. We talked about my work."

"Your work! But your work's never been a problem. It's
the one solid thing in your life."

"Thank you, Marsha."

"Oh, you know what I mean. What exactly did you say
about work?"

"I'll tell you later. I'm exhausted and I have to take a
bath yet."

"Listen, I have to be in L.A. on Monday to look at a
new sportswear line—so that play on Sunday is off. If you
can meet me for lunch tomorrow, I'll give you the tickets."

Marsha was a failed fashion designer who had become
a successful fashion buyer for one of New York's most
prestigious women's clothing stores, and because she had

to travel constantly—often on short notice—there were frequent cancellations of plans she and Fay would make.

"I'll meet you for lunch when you get back. Give the tickets to someone else. I just want to relax at home this weekend."

"All right." Pause. "I think it would be nice if you had a man to relax *with*."

"Well, one of these days. My bathwater is getting cold."

As soon as she settled into the tub, the other telephone—the one in the bedroom—rang. After the third ring, the answering machine intercepted.

She sipped at her spritzer and eased farther down until the water touched her earlobes. Trying to blot out thoughts of the evening, she took deep breaths for relaxation. But her father's eyes remained before her, urgent and almost supplicating. She hated seeing him as a supplicant; that only roiled her emotions, confusing them, and tapped at the armor it had taken her years to build to protect herself from Curt Colby.

The telephone rang again, three times, and stopped. Two calls. The wanted one would be Sam, the unwanted one Kevin. She wished it could be Andrew instead of Kevin but Andrew was on vacation in Barbados.

She dried off, put on her robe, brushed her hair, then walked over to the answering machine and rewound the tape to the first message: "Hi, it's Sam. I'm coming to New York on Wednesday, and naturally I'd like to see you. Although tomorrow's Saturday, I'll be at my office until four-thirty and then at home after six-thirty. Please give me a call. Collect. Good night."

A brief pause and then the second message: "Hello, Ann, this is Kevin. It's Friday, ten P.M. I'm a little disappointed you haven't returned my last two calls. I got a writing assignment and have to go to Charleston for research. Be back Wednesday—please try to get away that night. Have a good weekend."

She removed the cord from the wall jack, then turned out the lights and got into bed.

3

IT WAS SAM SHE WANTED TO SEE, BUT KEVIN SHE *HAD* to see—for the most unpleasant reason.

Sam had understood completely when she called him and said that she was embroiled in family matters. He would be coming to New York again in two weeks, and his spirits seemed to lift when she promised to meet him then and assured him that she was anxious for their rendezvous.

At eight o'clock on Wednesday night she took a taxi to the Village and got out at Perry Street. Kevin lived in the largest building on the block, stately and solid on the outside but, due to renovation twelve years ago, modern and ordinary within. She pressed the button next to "K. Ivory," then, when the buzzer sounded, pushed open the security door and proceeded to the elevator.

He opened his door the second after she rang—and the second after he'd closed it he pinned her against the wall and fumbled for a kiss.

"Kevin, *please*," she protested, the rigidity of her body

fending him off even more effectively than her hands. "I'd like to sit down. and I'd like a drink."

"A drink?" His face registered amazement at this change in the usual; he always kept white wine especially for her. "Uh, what kind?"

"Whatever you've got."

"Scotch, vodka . . ."

"Vodka's fine. On the rocks, please."

From the sofa in the living room she was able to view him through the cut-out square in the kitchen wall. She saw that already he was apprehensive, his eyes flicking up from the drink preparation every now and then in a way that suggested surveillance. And she knew why: the change in their lovemaking, the change in her willingness to meet him regularly, and now this small change—the request for liquor. With his wide all-American face and blond curly hair, his firm long-waisted torso and powerful legs, he was by far the best-looking of any of the men she visited. Perhaps that was the reason he had grown so demanding and jealous, so full of questions as to why she couldn't be available more often. He yanked up the lever of the ice cube tray, and she watched his golden-haired arms—arms that had once, with gentleness now lost, had the remarkable power simultaneously to excite and soothe her.

He brought in her vodka and his bottle of German beer. Sitting next to her, he nodded at her glass and said, "Tough day?"

"Well, yes, in fact it was."

"Then all the more reason to relax." He began stroking the back of her neck.

She had eaten a light supper—a small chef's salad— and so the vodka burned her stomach with each swallow. Almost instantly it began to do its work.

He leaned over and nuzzled her ear. Resisting the desire to pull away, she said softly, "Kevin, we have to talk about something."

He sat back and waited, his eyes steady, unblinking, and, it seemed to Fay, bluer than they were a minute ago.

"We ... can't see each other anymore. I'm going back with my husband."

He looked her face up and down. "You mean you're going to remarry him?"

"We're going to start off by living together and see what happens."

Again he waited, forcing her on.

"I didn't want to have to tell you on the telephone — that's why I've come here tonight."

"You thought I deserved better than a phone call?"

"Yes."

"You're right. I do." He smiled without parting his lips, a warm smile. "And I deserve something else. If this is going to be the last time, I think you should give it to me without that alarm clock in your head ticking away. That is to say, no time limit."

"That's just it, Kevin. Now that I've made this decision, I don't think it would work well between us."

"Sure it would. You don't have to feel guilty about me. I mean you're not back with your husband yet." He paused. "Take this the right way, Ann—don't you think you owe me more than just good-bye?"

Her stomach did a little flip-flop in recording the truth of what he said.

She accepted another vodka and then half of a third one, which enabled her to accept his strokings and deep-tongue kisses.

In the bedroom she allowed him to take her twice. At the end of the second round, as she was climaxing, he put his lips to her ear and whispered through clenched teeth, "I think you're going to miss this, baby. And anytime you do, just give ol' Kevin a call." She was flooded with relief that her orgasm had begun before he spoke.

He offered another vodka, which she declined, then told

her, "Don't go into the bathroom yet. Stay right here. I want to bring you a little farewell gift." Smiling, he smoothed the hair back from her forehead, got up and put on his shorts, and disappeared into the living room.

She closed her eyes and groaned at the aftereffect of the vodka thumping at her temples. Aspirin, she hoped, would be sufficient antidote: she did not need a hangover at work or at lunch with Marsha.

Not hearing him but sensing his presence, she opened her eyes to find him leaning against the doorway, his hands behind his hips, one side of his mouth turned up in a mockery of a smile. He approached the bed and extended one hand, which held a small pink-papered box; the other hand remained hidden.

"Just a little something I picked up for you in Charleston. Go on, open it."

It was a magnolia-shaped bottle with three glass leaves forming the base. She removed the cap and found the perfume overly sweet but told him she loved it.

"While I was in the living room I happened to think that you should give me a present too. Since you won't want me to call you anymore, you can give me your address so I can drop you a line now and then to let you know how I'm doing."

"You know I can't do that."

"Well, you already have. *Fay.*"

He now revealed the other hand and, in front of her face, unfolded the plastic packet containing her driver's license and credit cards.

Her purse! He'd gone through her purse! She had always been careful with it when she was with a man, just on the off chance that one of them might suspect her and try the very stunt he had just pulled. But tonight the vodka, the tension, her eagerness to get everything over with, had made her careless.

His grin widened, yet smoldered. "Fay Colby, is it? Well,

how do you do, Fay? And what about poor Ann Decker who lives on the upper West Side, and who's just all broken up over the sa-a-ad end of her marriage and can only see me every two weeks because she really still loves her dear hubby and can't make up her mind if she should take him back and put up with his compulsive gambling." He paused to catch his breath. "You really ought to be writing for the soap operas, Miss Colby of *East* Seventy-fourth Street. That would make you more money than playing *me* for an asshole."

She started up from the pillow, but he pinned her back by her shoulders. "Uh-uh, baby, not yet. We've got a few things to settle."

"I haven't been playing you for anything, Kevin. What I've done is *my* problem."

"When two people are involved, your problem is *their* problem."

"You and I are not involved."

"Oh, yes, we are—although you're probably a grasshopper jumping from bed to bed. Well, you're not jumping out of *my* bed."

Anger, fear, regret, raced through her, creating panic that had to be subdued. "I'm going back with my husband," she said calmly.

"Your husband..." His eyes raked over her face. "If there *is* a husband, it's not going to make any difference between us, none at all. He doesn't have to know anything."

"Kevin, you're decent enough to realize why I could never do that."

"Am I? Decent as you are?" He let the question hang for a second. "No, we're going on like before, whether there's a husband or other Kevins in the wings."

"Please let me up. I have to go."

"I'll let you get up, but before I do I want you to repeat after me, 'We're going on like before. I know you mean business.' Say it."

"I know you mean business," she answered dully.

"The rest."

"We're going on like before," and to keep herself from grimacing she mentally corrected his grammar.

He moved up and out of the bedroom. She dressed in a flash, like a soldier hearing reveille, and even forwent a trip to the bathroom.

He stood at the front door, waiting to open it for her. She would not look him in the face. Before turning the knob he said softly, almost gently, "I do mean business. Don't make me have to prove it."

"Kevin, there are other women—"

"Not like you, there aren't. See you next week."

She made her bath hotter than usual and soaked longer than usual, but the water wouldn't ease the revulsion she felt toward Kevin—and herself. In the beginning he had seemed so shy, her chief prerequisite in a man, and during their first six months she had flattered herself as being responsible for his flowering self-confidence. The confidence turned to assertiveness, and then the assertiveness crossed the line to an aggressive possessiveness. The meeting that irrevocably changed her attitude was the one during which he told her that if her estranged husband ever gave her any trouble, he himself would "take care of him." She knew now that the very next day she should have had the number changed on her "second" telephone and written him a *letter* of farewell. And now he had her address.

Don't make me have to prove it. She despised him the more for his choice of words. "Don't make me have to—" was the exact phrase her father used to employ with her; and living in his home, she'd heard him use it against others, too.

But what could Kevin possibly do to her except make himself a temporary nuisance? The moment she asked herself the question, looming up before her mind's eye were those tabloid stories whose headlines screamed violence from the front pages of the New York *Post* and *Daily News*. Incidents of jealousy that led to maimings, mutilations, murder. The case of the man who had thrown acid in the face of a fiancée who jilted him. . . .

She swallowed four aspirins, took the second telephone off the hook, and got into bed. Five minutes of deep-breathing exercises calmed her into drowsiness.

A little after two A.M. she awakened with a jolt and in a sweat. She had been falling. Falling. Falling away from Kevin's menacing reach but also away from Joe Blakis's *rescuing* reach. So vivid was the dream that she instantly stretched out both arms for reassurance from the mattress. Solid ground. Years ago she had found that even a queen-size bed was not sufficient to provide her with the necessary feeling of safety, and so she had bought this one, a king-size. She always slept squarely in the middle of it.

Her eyes closed; sleepiness returned. But before she went under, memory spun out another night when she had been in bed. She was four years old. The muffled voices in the bedroom next to hers had woken her, voices low and seething with vindictiveness, and then they moved farther off, down the hall to the living room. She had drifted off and woken again, so she never knew exactly how much time elapsed between the sound of the voices and that of the howl that spiraled downward outside the apartment building. It wasn't until the next day that she was told, by Claire, that the broken body the police had picked up off the sidewalk was her mother's.

Trotter's was a new restaurant on Second Avenue in the high Fifties, understated and expensive, popular at dinner but not at lunch—which suited Fay and Marsha just fine. When Fay arrived she found Marsha seated at a table next to the oak-paned window with a Bloody Mary in front of her. Fay ordered a club soda and a half-dozen clams to begin with.

"We're looking pretty shot-down. Big night last night?" Marsha hinted.

"Just a sleepless one."

"Anxiety?"

"No, Bright's disease," Fay said archly.

Despite her involvement in analysis, Fay always winced at clinical terms, even though she acknowledged that *anxiety* had its place in the vernacular. But Marsha used the word clinically, as she would use others in her probing. Marsha had been Fay's best friend since their senior year of college; in the past year and a half the friendship had made a turn that discomforted Fay. When she and Marsha first met, Marsha was engaged, and self-absorbed with wedding plans and career considerations, so the footing they started on suited them both: Fay was the introverted listener whose unwavering steadiness worked in counterpoint to the other woman's unpredictable and effusive ups and downs and almost daily advice-seeking. The tacit terms of the relationship continued through the rocky marriage, the even rockier divorce, and Marsha's nervous breakdown. Three years of analysis with Dr. Maxson was Marsha's ladder up from the emotional pit, and as she began to near the top, she also began to scrutinize her friend's life as carefully as her own—and found it lacking. Fay had brushed aside Marsha's suggestions that she too go to Maxson, or to anyone who could help her resolve her past and pry open her shell. The refusal was steadfast until Marsha's end-of-my-analysis party: Fay's fears and prejudice dissolved after talking to Maxson and watching her socialize, and the following Monday she called for an appointment. Ever since, Marsha wanted the role of the listener, and sought out progress reports. Although Fay recognized the good intentions and genuine concern, she had not yet reached the point of security from which she could reveal her sex life to anyone but Maxson.

"If you're not sleeping well," said Marsha, "maybe you should see Maxson twice a week. Insomnia is usually an indication of unresolved—"

"It was one sleepless night." She didn't admit that the suggestion about "twice a week" was exactly what she was contemplating. To change the subject, she said, "I'm thinking of taking a course at the New School."

"Oh, come on. You did that last year and dropped out halfway through the term. Taking classes is just your escape from real problems."

"All right," Fay said resignedly, "what's on your mind today?"

"Just this: are you seeing anybody?"

"Anybody?"

"A *man*." Marsha said impatiently.

"I . . . I've started. But I don't know if it's going to work out."

"Yes, yes, the usual disclaimer. Look, Fay, I know you haven't had a long-term relationship since you came back to New York after college, and I would imagine that's the major thing you're working on with Maxson. But tell me why, out of all the short-term men, you've introduced me to only one."

"Exactly because they've never lasted long enough. Marsha, this is not my favorite kind of lunchtime conversation."

"It's not your favorite kind *anytime*. I'm concerned and I'm curious; I think that's normal. You haven't been happy in a long time—I'm not blind—but you never admit it, never talk about it."

"Most people talk too much about their unhappiness. After a while it gets boring."

"You're not 'most people,' and you're never boring, certainly not to me. You've got this superwoman complex stiff upper lip at all times, total invincibility. From everything you've told me about your father, it sounds as if you're a lot like him."

"I'm not *at all* like him."

"Such an angry denial would indicate that you are."

"It was firm, not angry. I find all of this annoying."

"You're annoyed when I ask you questions, and I'm annoyed when you tell me nothing, when you don't have enough trust in me to confide—"

"Marsha, don't say I don't have any trust in you. My . . . exaggerated privacy has nothing to do with your character. It's *my* problem." Suddenly, Kevin's words from the night before came back to mock her: "When two people are involved, your problem is *their* problem." To blot him out, she hurried on, grasping for a defense. "You recommended Dr. Maxson, and now I'm going to her. Isn't that a show of confidence in your advice and judgment?"

Marsha smirked. "Let's keep the record straight. You didn't go to her on my recommendation. You went to her after you had firsthand exposure to her at my party. Even though you have to talk to her now, you can still afford a little more intimacy with me."

"I'm trying. I really am working hard."

"All right. A last word. You're gorgeous, you're smart as hell, you have a job that you love and pays you well— many blessings, and the best way to show thanks is to let them make you a little bit happy." With one hand she comically fluffed her hair. "The way I have."

Fay pounced upon this shift to levity. "*Your* biggest blessings were the invention of the girdle and Miss Clairol."

"Bitch. I'll have you know I'm down to a hundred eighteen pounds. And on the way over here I was whistled at twice."

"Grocery delivery boys whistle at every blonde."

"One of these days, dear heart, I'm going to be wearing

a cast on my knuckles, and you're going to be wearing dentures."

Fay got onto the topic of her trip and the line of women's sportswear she would be appraising; but she listened with only one ear, while the other echoed Kevin's threat.

Curt Colby left his office at three-fifteen and walked ten blocks toward his three-thirty appointment. On his way, without pausing, he glanced up at the eighth-story windows of the building that housed Mayhew Advertising and wondered what his daughter was doing at this moment.Ever since she had come to dinner the previous week she had dominated his thoughts, so much so that his customary speed and precision at his job were cut nearly in half. He'd been deliberating, and the deliberating had led him to a decision and, in turn, to his present destination.

The agency was on the fourth floor of a narrow structure off Madison Avenue whose lobby had the dimensions of a walk-in closet. As Colby rode the elevator up he braced himself—against what, he couldn't quite determine. The door opened directly onto the waiting room; at the head of it was a rectangular plexiglass panel through which the secretary-receptionist eyed Colby with professional coolness. He speculated on the possible presumptions she was making about his having come here; suddenly defensive, he found himself speaking rather imperiously: "I'm Mr. Colby. I have a three-thirty appointment."

She nodded. "If you'll just take a seat, Mr. O'Brien will be with you in a moment."

The two sofas and two chairs were upholstered in a dark gray tweed, a rather tasteful choice of material, although the furniture itself was cheap. The magazines on the small formica table were neatly arrayed and new-looking, but Colby found that most of them were back issues. Perhaps, he considered, clients who sought the services offered here were too distracted to thumb through the magazines; and perhaps, too, one was not kept waiting long enough to have to resort to reading material.

At three—thirty-six the woman answered the buzz from her telephone, then put her face to the hole in the plexiglass: "Mr. O'Brien will see you now." She nodded in the direction of the door, and when Colby reached it she pressed a buzzer that released the lock. He stepped into a small corridor that led to two offices. A tall man stood in the doorway of one and said, "In here, Mr. Colby."

They shook hands, and as O'Brien moved to the chair behind his desk, Colby did a quick appraisal of the room. The odor suggested that the walls had been recently painted. They were a very pale though soothing yellow that also pointed up the age of the contents: the gray desk and file cabinets were laced with scratches, and here and there showed nicks where the lamination had come off to reveal the raw metal; the carpeting, unpadded and probably glued to the floor, was literally worn to reveal its stitching; the chair Colby sat down in answered back with its springs. Offsetting the look of wear was a white poinsettia, and a newly installed brown-tinted window was open about two inches to admit fresh air.

O'Brien set about explaining his fees—which varied according to the difficulty and danger of the work. Watching this tall, lanky "black" Irishman, Colby thought of how the man fulfilled, physically, the stereotypical picture of an intense, driven "serious" writer. O'Brien was probably in his early forties, with penetrating dark eyes, three deeply cut worry lines across his forehead, nicotine stains on the thumb and first two fingers of his left hand, a ballpoint ink mark on one finger of his right hand; the knot of his tie was loosened, and his shirt-sleeves were rolled up to just below the elbows. The timbre of his voice wore a slight raspiness that was most likely the result of excessive cigarette smoking. He was clearly intelligent, sounded and looked discreet, and yet Colby had the distinct feeling that this was not the kind of man you would chance introducing your wife to: he had that brand of confidence and unconscious charm that might seduce even the most faithful of women.

"Now," said O'Brien, "if all that is clear and you have no questions, we can get down to the nature of the assignment."

Colby hesitated, then said, "It's not that easy to explain. This—this is the first time I've done anything like this."

At once, O'Brien began his list of silent notes: Colby was a normally articulate man suddenly fumbling for words— like someone speaking to the first hooker he's ever hired, trying to convince her that he's "not like all the others."

"I want to know my daughter's habits. Where she goes, whom she sees."

"Yes?" O'Brien waited, but Colby only stared. "How frequently do you want her followed?" This last word made Colby wince.

"That will depend on how often she goes out. I mean, she's employed during the day, so it won't be necessary to—" His eyes shifted to the wall lined with file cabinets. "Well, I suppose you should watch her during her lunch hour. Yes. And then if there's nothing, uh, significant about that time period, we can dispense with it."

"All right." Again O'Brien waited, but there was nothing. "Mr. Colby, what is it exactly that you want me to look for?"

Colby's collar felt strangulating, but he resisted pulling at it. "I've told you. Just her habits."

"What specific habits do you suspect?"

"I don't 'suspect' anything specific," he replied adamantly, almost rudely. "I just want to know how she lives."

"People don't hire private investigators unless they suspect *something*. Now what is it? Infidelity to a husband, general promiscuity, lesbianism, drug addiction, drug selling, kleptomania?"

"None of those. I just want to know how she lives."

O'Brien sighed. "If I weren't an honest man, Mr. Colby, it would be very easy to cheat you on an assignment as vague as this one. I could pretend I found a pattern that doesn't exist and lead you down the garden path for quite a while."

Colby didn't respond.

"How old is your daughter?"

"Twenty-eight, almost twenty-nine."

"Does she live alone?"

"Yes."

"Do you have a recent photograph?"

He withdrew it from his jacket pocket. "It was taken this past Thanksgiving."

"Um-hum." Very nice, O'Brien thought. Following her would be simple: walking along the city's streets, she would undoubtedly be subject to whistles, lewd remarks, smooching and sucking sounds, and for protection would keep her eyes straight ahead and never glance backward. He could divine, even in his snapshot, a remoteness in her unsmiling face.

"Is one of these women her mother?"

"Aunt and stepmother."

"And her real mother?"

"She's been dead for years."

O'Brien wrote down all the necessary information and accepted the cash retainer. Like most of O'Brien's clients, Colby didn't want to do any check-writing.

As the money was being laid on the desk, one of O'Brien's two assistants opened the door just far enough to stick his head in and say, "I'm going home." Seeing Colby, Les Beckhorn apologized to his boss: "Sorry, Rhoda didn't tell me you were with someone." When O'Brien introduced the two, Colby looked like a man reluctantly shaking hands with the devil.

Left alone, O'Brien studied the snapshot, but his mind

worked at assessing Colby. Debonair, disciplined, rigid, taciturn, quietly arrogant, probably a great snob. Beyond these qualities was something else that he couldn't quite put his finger on—something that he might discover as he worked on the case; something that would continue to itch at him until he discovered it.

For the time being, however, his instinct told him that Colby was what used to be called "a wrong guy."

4

Dr. Maxson had already taken her position in the chair behind the couch, but Fay remained standing at the window, staring out at the languid snowflakes that were collecting on the window ledge, and longing to scoop up a handful to press against her face.

"I'm glad you're enjoying the snow," said Dr. Maxson, "but it's not very economical of you. We've just lost seven minutes already."

"You think I'm stalling."

"I can only presume. Are you?"

"I suppose." She turned to look at the woman, who was probably close to her father's age. Dr. Maxson had a thick head of hair, chestnut flecked with gray, which she wore parted in the middle and shoulder-length and which at certain angles made her head seem just a bit too large for her long, sleek body. In clothing, she made no concession to trends; the understatement rendered her appearance a perfect match for her quietly commanding voice. Today she wore a beige wool dress belted at the waist, a brown sweater draped across her shoulders, brown medium-heeled shoes. The only jewelry was a narrow gold watch on her left wrist.

Twenty minutes into the session the topic still resided with that evening the week before when she had had dinner at her father's. "I was on pins and needles, as usual. Somehow I always feel I have to keep the ball rolling, and sometimes I just refuse to do it and sit there gritting my teeth through the silences. No one seems to mind as much as I do."

"What do you think about during these silences?"

"The time. How much longer it'll take till I can leave."

"Nothing personal is discussed with you or among them?"

"My father isn't a personal man, and he sets the tone. Sheila seems quite content with her bourbon and cigarettes, and Claire—well, I can never really tell what Claire is thinking. She doesn't exactly cater to my father, but sometimes it seems rather as if she collaborates, or at least cooperates with him. If they have any disagreements, they must haggle them out in private."

"Do you love Claire?"

"I like her. I don't love anybody. You know that."

"She's never told you she loves you?"

"Never."

"Do you feel perhaps she does?"

"I don't know. I think she's fond of me, if only because she has no children of her own. As I've told you, she helped to raise me after my mother's death. And over the obvious disapproval of her husband."

"He disapproved openly in front of you?"

"Just with looks. There must have been arguments, but they took place behind closed doors. I remember him once saying, 'She'—meaning my mother—'probably should have taken the poor kid with her.'"

"Was this about the time you began to be afraid of heights?"

"I can't remember. All I know is that after Claire told me what my mother had done I never wanted to go out onto a balcony or terrace again. Anyway, my father lost little time in moving himself and me to another apartment that had no terrace, and Claire and Herb's didn't have one either."

"Did you spend most of your time at Claire's?"

"One or two nights a week, sporadically. An occasional weekend. She came to our apartment a lot. Until my father married his second wife, Lenore."

"How did you feel about his remarrying?"

"I think . . . relieved. It took pressure off our having to talk to each other, and Lenore was kind to me. She lasted five years. They separated when I was thirteen and divorced soon after, when I was sent off to boarding school."

"They had no children?"

"No."

"And there was no pregnancy?"

"None that I know of."

"Whose idea was it to send you to boarding school?"

"His, of course. At first I protested. I was going to a good private school here in the city, and I had friends I didn't want to leave. But when Claire took me up to Connecticut one weekend for a tour of the place, I began to warm up to the idea."

"Did Claire indicate how she felt about your going away?"

"She said something about hoping I'd like it, that my father was doing what he thought best, and that he'd put a lot of time into investigating different schools. After the first month I was glad to be there. Claire wrote me or called every week."

"Then you liked communal living?"

"Yes, very much. I was the quiet type, but for some reason quite popular—I guess because I was always interested in the other girls' problems. Pretty soon I was the Ann Landers-in-residence."

"And were any of them interested in *your* problems?"

"At the time, even I didn't think I had any. I didn't talk much about myself."

"So you were a kind of mother figure—revered and wielding the upper hand."

Fay's laugh was forced. "Is that a criticism?"

"No. Neither is it a judgment. It's an attempt at clarification. If I'm drawing the wrong conclusion, please correct me."

"I suppose I was an elected authority. Often you're given that position simply for being a good listener. And because I was considered pretty and clever, no one thought I had any problems."

"How did you feel about always being the listener?"

"I liked it. It was . . . entertainment. And it was reassuring to learn that one or two girls had worse parental problems than I did." She paused. "And naturally there were problems with boys. The headmistress was very strict and approved of boys only from the neighboring academy—on that issue I think she was encouraged by most of the girls' parents. Still, a girl couldn't be prevented from dating a boy from town. But she could be discouraged. Somehow the boy's family would be investigated, and if in any way it didn't meet the unspoken standard, the girl's parents would be notified and would make a surprise visit. Of course, this bred resentment and some sneaking around."

"Did your father ever make a surprise visit?"

"No, but he was called up for a disciplinary hearing. My roommate was seeing a boy from town, on the sly, and one night she sneaked off to be with him. A telephone call came through from her grandmother, and I begged the house-mother not to disturb Patti—I said she'd been suffering from insomnia and that on this particular night she'd gone to bed after dinner and was sleeping soundly for the first time in weeks. Patti was caught coming through the garden after midnight."

"Was this cooperation of yours with Patti strictly voluntary?"

"Yes, I . . . I wanted to get Patti off my back." She closed her eyes. The session, up to this point, had been painless, but now she had to reveal one more example of Fay the User, Fay the Coward. "Patti and I had had a—well, an infatuation. It lasted about four or five months, and then I became tired of it but she wanted to continue. I had to keep trying to convince her I liked her but not *that* way. The atmosphere became quite strained. So when she met this boy and seemed to fall for him, I did everything I could to encourage her, without overencouraging. She ended up marrying him in college. Happy ending."

"Who initiated this infatuation, and what physical form did it take?"

It seemed to Fay that in spite of Dr. Maxson's clinical and propitious phrasing, her tone was suddenly softer, perhaps to make admission easier. "I initiated—I guess at first unconsciously. I used to braid her hair, and sometimes I'd rub her neck. One night I had a bad dream and she got up and shook me out of it, then got into my bed and held me. We stroked each other, and I kissed her on the cheek. We slept together from then on until I began to feel pressured. She wanted to be together all the time, not just in bed, and she became jealous of my other friends. One Friday afternoon we had a huge fight, and she got hysterical and called her parents to come get her for the weekend. For two days I couldn't eat—I was frightened to death she'd make a spectacle of us by telling her family. But she came back much calmer and we were able to have a sensible talk. A while later she met the boy from town."

"Did you actually tire of the physical relationship, or was it simply her possessiveness?"

"I think it was both. After Patti, I wasn't attracted to any other girl in that way. I started dating boys. From the academy."

"Go on."

"There was nothing serious. Simple dates, simple kisses, a little petting, nothing more. No drugs, not even pot— well, just once, but I didn't like it. I think it was laced with something—I felt blurred and out of control."

"Did a boy give it to you?"

"Yes. I never went out with him again, and I warned the other girls. After that, of course, there were those who couldn't wait to be asked out by him."

"Then there was no steady boy during your teens."

"No."

"And in college?"

"Only the one I've told you about, the one from Albany who came to see me on weekends. It took me a whole year to find out he was married, with two children. What a fool I was."

"One can be fooled without *being* a fool." There was a considerable silence before Dr. Maxson spoke again. "The men you now see, do you consider them fools?"

"Certainly not. I . . . could never be involved with a fool."

"Do you consider yourself 'involved'?"

You and I are not involved was what she had told Kevin. "There are degrees," she countered, miffed at having trapped herself. "Anyway, not one of them is a fool, least of all Joe. But Kevin has become possessive, so I've broken it off with him."

"Oh? When was this?"

"Last week."

"How did he react?"

"Angrily. His pride has a dent in it, but he'll have it bumped out before long."

"Our time is up."

Ritualistically, they both rose in the same instant.

"One last thing, Fay. At our last session you waited until the end to mention your dream, and today you did the same thing with this news of Kevin. Just think about it."

* * *

As soon as Fay left, Olivia Maxson went to the small,
box-shaped refrigerator that sat on the floor next to the file
cabinet. She took out a container of crab salad, an apple,
and a can of club soda. She sat in the swivel chair, ate, and
looked out the window, but she barely tasted or saw. She
was wondering to what degree she might eventually succeed
in rescuing this young woman from the emotional catas-
trophes she was most certainly heading for.

The handwritten envelope, lacking a return address, gave
Fay a premonition of the contents. At the corner of the flap
she inserted her nail and ran it slowly down then up the V.

> *Ann/Fay/Whoever-you-are-today (nice rhyme):*
> *What a sly girl, having your phone number changed.*
> *But what a silly girl for thinking that will make me go*
> *away. Call me soon. Very soon. I'm getting impatient,*
> *and I don't like the feeling.*
>
> *You-Know-Who*

The handwriting was exceedingly formal, studied; it
looked as if it had been lifted from an old Palmer penmanship manual. And perhaps it had been—an intentional camouflage. Camouflage would be necessary only if . . .

No return address.

She looked up from the note and saw herself staring back
at her from one of the two front windows of her living room.
After glancing out at the street, she closed the draperies.

At seven-forty she locked her apartment, descended the
staircase, and rapped on Mrs. Fleming's door. Inside she
heard the landlady's brisk, bedroom-slippered shuffle on the
hardwood floor.

"Fay?"

"Yes."

The cyclinder lock was turned and the door opened to reveal a small pink woman in a pinker bathrobe, the ends of her thin white hair wound in rollers. The partial dental plate on the right side of her mouth had already been removed for the evening.

"I'm going out," said Fay. "I'll be back around eleven. Is there anything you need for the morning—milk or juice?"

"No, thanks, darlin'. I'm all set. But if you pass a newsstand you can bring me a paper. If I'm asleep, just leave it outside the door here."

"Asleep?" Mrs. Fleming was consistently nocturnal, and watched just about anything that filled her television screen until three in the morning.

"I think I'm courting a virus," the woman reported, then eyed Fay's coat. "You sure that's warm enough?"

"Oh, yes. It's cashmere."

"You ought to get fur. Nothin' like it."

"People will mug you for fur."

"Well, that's true. Now you be careful, fur or no fur. You're taking a cab, aren't you?"

"Yes."

"Watch out for the drivers, too. Lots of them take dope. You know, half of them are foreigners, and most of them are just plain nuts."

"I'll be careful." The Palmer penmanship reappeared in her mind's eye.

She stepped out into the night, letting the heavy oak door close and self-lock behind her, and looked up and down the block. Not a soul. She would have preferred some population.

Her legs worked swiftly and her eyes canvassed all shadows until she reached Park Avenue, where she hailed a taxi. Twelve minutes later, she got out on East Thirty-eighth Street, in front of the Hotel Hanson, a tall, narrow structure whose Art Deco motif did not extend beyond the lobby and adjacent piano bar: the rooms themselves had been recently renovated and now embodied a sterility equaling that of any Holiday Inn. Still, great care had gone into preserving and maintaining the original material and appointments on the first floor, so that when one entered through the revolving door, it was indeed a spin backward into a more civilized and elegant period. Potted palms stood before the two black marbled columns that framed the two-steps-down archway to the bar. In front of one palm was a three-legged billboard advertising the entertainment:

11th Year...

Estelle Klein at the piano

playing

Sugar and Spice
Naughty and Nice

In an intimate register, Estelle—whose voice was mediocre, partly because it was so insistently sincere—was singing "My Man" when Fay came down the steps and paused to scout the tables and booths. In the far corner Sam raised his hand, and as she walked toward him, all eyes, including Estelle's, followed her course. His face beaming, Sam stood and pulled the table slightly away from the booth to admit her, then sat down and readjusted it. In her presence he had two kinds of smiles, and she privately classified them as clear and opaque: clear when he was just plain glad to see her, opaque when he was *too* glad to see her—his joy smudged with regret over their two-week separation and dread of their next. She was relieved to find tonight's smile clear.

He covered her hand with his large callused one. "'Good to see you' would be an understatement," he said. "The usual? Or would you like to break tradition and have a bottle of Dom Pérignon?"

"Oh, no. Somehow the bubbly always ends up as a sledgehammer in my head by morning. But I will have something different. Maybe, uh . . . a perfect Manhattan, up, with a cherry."

Sam ordered the drinks and said, "I wish you could've joined me for dinner. I had an excellent salmon."

"I wish I could've too. But I like to have dinner with the girls—it's a nice time to review the day and plan the next." The girls, of course, were her mythical daughters, with whom she had a solid rapport, as opposed to no rapport with her workaholic husband. Having heard the full story, Sam had once said, "It's so hard to believe that any man could put his work before you." "Writers are notorious for that," she had replied.

When the drinks arrived, they clicked glasses, sipped; and then she took his hand, turned it over, and rubbed the calluses with her fingertips. "How do you get these? Certainly not from your job." Sam had an executive position with an insurance company.

"Working at my house, in the garden."

"You have a *winter* garden?"

"No," he laughed. "This is wood-splitting season. Nothing like it for getting rid of tension."

Yes, she thought, he *would* split his own wood, dig his weeds, prune his shrubbery without assistance. She had seen pictures of the small stone house, an hour away from Hartford and the apartment living he disliked. He was a self-made man always working at self-improvement, measuring his progress by his own standard and no one else's. A third-generation Greek approaching Curt Colby's age, he had escaped his native Maine fishing town and its main profession to put himself through college, get married, and produce three children. When his wife died, three years ago, he sold the large house, took an apartment, and bought the small house out in the country, where he spent his weekends and vacations. In reference to his departed wife he had told

Fay, "I allow myself ten minutes of grief in the middle of every day, and that's all. I wouldn't survive if I did it in the morning or at night." This self-concocted remedy Fay admired; she wished that her own grief were as focused and specific as his.

Like Joe Blakis, he believed that she was "just a house-wife," doing the best she could to raise two daughters in the presence of their almost indifferent father. Consequently, she had little to say, only asked questions, and assumed her favored role of listener.

Estelle began "You Go to My Head," and as the woman's eyes flicked around the room, Fay was certain that they lingered on her and Sam. They'd had only three meetings here in the past six weeks, and yet Estelle already might be regarding them as regulars.

"You seem a little bemused," said Sam.

"I'm not, really."

"Everything's all right with your family? I mean those complications you told me about on the phone."

"Yes. As all right as can be expected. Since it has nothing to do with my daughters, it's not so terrible."

"I'd like to see a picture of them someday."

Panic iced her throat and shame dried her mouth. "Well, I . . . we're not much of a picture-taking family. But if I think of it I'll go through what we do have and see what I can find."

There followed a long pause, and then Sam suggested they have their second drink in his room. They waited until there was applause for Estelle, then got up.

From a distant booth O'Brien watched them cross the room, take the two steps up to the lobby, and head for the elevators.

When they entered the room the radio was playing softly, positioned at a station that offered bland instrumentaliza-tions of old standards. The bed was already turned down invitingly, blanket and bedspread gathered into a neat fold at the foot. On the dresser and nightstand were five votive candles, which Sam promptly lighted before slipping his arm around Fay and drawing her to him. Perhaps because of his size and strength—perhaps, too, because of his eagerness—his touch was halting, self-consciously gentle. Somehow, she unleashed the hibernating sensual animal in Joe Blakis; conversely, she seemed to tranquilize and domesticate the dirt-pawing bull in Sam. What thrilled her, closed the door to her troubles, and temporarily disconnected her general pessimism, was the obvious decency in both men— in most of the men she had ever chosen. Television—especially its ads—promoted sunglassed, slick-haired, chisel-chested, sullen pseudo-studs as the epitome of American masculinity, but any man who adopted that standard for himself had absolutely no interest for her. The large freckles mantling Joe's shoulders, his thinning hair, the ears that should have been flatter and closer to the head—these had become endearments. And with Sam it was the gap-toothed, playfully wicked, almost Mafioso-style grin; the thickening but not softening "handles" over each hip; the columned legs that barely narrowed at the ankles, legs so ample that his trousers whittled away the wiry hair on the front of his thighs, on the backs of his calves; the pungent but not repulsive sweat that always sheathed his shoulders and ribs soon after they began making love.

He held her softly now, as they stood before the bed, and kissed her eyelids, the bridge of her nose. Her breasts seemed to swell and her nipples hardened. When the lips traveled down her cheeks to her mouth, he pulled her closer so that, against her leg, she could feel the erection growing.

"Would you like another Manhattan first?" he whispered. "Or do you want to switch to your wine?"

"Another Manhattan," she answered, kissing his ear.

Another Manhattan, caution to the wind. It was what she wanted, needed, tonight: a carelessness that would be as safe with Sam as it had *not* been with Kevin. Bourbon,

Sam's body, Sam's very being, would blot out the note. At least for a time.

As usual, she went into the bathroom when room service rapped at the door, and came back out after the "Thank you, sir" and the exiting. Sam gave her a lopsided smile, and she answered it with "I know, I know. With a two-drink order, he has to figure there's someone else—"

"And with your coat on the chair."

"Nonetheless, I don't like looking at someone who's *presuming*—even if he's presuming correctly."

He bowed slightly. "The lady's prerogative."

They kissed, lingeringly; then he pulled away, carried their drinks to the high round table near the window, and sat down in the chair next to it. "Come here," he commanded softly, his arms outstretched. A rush of excitement passed through her as she moved toward him, about to do what she would be embarrassed to do with any man but him.

She sat on his lap, facing him, her legs curled under her.

He held her glass to her lips, tipped it so she could sip, put it down again. Within seconds the buttons of her sweater were deftly undone, the brassiere straps removed from her shoulders, one breast cupped in his hand and the nipple of the other trapped between his teeth and being teased by his tongue. She stroked his nape, and when his teeth parted and his jaws widened to pull in more of her flesh, her hand moved up to grip his hair in a fist.

In one fluid movement, without a groan or so much as a break in his breathing, he stood up with her in his arms, paused to suck her tongue in his mouth, then released it. "Say anything you want tonight, Ann. It's just between us." "Just between us," she knew, meant that she would not be held accountable for any words of affection, of need, she might utter. He carried her to the bed, lowered her onto it, lifted the glass once again to her mouth, then slowly completed the task of undressing her.

"Sam . . . oh, yes . . . oh, I love . . . you."

His strokes, as always, were smooth, deep, rhythmic: when she closed her eyes she imagined herself being carried over waves toward some isle of epiphany. After their arrival, she lay with her head on his shoulder and felt an undefinable reassurance from the mingling scents of his muted after-shave and her own hair.

"I wish," he said after a time, "someday you could come up to the house for a weekend. And bring your daughters. They'd love my aviary."

She would love his aviary, love to wake up to a country morning and eat strawberries for breakfast and watch the birds at the windowsill. But what an image, what fantasy, the makings of an idyllic ad—camera zooms past her and strawberries to focus on the latest high-fiber cereal next to the sun-splashed window. Good morning, America, how's your bulk, how's your regularity, how's— Stop, she told herself. Deprecating the scene was cheap and childish rebellion against the impossibility of her ever having it. Of course, she could find a way to get away from her "daughters" for a weekend, but two solid days with a man—even a man as good as Sam—opened the gates to impatience, silent criticism, disillusionment, mistrust. Fear. The old fear; fear that would take more time to overcome.

"That would be nice," she said. "But impossible."

"Just a wish," he answered reassuringly.

She waited, feeling, under her hand, his heartbeat returning to normal. "Sam, do I . . . does our situation keep you from having something you really want?"

"Like what?"

"A steady companion. Maybe a wife."

"No, not so far."

"I just don't want to cheat you."

"You aren't. And who knows, someday you might leave your husband."

"That's not likely."

"A lot of unlikely things happen to people. Here, turn over, I'll give you a massage."

"Don't you know that every girl's been warned about turning around for a Greek?"

With a laugh, he maneuvered her onto her belly. "Listen, when I was in college there was a girl who kept chasing me because she thought that was exactly what I *would* do." His hands went to work on the area between her neck and shoulders.

"And did you accommodate her?"

"I always try to accommodate a lady."

"Was she a lady?"

"Of course." His hands squeezed playfully. "Kappa Delta, like her mother."

Like her mother, *like* her mother, echoed his words to the rhythm of his hands, and memory served up the woman's face, often puffed from weeping, always haunted and wary. And her father's face, molded in a single expression that seemed to be fueled by an unwavering pilot light of rage.

She canceled them out by turning her own face from one cheek to the other on the mattress. And she gave herself up to this man who had perfect knowledge of her body, if not her mind.

Even the badly shock-absorbed ride in the taxi failed to undo the elixir of Sam's treatment. After six blocks she instructed the driver to pull over at a newsstand. She glided out, bought a *Daily News*, and glided back in.

Only when she handed him the money at the end of the trip did she feel a tremor of tension in her stomach. But it quickly passed as she closed the car door and spotted two well-dressed women, neighborhood women, standing some thirty feet away, talking and holding leashes with dogs at the ends of them. She hadn't noticed the taxi that had followed hers from the Hotel Hanson and passed by while she was paying her driver.

And as she climbed the front steps to the door, key in one hand and Mrs. Fleming's paper in the other, she didn't see the man who, for the past hour, had been sauntering up and down the other side of the street, keeping watch on her windows.

5

MAYHEW ADVERTISING WAS NOT AMONG THE LARGER
agencies, but it was solid and well recognized and sixty-
eight years old. Its accounts included home products, cos-
metics, pet foods, frozen foods, cereals, a coffee, baked
goods, soft drinks, remedies for wilted hair and weary feet,
neutralizers, naturalizers, and—most recently and thanks
to Fay—a line of paperback books called Stardust Sagas.
She had persuaded the publisher, a longtime acquaintance
of Curt Colby's and an avuncular admirer of hers, to let
Mayhew have an exclusive try at creating a television campaign for the new line of written-to-formula novels. Fay
read six of them, but the first two sufficed in giving her a
picture of their substance, or lack of it. Stardusty they were,
but by no means sagas, not according to Webster's defini-
tion. And one hardly needed Webster's at hand to read
them—fourth-grade skills would do. The heroines, inter-
changeable save for color of hair and eyes, were modern-
day "liberated" women plunked down in speciously

historical contexts, where they tamed their men and triumphed over poverty, parental rule, and prejudice; life-long love and wealth were signed, sealed, and delivered in the last chapter.

Fay knew, of course, that predictability was the main ingredient in selling this stuff, but the ad also had to offer transcendence, seductive mystery. After the client had enthusiastically approved Fay's storyboard, her boss, Jay Greene, granted her the final say in choosing the model. She insisted that this one must be truly different—exotic but not foreign, proud but with the slightest touch of latent guttersnipe. The videotapes were made, and the fourth young woman Fay looked at was chosen. The powers at Stardust were even more thrilled with the final product than they had been with the storyboard—"My God, where'd you find the girl? She's a young Joan Crawford and Maureen O'Hara rolled into one!"—and Jay Greene was thrilled to have the account firmly squared away in Mayhew's pocket. For the voice-over Fay purposely selected an elocution-school type, throaty yet feminine and of an indeterminate age. The ad ran:

FADE IN:

EXTERIOR—LONG-GRASSED HILL—SUNSET

Woman in long dress, free-flowing hair, climbs hill in profile.

OFF-CAMERA VOICE
This woman stands apart.

Cut to woman at top of hill looking out on lush valley below.

O.C. VOICE
She stands for independence, for passion . . .

Woman smiles faintly, almost smugly.

O.C. VOICE

. . . in a world you thought was gone forever.

Cut to woman's viewpoint: handsome man riding white horse at full speed up winding road in her direction.

O.C. VOICE

But that world can be yours again—it's alive, glowingly vivid, in every Stardust Saga.

Cut to extreme long shot of horse and rider galloping uphill toward the woman in profile.

O.C. VOICE

Stardust Sagas—where a woman's dreams become reality.

Cut to full-face close-up of woman. The man's face appears next to and behind hers. His hands grip her shoulders; he buries his face between her neck and shoulder. She responds with an upward tilt of the chin and an intimate, triumphant gaze into the camera.

O.C. VOICE

Stardust Sagas.

The logo writes itself at bottom of picture frame.

O.C. VOICE

Romance . . . *lower, huskier register* and so much more.

The ad was so successful that Stardust doubled its ad budget at Mayhew. In a matter of months Fay saw the sagas, in candy stores and news shops, usurp the shelf space from the earlier established romance paperbacks. Sometimes she felt the natural professional pride in her contribution to this boom; at other times she saw herself as a conspirator in launching a minor pestilence upon the reading public.

This most recent notch in her belt drew attention from other agencies, and she was courted anew, with one of them offering her twenty thousand more a year. Her refusal was polite, but she didn't volunteer the reason for it: since her beginning days as an assistant art director, the staff at Mayhew was the closest thing to a family she had ever experienced, Jay Greene and his wife, Nancy, regarding her as a kind of "genius" younger sister. When she got off the elevator every morning and passed through the reception area, she felt as if she had spent the night away from home. . . .

The morning after she saw Sam, she went directly to the shooting studio on Eleventh Avenue. Near the entrance a young black woman was half slumped against the wall, her eyes glazed, hair tangled, her thin cloth jacket cruelly inadequate against the saw-toothed wind off the Hudson River.

"Got a cigarette, miss?" The question came out between bloated, cracked lips.

"I don't smoke."

The woman nodded forlornly and looked away. It was less her appearance than her resignation that made Fay shiver. The change from her taxi ride was in her coat pocket, and when she withdrew it and held it out the woman looked disbelievingly at the four bills.

"Take it," Fay said impatiently.

She did. "Thanks. Honey, lemme tell you sump'n—"

"I'm late."

"Jes one thing. Stay away from men. Mine did this to me." She lifted her lip to reveal the naked gum—it looked like a red and purple picket fence. "Kep' on hittin' and hittin' till he knocked ever' one of 'em out."

Yes, Fay said silently and furiously, and *who* let him do it? Sickened, she reached blindly for the door handle and yanked it open with more force than was necessary.

The commercial they were shooting today was for MenthaRub, a liniment for aching muscles and joints. In making the presentation to this client, Fay had had to summon every means of persuasion to get the storyboard approved. The three men winced, frowned, grimaced, as she outlined the scenario of a young boy applying the product to his grandfather's shoulders after a backyard game of catch. "Sounds pervy to me," said one. "Some old goat grinning while the kid's rubbing him." "How're we supposed to show Gramps's bare shoulder without having him naked to the waist?" asked another.

Cynics and idiots, she thought, but she responded serenely, "My feeling is that we should deflect the emphasis from the clinical. The viewer has had it up to here with charts, illustrations, testaments from pharmacists—it's ho-hum time. We need to humanize the product, or rather the situation in which the product is used. In the first and last shot the man and boy are playing catch—that means the man is doing a favor for the boy in taking the time to help him improve a skill. Now, if you have the man apply the product to himself, you'll sacrifice a good emotional potential, that being a display of reciprocity. The suggestion is, each does something for the other—and the scene underscores the point that MenthaRub is doing something for the man—a thing that allows him to help the boy. Full circle. MenthaRub not only brings relief, but also allows you to do a good deed."

One man's face brightened with inspiration: "The boy can look on while the *grandmother* rubs the man's shoulders." Fay thought quickly and replied, "Terrific idea to include a grandmother, but let's have *her* do the looking-on in the far background, pleased by what she's seeing because—"

And so it went until she had them firmly convinced.

Because of the winter weather, playing catch was changed to building a snowman. Today, in the Eleventh Avenue studio, the interior shots would be done; the exterior shots had been completed the day before in New Jersey.

"I saw the rushes last night," she was told by Jim DeLuca, Mayhew's producer. "They're just fine."

In mock horror she widened her eyes and put a hand to her cheek. "What! Not 'great'?"

They exchanged grins. In a business where superlatives were cheapened through overuse, DeLuca was the rare person who never spoke them. His restraint and quiet humor impressed Fay as much as his work did.

With a twinge of apprehension she asked, "And how's the boy look?"

"Very good. Cute but not too cute."

She was relieved, but only until DeLuca spoke again.

"But this morning he looks like he just crossed Siberia. I'll bet he didn't sleep a wink last night, and his face shows it."

A sleepless night was very likely: the boy's bitch of a mother. "Does Edna have him made up yet?

"Yes, but the only remedy for listless eyes is sunglasses."

"That bad?"

"It's no catastrophe, but he's definitely not the perky kid he was yesterday."

"All right." She shed her coat and dropped it onto a chair. "Where is he?"

"Second dressing room."

Together they left the reception area and entered a long corridor that terminated at the studio door. On either side were dressing rooms, restrooms, rooms where film was developed, spliced, projected. DeLuca continued on his way as Fay turned in at the room where Edna was rehearsing lines with the boy.

"Good morning, Edna. Morning, Alan."

"Morning, Miss Colby," returned Alan in a tone he might have used with an awesome teacher.

Edna, middle-aged and a matter-of-fact master of her craft, had worked often enough with Fay for the two of them to communicate without speaking; the glance they shared indicated their mutual recognition of the problem at hand.

"I have some touching up to do on Roger's eyes," Edna said, and made her exit.

Fay looked down at the boy in the chair; he was studying today's script. Suddenly, his jaw shifted and his upper lip twitched in an effort to stifle a yawn. "Was I all right yesterday? Did you see the rushes?"

"I didn't, but Mr. DeLuca did, and he says you were just fine."

"But today's the hard part, isn't it?"

"Yes, interiors are usually harder—for us, but it shouldn't be any harder for you." She paused while he buried another yawn. "Tired? Didn't you sleep well last night?"

"I kept waking up. The pill didn't work."

"What pill?"

"The sleeping pill. My mother gave me half of one." Her face must have betrayed something, for he hastily said, "It's not barbiturate; it's safe. I think she just gave it to me too early, but she wanted me to sleep for ten hours. But I kept waking up, and now I feel groggy."

She looked into the young all-American face, which was slightly freckled, slightly precocious, and, now, overlaid with adult concern. How many nine-year-olds, she wondered, knew how to pronounce "barbiturate"?

He got up from his chair and went to the mirror. "I don't look so good, do I? I could tell Mrs. Tarpoff was worried when she was putting on the makeup."

Fay's pity for the boy, her rage at his mother, left her momentarily speechless.

The day of the videotape auditions, the reception area at Mayhew had been an anthill of little boys and their mothers. Passing through the area upon her return from lunch, Fay had heard a woman's voice shrilling just above a stage whisper: "We've been to four auditions in the last week and a half, and you haven't got a bit of work. You're as good-looking as any of them, so it's got to be your attitude. Now look sharp and smile—your smile is your ticket. It's the *one* thing your father gave you." Fay had stopped and glanced over at the woman, who would have been attractive if not for the hard eyes and harder mouth. And then she had looked at the boy. He had been folding, unfolding, refolding, a small wad of paper, his body angled away from the mother as a silent statement that he wanted no identification with her: Fay had had the same feeling about her own father enough times over the years not to misread it in the boy. Then, seeing the attention Fay was giving them, the mother had muttered at her son, "Sit up straight." Moving on to her office, Fay had found herself hoping that the boy's performance on the tape would qualify him for serious consideration.

And once he was chosen, Fay had politely banned his mother from the shootings, explaining to her that this was her policy. Fay had sensed that the woman was miffed but would never show it, so eager was she for her son to be bringing home the bacon....

A sleeping pill, thought Fay, and most likely a list of instructions and a final warning as he was delivered to the studio.

"They can always change their minds today, can't they?" Alan said to his reflection in the mirror. "It happened to me before when I did oatmeal—they didn't like me in the close-up, so they got someone else."

She wanted to soothe but not coddle him. "It does happen sometimes, even to adults, but that doesn't mean they won't work again."

"Yes, it does. My mother has a friend, and her daughter can't get—" All at once his shoulders began to twitch and his head tipped forward and to the left. Fay's muscles went rigid as she watched him cry uncontrollably yet noiselessly. The revulsion she felt in the face of this kind of misery dredged up her own fears and hatreds: she wanted to grip Alan's shoulders and tell him that one job wasn't worth it, drugged yet sleepless nights weren't worth it, even his mother wasn't worth it.

"Alan." She was surprised by the tininess of her voice.

His shoulders continued to shake. She started toward him, then checked herself; perhaps even at nine he had already developed that hard masculine pride that disparages feminine comforting. "Alan, you're going to do all right today. I'm going to leave you alone for ten minutes and then I'll be back. You won't be disturbed by anyone."

"You won't tell—" was all he could manage.

"No one." With that, she left him.

She moved quickly, down the corridor to the studio. Good—they were still setting up lights and marking the floor for the actors' positions. Then on to the first makeup room. "Edna, I'll need you in about twenty minutes." Fay saw the look of concern in the woman's eyes and motioned with her hand that all would be well. On to the receptionist, who informed her that delivery from the nearby delicatessen took longer than going out for oneself. So Fay threw on her coat and pushed open the door to the sidewalk. The black woman now lay on the concrete, muttering incomprehensibly, her body spasming from shoulders to knees. Fay reopened the door and told the receptionist to call the police, then turned and ran down the avenue toward Fifty-fourth Street.

The woman was gone by the time she came back with the Coke and two large cups of chipped ice. Good. In this neighborhood, the cops were never far away. She knocked on the door of the second dressing room, waited for Alan's response, and went in. He was sitting with his hands tucked between his knees, his eyes red and swollen and filled with shame. Countering his mood, she said breezily, "Here's a Coke, but drink it slowly—you wouldn't want to burp during the shooting." After allowing him a few sips, she instructed him to die down on the divan. "Ever had eye drops?"

"Sure."

She applied them, then wrapped two handfuls of the chipped ice in paper towels and laid them over his eyelids.

What to say to him? Her mind was full of trivial questions she could have asked, but she knew better than to talk down to a child in distress. "Relax," she said. "We've got plenty of time. Plenty of time." Pause. "Who cuts your hair?"

"My mother."

"She does a good job."

"It takes hours. I think she cuts one hair at a time."

"Does she cut your father's too?"

"My father's dead."

"Oh. I'm sorry."

"He drank a lot. And took pills. He drove his van over a guardrail in California. He burned to death. He didn't leave any insurance, so we couldn't go to the funeral."

One simple question, thought Fay, and out comes this grisly flow. "Burned to death": why couldn't the mother have said that the boy's father died instantly? "Couldn't go to the funeral": her father hadn't allowed her to go to her mother's.

For the boy's momentary well-being, she thought it best to terminate these confidences. Perhaps for her own well-being too. She herself, who had dreams of falling, did not like to imagine Alan dreaming of burning.

She wiped away the dampness from his eyes when Edna came in. At once the boy apologized.

"It's all right, honey. You actors do retakes and I do reapplications. It's all the same game."

The blocking of positions, the rehearsal, the shooting itself, proceeded without undue difficulty after a burned-out light was replaced. During the rehearsal Fay made sure that she stayed within Alan's view after one glance of supplication from him; during the shooting she stood just behind and to the right of one camera and watched him give a more than adequate performance.

His mother showed up at four o'clock and in the reception room instructed him to say good-bye to Mr. DeLuca and Miss Colby and to say how much he enjoyed working with

them. In rote, he delivered what he was told to; but before
he left Fay he paused, looked briefly at her face, then lowered his gaze to the level of her forearm and added, "I wish
you were my aunt or my cousin or *something*." She wanted
to say, "Maybe we'll be working together again soon," but
she couldn't return an unlikelihood for his sincerity.

"Thank you, Alan," she answered.

She could have gone directly home after the shooting,
but did not. There being no plans for the evening, why start
it early? A taxi delivered her to Mayhew, where she had a
brief conference with Josie, an account executive, about the
print layout for a hair relaxer. Josie was right when she said
that an exhaustive discussion of the problem could wait until
tomorrow: she and her husband had theater tickets, and they
wanted a leisurely dinner before the show.

At five–forty-five Fay closed her office door against the
last voices making their exodus to the elevator. For twenty
minutes she stared at the print ad on her desk, but her
thoughts were worlds away from hair beautification.

Fay Colby, Vice-President, Creative Director. But she
could not create a new life for herself, much less one for
Alan.

She could not rid herself of his face, which led her to
aligning his mother's image with her own father's. She tried
focusing on Joe, Sam, Andrew; but Kevin and his note
appeared, blurring all else into the background.

She stuck the ad into her briefcase and left.

Taxis were scarce on Third Avenue, and she was too
involved in trying to find one to notice the man watching
her from the bus stop a few feet away. He was not exactly
conspicious, and his eyes could easily dart away before hers
turned in his direction.

"Good evening," the driver said cheerily.

Was she hearing right? The driver who took her to the

studio this morning had said, "Where to, babe?" and then managed to hit every pothole getting there.

"Uh, good evening. Seventy-fourth and Madison."

His radio was softly playing classical music, and he maneuvered the car with ease and caution. The heater worked beautifully, quickly taking the chill out of her legs. Six blocks from her destination she said, "Let's change that. Go through the park and just drive around for a while."

He looked into the rearview mirror, his eyes as suspicious as his voice. "Drive around?"

"I'm not dangerous, and I can pay. Here, I'll give you a twenty right now for security."

He took it.

She settled back into the corner of the seat, warm, snug, the most relaxed she had been all day. For a few minutes she enjoyed the fantasy that her father and Kevin had moved out of town and out of her life.

6

COLBY APPEARED AT NINE A.M. SHARP, LOOKING GEN-
erally dapper but a bit haggard around the eyes. O'Brien
disliked the man; perhaps one of the things that put him off
was Colby's too perfect appearance. It was something off
the page of a magazine: gray pinstripe suit, size forty, the
jacket descending in uninterrupted vertical lines from his
squared shoulders; the red-flecked navy-blue tie knotted in
a way that would have taken O'Brien himself half the morning to accomplish; shoes polished and buffed to a subtle
luster that only the best leather can provide. The dark brown
hair would never look just-cut—the guy probably had it
barbered every week. O'Brien presumed that Colby cashed
in on his good looks whenever possible; presumed further
that he generally succeeded. He wondered if Colby ever
ruffled those looks, if he allowed himself to sweat during
sex. His beautiful daughter lacked not only a physical resemblance to him but also, it seemed, his buttoned-up vanity.
Just the night before last, while she was trying to hail a

cab, he saw that she had not bothered to comb the drooping hair that signaled a taxing day.

O'Brien began his report, and, at once, the haggardness lifted from Colby's eyes, replaced by an anticipatory glitter.

"Tuesday night your daughter met a man in the lounge of the Hotel Hanson on Thirty-eighth Street. After a drink she went to his room, where she remained for nearly two hours. Then—"

"Are you certain she went to his room? Perhaps there's another lounge on an upper floor."

"There's no other lounge. My assistant was in the lobby, and he watched them get into the elevator alone. He noted that the elevator stopped on the seventh floor and then returned to the first. The man was registered in seven-twelve."

"How do you know that?"

O'Brien overlooked the challenge in Colby's tone. "Room service. They ordered drinks. She had a Manhattan in the lounge, and that was one of the drinks taken to the room."

"How did you find that out?"

"The usual way. By bribing. Generously."

Colby appeared to stifle a wince.

"Of course," O'Brien continued, "it doesn't always work. And it can be dangerous to make an offer to the wrong person, a person who can blow your cover. I'll elaborate in a moment. When your daughter left the hotel she stopped at a newsstand, then went directly home. The man she met was registered under the name of Sam Telias. Hartford, Connecticut. I can check out his address and place of employment if you want."

"That won't be necessary," Colby answered crisply, as if the suggestion were insulting.

"The next day she didn't leave Mayhew to go to lunch, and that evening she left work late, at six-forty. She took a taxi uptown and through Central Park, but as soon as it reached the West Side the route became a random zigzag. Although I doubt she suspected being allowed, I dropped behind. I went to Seventy-fourth Street, waited half an hour, and she returned. In the same taxi. My assistant took over for me at eight o'clock. He reports that she didn't go out again and her lights were turned off at eleven-ten."

"You say she returned in the same taxi after half an hour. That would suggest some kind of errand, wouldn't it?"

"Maybe." Possibly a drug pickup, thought O'Brien. This Telias from Hartford could be a pusher, ditto the Colby girl. Was this Colby's real suspicion, he wondered, and the motive for having her watched? But Colby's face revealed nothing except an eagerness to get on with the report.

"Yesterday at twelve-fifteen she didn't go to lunch—she walked over to Fifth and took a taxi down to Eighth Street. She went into number Two Fifth Avenue and stayed fifty-five minutes, then walked to University Place, picked up a sandwich at a deli, and took the Lexington Avenue subway from Astor Place to Fifty-first."

"Subway?" This seemed to scandalize Colby more than any other information in the report.

"From Fifty-first she returned to her office. Last night she didn't leave her apartment. Now, about this business of buying information—the building she went to on lower Fifth Avenue is a high-rise with an excellent security system. I've had experience with the place before. Expensive as the rents are, there's a very low turnover rate of tenants. Every visitor is announced by the doorman and then is given a slip of paper with his or her name on it, the time, and the number of the apartment being visited. And then the visitor turns the paper over to the elevator man. While I waited for your daughter to come out, I watched the doorman from across the street. During that time several tenants came and went, and he was very chatty with some of them. One woman was returning from the supermarket and bought him a small package of something, which he paid her for. Now, if a tenant is doing an errand for the doorman, I suspect he's on excellent and faithful terms with just about everyone.

In short, I doubt very much he could take a bribe, but I'm sure he'd report the offer to the person your daughter went to see—who in turn would tell your daughter."

Colby nodded. "I believe that building also has professional apartments. Doctors, dentists."

"Yes. Then you've been there too?"

"No. I just know someone who used to live there." He knew someone who still lived there—a literary agent, who had converted her second bedroom into an office. "Perhaps her doctor or dentist is in the building. Or one of Mayhew's clients—she's told me that the ones from out of town often keep apartments here."

"That could be," O'Brien agreed convincingly.

Colby reached inside his pocket and laid the bills, most of them fifties, in front of O'Brien. "Let's continue on for another week. In fact, I'd like to take it week by week, if that's all right with you."

"It's quite all right. Uh, from the information I've given you there's still nothing in particular you want me to look for?"

"No, nothing." Colby paused and looked down at the pair of kid leather gloves that he was squeezing with both hands. "My reasons for having my daughter followed are personal—and not very interesting." He stood and walked to the door, then turned. "I'm very satisfied with your work thus far. And with your judgment in not approaching the doorman. Good-bye."

Left alone, O'Brien paused to smile at the thought of his own vanity. For despite his dislike of Colby, the man's praise had pleased him.

On Saturday O'Brien followed her to a supermarket, a dry cleaner's, a flower shop; Saturday night she had dinner and saw a play with a woman, a blonde about her own age who appeared to be a close friend, judging from their facial expressions during conversation. On Sunday she took a very long walk, through Central Park to the West Side and back again. The only detail worth noting was her stop on East Sixty-sixth Street: for nearly five minutes she stood on the sidewalk and stared at the building on the opposite side. As she did so, the angle of her profile suggested that her gaze was trained upon one apartment in particular.

By Monday he had decided that this case would most likely turn out to be a rather dull one. But by early that evening his opinion was more than slightly altered.

It was snowing when she left Mayhew at four-forty and started south on Third Avenue. O'Brien's legs were still a bit weary from following her across town the day before; nonetheless, he was grateful to be traveling by foot. It was simpler than scrambling for a taxi and then trying to keep hers in sight, less chancy than getting on and off a subway when she did.

She led him to an apartment building on Thirty-fifth Street, where the doorman nodded in recognition. When she disappeared inside, O'Brien watched the doorman for the next hour as the just-getting-home-from-work inhabitants entered the lobby. There was a measure of congeniality between them and the man in uniform—but not the warmth he had seen at the building on Fifth Avenue, whose doorman was easily in his late fifties and could be a proud long-term holder of his position. This man across the street was no more than thirty, Hispanic, poorly postured, and quite aloof when he opened the door for some—probably those who hadn't been generous at Christmastime. O'Brien decided that an offer of money was worth the chance.

From the coffee shop on the corner, where he could keep watch on the lobby, he phoned his assistant and told him to come at once.

The two of them sat in a booth next to the window and ordered dinners. When Les Beckhorn's once-a-week treat of corned beef and sauerkraut was delivered, he cupped his hands around the plate, inclined his head a few inches toward it, and inhaled deeply several times.

"Mother of Jesus, this must be what heaven smells like. And up there, you must be able to eat as much as you want without your stomach ripping you apart all night."

Beckhorn's stomach was an ex-policeman's cliché, riddled with ulcers, and the plumbing below it was subject to severe bouts of colitis. After twenty years with the Jersey City force he had retired to what he called vacation work. But still his digestion refused to improve, and it seemed that a thoroughly bland and nondrinking diet was to be his lasting reward for having once taken a bullet in the left shoulder, for having had three teeth knocked out with a piece of pipe, for having breathed the heavy air of hopelessness generated in ugly industrial towns, tolerant of violence. At fifty-two, ten years older than O'Brien, Beckhorn knew that even total retirement was unlikely to change his health, and so he continued working to contribute toward his youngest daughter's tuition at Vassar. O'Brien valued the man's dependability and proficiency—and his humor. Beckhorn made his stomach a joke, although it was the source of his wan complexion, the straitened smile, the alternating anger and sadness to be read in the eyes of one who knows that physical well-being is gone for good. But his appearance was so carefully attended to that the man in the morning mirror had to possess a fair amount of day-to-day optimism.

"Edith's going to have a nice boiled chicken waiting for me," said Beckhorn with sarcastic cheerfulness. "Dullicious."

"And what will Edith have for herself?"

"The same. She eats the good stuff for lunch, except when I'm around. Waits till I go to bed to have her snack. Can't ask a wife to do much more than that."

"No, you can't." Although O'Brien liked Edith enormously, he didn't like the subject of wives in general. It brought unwanted and enervating thoughts about his own.

Beckhorn sipped from his glass of milk and looked out the window. "You followed her here from work?"

"Yeah. You'll tail her when she comes out. I'm going to try my luck with the doorman."

Beckhorn's eyes narrowed slightly, professionally. "Right, he looks like he'd welcome a few extra pesos. Look at him—snapping his fingers and tapping his foot. Only thing between the ears is rhythm."

At six-forty the counterman began putting chairs up on tables, cueing the stragglers to make an exit. O'Brien and Beckhorn left, and stood talking in the tapering snowfall, neither one allowing his gaze to shift from the lobby across the street.

"She could stay in there quite a while."

"She could," O'Brien agreed, "but I'm riding the hunch she won't stay much longer than she did with that guy in the hotel."

"What about Fifth Avenue?" said Beckhorn. "Was that a short visit too?"

"It was the middle of the day. She was on her lunch hour. Anyway, we'll see."

"You think she's dealing?"

"Good possibility. Nice extra income. She could be supplying the place she works at."

"Ummm. I wonder how much her old man really knows or suspects."

"Hard to say. Drug dealing would shock him, but I get the feeling he's more interested in the status of her sexual virtue."

"Oh?"

"It's just a feeling."

"Maybe she's hooking."

"Maybe. With her looks, she could get top price. Combine that with her legit income and she can retire in ten years."

"She ever been married?"

"Colby didn't say. Just said she was single." O'Brien lighted a cigarette. "She *is* strange."

"Strange interesting?"

"We'll see. There's something . . . guarded about her. Her face, the way she walks."

"Guarded like she's on to us?"

"No, not that."

"Well, if you're a woman in this city you have to—"

"Hold it. That's her."

At once, Beckhorn hailed a taxi from Third Avenue, signaling it to turn onto Thirty-fifth. He got in and instructed the driver to wait. O'Brien leaned down at the open window and together they watched the Colby woman try to get a taxi for herself. Beckhorn sighed and said, "Earl, why don't we go to work in L.A., where we can enjoy the comfort of our own cars."

"You watch too much television."

Fay Colby was opening the door of the taxi that had stopped for her.

"Driver," said Beckhorn, "there's ten bucks for you if you can follow that cab without their knowing it."

"Fifteen, and they won't know *nothin'*."

Beckhorn groaned his assent. "Let's go."

O'Brien waited until both taxis disappeared. Then, fingering the bills in the pocket he called petty cash, he crossed the street and headed for the doorman, who was cleaning his nails with a toothpick.

By eight-thirty, O'Brien, in his robe and slippers, had settled back into his recliner with a drink—a glass of beer spiked with a shot of vodka. The television was on, a half-finished paperback and three unread magazines at hand, but he only nursed the drink in celebration of his success.

Joe Blakis, librarian, Fifth Avenue branch. "Mrs. Decker" comes to see him every other week. Days vary, but the time rarely does—usually around five o'clock.

The doorman had given value for the money.

Mrs. Decker. If she was hooking, why bother with a *married* alias. But a coke dealer might want to—what? Improve her credentials with a "Mrs."? Strike a note of respectability in a disreputable business?

He thought about what he had said to Beckhorn earlier, that the woman was strange and guarded. Guarded, indeed— evidence this left-field alias. But was she dangerous too?

This became a disquieting consideration as time passed and Beckhorn had yet to report back. "Guarded like she's on to us?" Les had asked. Had she known she was being tailed and purposely led Beckhorn into a trap, to some desolate spot by the river where some drug thugs could leisurely work him over? That very thing had happened to *him* when he was a detective with the sixth precinct.

His celebration was now soured by his apprehension over Beckhorn's delay. And when the phone sounded he picked it up before the first ring ended.

"Earl? My, that was quick."

"Hello, Joy." Christ, it *would* be her, of all nights. But she always did have perfect bad timing. "Listen, I'm expecting an important call."

"I won't keep you. I just wanted to tell you that my folks are coming to town this weekend and they'd like to have dinner with the two of us. I thought—"

"I can't this weekend."

"Can't or won't?"

"Can't. I'm busy."

"You were busy the last time they came."

"Yes, well..."

"I'm beginning to see the advantage of working unconventional hours. It gives you plenty of excuses."

"Joy, the call I'm waiting for is very important."

"All right, all right. But they'll be disappointed, especially Mother."

"I'm sorry."

"Shall I tell them you said so?"

"Yes."

"You know, Earl, just because we're divorced doesn't mean we can't be friendly. This is the eighties, you know—and I *do* refer to the nineteen-eighties."

"Let's talk about it another time."

"Fine. Give me a call when you're not so busy. And afraid." She hung up.

He sat quaking with anger. How he could allow himself still to be affected by her was beyond all reason. But he was spared a lengthy deliberation over the question by Beckhorn's call.

"Our little girl sparked some fireworks tonight. Got her face slapped on a street corner."

O'Brien leaned forward in the chair as if this would bring him closer to Beckhorn.

"There was a guy waiting for her when she got out of the cab at her place. I continued on to the corner, then walked up the other side of the street. The guy was yelling, and she kept trying to shush him. She went to a bar with him and they had this tense tête-à-tête in a corner. Then she flounced out and he followed and gave her a smack. And get this—she told him her *husband* would break his legs. He said he wasn't afraid of her husband *if* she had one. But he let her go home by herself. He took the subway to Union Square. We're at the Cedar Tavern on University Place. He's getting smashed at the bar and I'm at a table by the window. Earl, my stomach's crying out for my boiled chicken, and this artsy place won't give it to me. Come save a dying man."

"Twenty minutes."

"She called him Kevin. He's blond, well-built, tanned, about thirty."

"Got it, Les."

"If he leaves, I'll stick with him and then meet you back here."

"If this beach boy takes you out on another stroll, Edith will have my head on a platter," said O'Brien.

"As long as she doesn't serve it to *me*."

O'Brien was dressed and out of his West Sixteenth Street apartment in eight minutes. When he entered the Cedar Tavern, he exchanged a brief glance with is assistant; Beckhorn made a small nod in the direction of the target.

After Beckhorn left, the blond man had three more vodka sours before scooping up his change from the bar. He walked west on Tenth Street, weaving when he had to circumvent a couple talking in the middle of the sidewalk. O'Brien trailed a discreet twenty yards, although, given the man's condition, he would have been safe at five. Their journey ended at Perry Street, where O'Brien quickened his pace as soon as the man turned in to the lobby of his building. The fumbling, dropping, retrieving of keys gave O'Brien a choice opportunity: by the time he arrived for a view of the lobby, he saw the hands working impatiently at removing the jammed-in contents from a typically inadequate mail-box. Top row, second from the end. O'Brien walked around the block and came back.

The name on the box was K. Ivory, and O'Brien quickly matched it up with the one next to the bell for apartment 5G.

Walking home up Seventh Avenue, he couldn't account for his confused feelings about Colby's daughter—there was no reason he should have any feelings at all. He was doing what he was paid to do, what he enjoyed doing—the tracking, the coming up with answers. It was the report-ing that he often failed to enjoy, and his lovely quarry had given him an evening of messy information to report to her father. The Hotel Hanson, the lunch-hour visit to Two Fifth Avenue, and now two men in one night. She certainly got around. The way his ex-wife did. Ah yes, there it was.

The instant Fay entered the hallway after leaving Kevin, she knew he had done something he hadn't told her about. Seeing Mrs. Fleming's door open sent a needle of panic into her chest, and when the woman called out her name in a tone Fay had never before heard her use, she felt a wave of shame that at that moment made her want to erase her very life.

She stood in the doorway and heard the volume being lowered on the television, then saw Mrs. Fleming advancing with as yet unfocused censure in her face. "Fay, there was a man here a while ago."

"I think I can guess who it was," she answered as calmly as she could. "Was he ... nasty to you?"

"It wasn't so much that as what he said. About you."

"I can imagine. I've just spent half an hour warning him that if he ever comes around here again I'll have the police after him." Mrs. Fleming said nothing, and waited. "What *did* he say?"

Watching Fay's eyes for a reaction, she recounted the man's accusations and concluded, "He said you told him you were married. He said you had a ... a 'stable,' and you use the name Ann Decker. Is any of this true?"

"No. He's deranged. He's angry because I won't see him."

"Have you slept with him?" the woman asked flatly.

"I—yes. I was seeing him and then I broke it off. He's gone wild. He's been saying the craziest things; he just makes things up."

"In all of our talks you never mentioned him."

"I know. I guess because I hadn't made up my mind about him."

"Times have changed. In my day, *if* you slept with a man who wasn't your husband, it was just before you married him. But I guess the world was simpler then."

"I'm sorry he involved you in this. He won't do it again, I promise you."

Mrs. Fleming nodded. "The next time you meet a man, get to know him a little better before you get so . . . carried away."

As soon as Fay was inside her apartment she began to tremble with the onset of delayed shock. The invasion of one side of her life into the other had come at last, just as Dr. Maxson had warned her it would, and Kevin was the enemy general. The slap on her face was nothing compared to the poison he had put in Mrs. Fleming's mind. Poison that was truth, truth he had only guessed at—but correctly. At this moment she wanted him dead.

She drew her bath. Watching the water ripple, she recalled the half-hour or so she and Joe had spent together in front of his fish tank earlier this evening, their customary bottle of wine in an ice bucket between them. But now even the memory of that was sullied.

The bath did not soothe her.

About the time Earl O'Brien was heading for the Cedar Tavern to relieve Beckhorn, Fay picked up the phone and dialed Maxson's number. Her service took the message: "This is Fay Colby. Ask her to call my office first thing in the morning. Please tell her it's urgent."

7

To O'Brien, Curt Colby looked more haggard than he had four days ago. Haggard and haunted. Keeping his manner coolly businesslike, O'Brien concealed the hawkish attention he was paying to Colby's reactions.

"Your daughter has a lot of energy and is in very good shape. She did a variety of errands on Saturday, and on Sunday she took a two-hour walk to the West Side and back again. One note of interest there. She stood on East Sixty-sixth Street for several minutes and stared at the building across the way. It seemed to me she was looking at one apartment in particular." He gave the address and asked, "Do you know anyone in that building she might know?"

"No one."

He was lying, O'Brien could tell at once. Colby's eyes came to life at "East Sixty-sixth" and turned away at "one apartment in particular"; he made no attempt to learn the exact address, because he already knew it.

"Yesterday—rather, last night—she visited one man and

had an encounter with another. She went directly from work to East Thirty-fifth—" O'Brien told all that he and Beckhorn had seen and supplied the two men's names and addresses. It was apparent that Colby recognized neither. The only reaction he gave during the account was a quick involuntary parting of the lips when he heard the alias Mrs. Ann Decker.

"Mrs.?"

"Yes. I asked the doorman if he was sure about that. He was very sure. And during her spat with Kevin Ivory she threatened him by saying her husband would break his legs." O'Brien thought he saw panic race across the man's eyes, and the long silence that ensued seemed to confirm the impression. "I hope this information will help you to know your daughter better."

In this Colby heard a finality and protested. "I don't want you to quit just yet. I'd like you to stay with her for another week or two. Perhaps she has other . . . acquaintances."

When Colby left, it was not for Dowd & Dunay; instead, he hailed a taxi and headed home. Two fingers of whiskey, neat, would slow down his heart and blood, which had begun racing minutes ago. "Ann" was Fay's middle name, "Decker" her mother's maiden name, the "Mrs." a demented flourish.

Two weeks ago Claire had told him, "You're going through some kind of déjà vu." What unknowing accuracy, except that he was not merely "going through" it—it was being paraded before him in O'Brien's reports. Fay possessed a string of men, just as her mother had. But she could not be duplicating her mother's behavior by imitation, for he and Claire had kept her ignorant of it—and of the other things as well. Yet O'Brien recounted Fay's pausing on Sixty-sixth Street and seeming to look at "one apartment in particular." Indeed. The apartment they lived in when

Rosemary died—at twenty-nine: Fay's own age in a matter of days.

Had all these elements been tossed into a manuscript and placed on his desk, he would have derisively chuckled them away. This, however, was no manuscript. This was the past being exhumed, a past he despised for all its humiliations.

In the lobby he met Sheila, who was on her way out.

"Curt? Are you all right?"

Were his thoughts so apparent in his face?

"I got to the office and found I'd left some material here. I think I'll just work at home today."

"You look feverish. I could come up and make you some tea."

He pressed her hand. "No, you go on. I have to start working right away. Is Claire in?"

"She's gone to the new exhibition at the Metropolitan. She just left."

He calculated that his sister would be out for at least a couple of hours.

"I have some shopping to do and then bridge, if you're sure there's nothing I can help out with. I'll be back around four."

Inside the apartment he went straight to the bar, poured his whiskey and drank it, then stood at the French doors in the dining room and looked out at the roof garden. The potted evergreens, plump with health, were stationed evenly along the wall like sentries to ward off the city below. But it was the wall itself that commanded his attention: chest-high and a forearm-thick, it reassured him that going over the edge would never be quick and simple.

He turned, walked to the kitchen and down the short hallway to his private office. Behind the louvered door of a wall cabinet was a compartment whose contents Claire knew about (and disapproved of) and Sheila did not. He took out his key ring and opened the punch-button lock.

The mementos were stacked neatly, the way he had left

them the last time he looked into the compartment. His hand approached them, then hesitated. They were sacred or lethal, or both.

Sitting at his desk he began the all-too-familiar review. The first item was an eight-by-ten photograph of him, Claire, and Claire's husband gathered around the baby grand piano Rosemary was seated at; she was looking at the sheet music, and the three of them were looking at Rosemary. Naturally. Wherever Rosemary had happened to be, she was the center of everyone's attention. And if a man was weak and addicted like Curt himself, she would be the center of his existence. She looked so much like Fay that the information O'Brien had supplied began to revolve in his head. Joe Blakis, Sam Telias, Kevin Ivory.

He flipped the picture over and several others with it to arrive at four newspaper clippings, in various stages of yellowing, that reported her death. The then popular now defunct *Journal* had made it a page-one headline:

10-STORY PLUNGE TO DEATH
WOMAN LEAPS FROM EAST SIDE BALCONY

The last clipping terminated public scrutiny and hopes for something more sensational:

COLBY INQUEST RULES SUICIDE

This material put aside, he was confronted with the worst remembrance of their life together, and he got up to get another drink. Instead of pouring one, he filled a glass with ice, picked up the bottle, and carried both back to the office. After two long swallows he sat down to face the notes to Rosemary from her admirers.

* * *

Claire came home early, having found the museum full of rowdy day-tripping teenagers whose teachers could barely control them.

She went to the kitchen to make coffee and heard a ragged noise alien to this time of day. Down the little hallway she walked; quietly she turned the knob and cracked open the door. Her brother lay on the daybed snoring, tie still knotted, shoes still on. Formality even in repose. Had he come home ill?

Then she saw the glass and its copper-colored contents, the bottle next to it. She opened the door farther until the other side of the desk and the mementos came into view. Inside her a shiver of fear collided with a wave of sadness. Something had set him off.

Those damned things, she thought. If only she had the courage to dump them into the incinerator. But then, the memories would not go with them.

Without warning, tears filled her eyes and blurred the pathetic scene. Curt and Rosemary: for a time, her own world, their friends' worlds, had orbited around those two. They had been sought after, revered, resented. Their passion for each other had been envied, and no one, least of all Curt and Rosemary, had dreamed that that passion was spinning the web of their undoing. A single indiscretion and the battle was on to the finish.

If only Rosemary had left him a broken man—that would have been a blessing. But she had left him a twisted one.

Claire held her breath as he stirred, frowned, and rolled onto his side. Whenever she compared the man he was now with the man he had been, she told herself she was merely observing, not condemning. Because in regard to Rosemary's death, she was almost as guilty as he.

*   *   *

A few minutes before Claire arrived home to find her sleeping brother, Fay entered Dr. Maxson's office, grateful to have been given an appointment on such short notice.

"A matter of luck. I had a cancellation shortly before your call last night." She stood up from her desk, nodded in the direction of the couch, then walked around it to take her station in the chair behind. As always, Fay made special note of the woman's attire, because it was soothing, seemingly chosen to calm the observer as well as to enhance her own attractiveness. Today she was all in the softest gray—cashmere sweater, straight skirt, open-toed suede heels. Funny, thought Fay, how people disliked gray skies; in clothing, the color was so comforting.

Knowing that a single session provided so little time for all she had to say, she began: "Kevin has threatened me again," and blurted out all the ugly details. "I was so ashamed with Mrs. Fleming. I'm ashamed *now*." She stopped, in tears.

"You mean with me?"

"Yes."

"Why is that?"

"Because you warned that the two sides of my life would clash someday."

"I don't think 'warned' is the word you mean. I believe what I said is that these two lines of behavior—which you strive so hard to keep separated from each other—were likely to come closer together until there was a meeting point. At which time, of course, you would experience a crisis. As for this 'shame,' it's a natural result of your doing things at odds with what you really want. But you needn't feel that way with me. I don't judge you; you're here because you *want* to remove these barriers."

"Yes," she murmured.

There was a long silence, finally broken by Dr. Maxson. "What do you think you should do about Kevin?"

"Just wait, until—oh, he's clever, though. He guessed

about the others; he told Mrs. Fleming I have 'a stable.' It's such a callous term, but maybe it's accurate. 'Fay goes down to the stable to pet and ride one of her nice horsies whenever she gets lonely,'" she said in a self-deprecating little girl's voice. After a pause she spoke defensively. "But I do feel something for them. Affection and respect."

"So long as they keep their distance."

"Yes, but I try to be fair. If they find someone they're serious about, I'll encourage them in that direction and stop seeing them. I never want to be in anyone's way when they have a chance at something . . . fuller and more permanent."

"Not in their way, as you feel your father has been in people's way?"

"Yes," was the accurate and miserable reply.

"This circumstance of retaining respect for a man by keeping your distance—let's think of it for a moment in reverse."

Fay was familiar with the variety of silences between the two of them; this one called upon her to develop the conjecture herself. "You mean keeping the distance so *they'll* have respect for *me*? I suppose it's possible. It could work both ways."

The lack of reply said, "Continue."

"After a while they would see my faults. They would see how"—she swallowed hard—"afraid I am of being out of control. I . . . I'm behaving like my father. He couldn't exist if he couldn't control everyone around him. I don't know why he divorced Fiona—I was in boarding school during most of that marriage—but I know Lenore divorced *him* because he gave her everything but his time. And my mother, taking the coward's way out, letting him drive her to the point of—I don't want to be like either one of them!"

"And you think you are?"

"Not as long as I'm alone." Her own words caught her up; it was as though they'd been spoken by someone else.

Someone she trusted, someone wiser than she. "But if I got involved . . . I don't know. I just don't trust myself. Yet."

"And now Kevin is trying to control you."

"Yes."

"Consider this: would you have called for this appointment if Kevin *hadn't* spoken to Mrs. Fleming, if there had been just the encounter between you and him?"

"I don't know. Maybe not."

"When you first came in, your anxiety seemed rooted more in shame than in fear of Kevin. We go back to that clash you mentioned. Kevin, a now undesirable friend, invaded your home and tattled to your 'mother,' Mrs. Fleming, accusing *you* of undesirable behavior. He forced you from the passive role of being silent about your life to the active role of lying to her. He broke that safe distance between you and her. Your choices were either to accept the break by admitting the truth or repair the break by lying. You resent his having forced your hand."

"Yes. And I resent my having been so stupid and careless that night he went through my purse."

"How would you feel if he found access to your father?"

"I'd kill him! I mean, I'd find a way to make him so damned sorry."

"Because your father's opinion matters to you?"

"No!—Yes! And that's what I hate! I hate the—the confusion. I don't love him; he doesn't love me. He hasn't loved me since my mother died and maybe not even before. Maybe he never wanted me—he never had any other children; he got me into boarding school as fast as he could. . . . I certainly don't like what I see of *him* in the books he publishes. But oddly, I've liked his wives, especially Sheila. All those years I wanted him to talk to me, and now that it seems *he* wants to, I don't want to hear from him—"

"He wants to talk to you?"

She told Dr. Maxson about the urgency she had sensed

in her father the past few months. "I thought I'd mentioned it."

"No, you haven't. And our time is up. You're a true copywriter, Fay, the way you save these important 'tag lines' until the end of a session."

At the door Fay turned and said, "All this talk we've had about respect—I want to say that I respect *you*."

"Thank you," Dr. Maxson answered with a nod, and then added with a teasing, friendly lilt, "After all, we have our necessary distance."

Pleased by this parting note of levity, Fay walked to the elevator and rode it down without a thought of Kevin and his threats.

BOOK TWO

Bad Girl

8

THAT EVENING, DINNER IN THE COLBY APARTMENT PRO-
ceeded with a charged solemnity worthy of an Ingmar
Bergman movie. Colby was withdrawn, practically in a
stupor; Sheila, puzzled, was watchful, and so guarded she
barely touched her bourbon; Claire made punches at conversation that proved to be mere shadowboxing. Refusing
coffee and dessert, Colby retired to the living room, and
Claire went upstairs to read. And wait. When Sheila came
up and closed her bedroom door, Claire descended the stairs
noiselessly, walked through the kitchen, and tapped on the
office door.

"Yes." The very tone of his one-word response indicated
that he knew it was she and not his wife.

Claire entered and leaned against the wall with her arms
folded. "What happened to you this morning after you left
for work?" she asked point-blank. He didn't answer, and
kept his eyes on the manuscript in front of him. "You were
fine at breakfast, but when I got back from the museum

you were asleep in here and"—she looked at the cabinet that hid the compartment—"you can guess what I saw." Again, silence. "A little relapse, Curt? What brought it on?"

He stacked the manuscript, squaring the corners brusquely. Then, his voice at the edge of a rasp, he announced, "She is her mother's daughter."

"What do you mean?"

"She has a string of men. Definitely three, maybe four." The latter referring to the Fifth Avenue visit.

"How do you know?"

"I've had her followed."

"Followed? By whom?"

"A detective."

"A detec—! For God's sake, how could you!"

"I told you, I wanted to know how she lives."

"But having her followed! Don't you realize what a breach of trust that is?"

"She would never have told us herself."

"And why should she!" Claire hissed. "What have *we* ever told *her* about us, about Rosemary?" She breathed deeply for control. "So now you know how she lives, so what?"

"So, nothing."

"I know you, Curt. And I'm warning you: stay out of her life. You certainly stayed out of it when she was a child, when you might have done something for her. There's nothing you can do for her now. Whatever regret—and guilt—you may feel, you're just going to have to live with it. The only way you can make anything up to her is to leave her alone."

Silence.

"Are you listening to me?"

"Yes, Claire, I'm listening. Now, I'm tired and I want to go to bed." He rose and turned away, waiting for her to leave.

His evasiveness—his eyes had refused to meet hers during this encounter—made her speak once more: "If you do anything rash, Curt, I want you to know that I won't be a party to it. I'll be on Fay's side."

The next morning he went to hear the final report of his daughter's activities—final because he informed O'Brien that his services were no longer needed.

Fay's regular session with Dr. Maxson on Friday went very well, because she came to it with a resolution. Maxson was at once supportive and cautionary.

"This is a step in the right direction," Maxson concluded. "The only danger is expecting too much all at once."

Immediately afterward, Fay stopped at a public phone on the street and dialed information for the number she wanted, then called the library and asked for the Art and Architecture Division.

"Joe, I know this is short notice, but I thought if you weren't busy tonight we might go to a play."

"Yes—I mean, no, I'm not busy."

"I can get the tickets right now."

What would he like to see? It didn't matter. Would he rather have dinner before or after? That, he said, was up to her.

She called back in an hour. She had got good seats for that new play at the Westside Arts Theatre on Forty-third Street. Why not meet at the Gardenia, a restaurant in the same block, at six-fifteen? She would make a reservation.

At five-fifty he left his apartment to walk to the restaurant. Their first meeting in public since the night they met. His first meeting with her in months without the benefit of marijuana to calm him down.

She was seated on a sofa in the restaurant lounge, a glass of wine on the small table in front of her. "Am I late?" he asked, knowing he wasn't.

"I'm early." She smiled. "Shamefully."

They went immediately to their table. After his drink

they talked about the weather and the urban horrors of the day. Gradually, the stiff politeness between them relaxed.

"Joe, I think it would be nice, *good* for us, to go out together once in a while. It doesn't always have to be an event, like a play. Just 'out.' What do you think?"

"Of course, I'd love it. But what about your husband? You said it was important for you never to be seen with me."

She couldn't reveal the whole truth to him now; besides, it would have to be done in private. This first step would be enough for tonight. "I've decided I've been too cautious. We could say we know each other from college if we're ever seen together. Something like that."

In establishing the fiction of past acquaintanceship they talked about their college days. Both had majored in art and both admitted to mediocre talent at it. He, wisely, had gone back to school for a degree in library science; she, still pretending to be a housewife and mother, didn't mention that she had begun at Mayhew as an assistant art director, that Jay Greene had discovered that her real aptitude lay in copywriting. They ended dinner by playing "If you had to choose just one favorite." His was Turner, hers Vermeer.

After the play, she said, "Since you can't walk me home, *I'll* walk *you*." And as she did, her arm looped around his, she silently recounted his attractiveness this evening: the unself-conscious, softly spoken thank-yous each time the waiter brought something to the table; their exit from the restaurant, his holding the door for her and remaining momentarily to hold it for the couple entering; the "Excuse us" he gave to the people at the theater who had to stand up from their seats so they could get to theirs in the middle of the row. In a city where too many men were preening peacocks, this man was a rare dove.

The success of the evening, based so much on who and what he was, impelled her to parcel out a portion of the truth. She would give it and go, delaying detailed explanation until the next time. "Would you mind if I didn't come up for that nightcap? All of a sudden, I'm tired."

"Sure. I'll get you a cab."

"Wait. Joe, I have something to tell you. I work. I mean, I have a job. You can call me there."

His face clouded over, a reaction that was less than she had feared, but disturbing nonetheless.

"I'll tell you more about it next week. I don't have one of my cards with me, but we're in the book. Mayhew Advertising. Would you call me, say, on Wednesday?"

"Yes. Mayhew."

"Ask for Fay Colby. Professionally, I use my first and maiden names."

"Fay Colby," he murmured, blinking twice.

She turned, raised her arm, and prayed for an available taxi so nothing more would have to be said right now. The answered prayer glided up next to them.

"Thank you for a lovely, lovely evening. You'll call me on Wednesday?"

"Yes."

She kissed his cheek.

Stunned but tingling with pleasure, he remained where he was until the car became indistinguishable in the snarl of traffic.

That night his sleep was fitful, and the next day, Saturday, he ate no breakfast and only an apple for lunch. His stomach was knotted with euphoria and apprehension; euphoria over this new footing with her, apprehension about the husband finding out and shaming her back into fidelity. But what if she would *not* be shamed? Suppose the marriage ended? Joe Blakis named in a divorce petition—who would believe it? There would be a custody battle for her two daughters and she would lose, but only temporarily. He himself would search out the best lawyer in the city and together they—

He had to keep yanking himself out of these Walter Mitty

dreams. It was only one date, one joyous evening. Yet she *had* said, "lovely, lovely."

He went jogging for an hour, twice as long as he normally did. Aferward, soaking in the tub, he told himself this was the beginning of the task of remaining calm until Wednesday.

Fay Colby, Mayhew Advertising. Only a few blocks away from the library. Maybe they could have lunch together one or two days a week.

At nine-fifteen he walked to Second Avenue for Chinese takeout and the Sunday New York *Times*. As on so many previous Saturday nights, the food and the paper would tranquilize him, firmly reassure him that solitude was preferable to the madness of a singles bar.

With the bag of food in one hand and the *Times* in the other, he walked briskly. The day had been unseasonably warm, and he had come out with only a light jacket, unzipped. But now a vicious wind blew from the west, penetrating his flannel shirt and making the jacket billow out behind him.

"Joe Blakis?"

His shoulders jumped, then he turned and looked into the face of the stranger. "Yes?"

"Ann Decker," the voice whispered.

There was a flurry of movement, and for a second or two Blakis thought he had been punched. He staggered backward, his vision suddenly darkened, his hearing closing down on the receding footsteps. Only when his knees gave out, bringing him to the concrete, did he realize what was taking his breath away. Protruding from his chest was the handle of a knife whose blade rested squarely, securely in the middle of his heart.

Fay had Sunday brunch and a movie date with Marsha. Over Bloody Marys they talked about their past workweek, and during the eggs Benedict Fay mentioned Joe.

"I want you to meet him. Maybe next week."

Marsha put her fork down. "Well!" The broadening smile, the beaconlike light in her eyes, registered her surprise and approval. "Tell all."

She, of course, did not. She provided only a few details—his age, his occupation, a description of his apartment.

"A librarian, huh? I've always wondered what those quiet types are like in private. Have you slept with him?"

"Yes," she admitted grudgingly.

"And? Is he good?"

"I'm sure everyone has a different idea of what's good."

"Not *that* different."

"He's good for *me*."

During the movie she knew that Marsha was paying scant attention to the screen; at roughly five-minute intervals her eyes would turn in Fay's direction.

On Monday she had plenty of work to do, but she allowed herself occasional lapses in concentration to recall the pleasantness of Friday night and to begin planning how she would tell Joe the whole truth. And, she had to admit, she was more than a little excited by the prospect of introducing him to Marsha. Lost in her own thoughts, she only half listened to Jay Greene's story about Saturday night, about how he and his wife had had dinner in a restaurant just a block away from where a man was stabbed.

Her high spirits collapsed when she arrived home from Mayhew and opened her mailbox to find the plain white envelope with no return address. This time, instead of the Palmer penmanship there were printed block letters.

She closed the door of her apartment, tore open the flap, and unfolded the paper. A muted noise, somewhere between a gasp and a moan, escaped when she read:

FRIDAY NIGHT.
BAD GIRL.

9

Unlike the Colby business, O'Brien's new case held presumed danger for him, Beckhorn, and Dan Hoag—the second assistant—dealing as it did with suspicion of embezzling and drug dealing in a commercial bakery in Queens. The client himself was none too savory, and was probably as guilty as the employees he wanted to expose. O'Brien hoped the next assignment would be simpler, one that Beckhorn and Hoag could manage by themselves. Then he would be off to parts tropical and let the sun banish his urban pallor, burn away the lingering resentment of his ex-wife and, he had to admit, the clinging memory of Fay Colby.

Over the years many clients had terminated his services abruptly, unexpectedly, and he knew better than to waste his energy speculating why. But Curt Colby's sudden withdrawal troubled him: it came on the heels of Kevin Ivory's fracas with Fay on a street corner. O'Brien thought if *he* were Colby, so interested in his daughter's private life, he would want to know more about the man who had slapped his daughter in public, would be curious whether she knew others like him. Would be worried about her safety, for God's sake. Something, O'Brien felt, was amiss.

It was on Thursday, a week and a day since Colby's final appearance, that Les Beckhorn entered the office looking excited and worried. "I have some news. Very late news."

He uncapped a Styrofoam cup that contained less tea than milk.

"Something, I hope, that's going to bring current business to a swift close so I can fly the friendly skies."

"Afraid not. This has to do with our last bit of business." He sipped and winced. "The taste of this makes you feel you're in your second childhood." He settled back into the chair and pulled from his pocket a ragged-edged newspaper clipping. "We get the *Times* delivered at home and we read it over breakfast, then Edith gives it to the old man next door. So she brings the *Daily News* home from the office for starting the kindling in the fireplace."

"Les, this is just too fascinating at this hour of the day."

"Hang on."

"I'm breathless."

"Last night, I was starting the fire, using Monday's copy. I'm rolling it up two pages at a time and *wham!*—this hits me smack in the face." He handed over the clipping.

MAN STABBED ON 35TH ST.

After the victim's name, address, the time of the killing, came a description of the weapon, a carving knife with an eight-inch blade. Three dollars and change had been found in the victim's pocket, but no wallet; the inexpensive watch was not taken.

"Blakis . . . quite a coincidence," O'Brien breathed.

"Sure is," Beckhorn answered.

"They got the wallet. Maybe he resisted."

"If he had a wallet. The Chinese food and the paper—a short errand, especially at night. You might leave the wallet at home and take just the money you're gong to need."

"Possible."

"Or it could be a crime of passion if Blakis was involved with another woman who found out he was playing around."

"Mmm."

"Or it could have been Kevin Ivory."

"Or Curt Colby, or even his daughter."

"According to the clipping," Beckhorn continued, "it must have happened right near his building. You can bet the cops questioned the doorman, and I'm wondering if it was our friend who was on duty."

The "friend" would remember O'Brien and the bribe. Beckhorn's allusion to him was quiet but concerned, for he knew the depth of O'Brien's fear of the police, of possible publicity—both fears stemming from his having been thrown off the force.

"We'll just wait and see what happens," said O'Brien. "Now let's get on with the paying job."

While O'Brien and Beckhorn split up their duties for the morning, Fay arrived at her office in a state of high-strung anticipation. Since Joe hadn't called yesterday as he'd said he would, it would be today—and with a good reason for the delay.

In the afternoon she left Mayhew with a storyboard to make a presentation to a client, and when she returned at four o'clock she checked with the receptionist for messages. Still none; in view of their past secrecy, maybe he'd been shy about leaving his name with any third party. Still, no calls came through to her office before the switchboard closed down for the day.

Despite the twenty-degree temperature she walked home from Mayhew, thirty-two blocks. But the chill lashing at her legs and face failed to numb the humiliation, anger, loss. She wished she were on her way to meet Maxson in some cozy corner for some woman-to-woman, not doctor-to-patient, talk.

That cloudy, puzzled look on Joe's face last Friday night when she had told him her name, where she worked: he had had a week to ponder the information and very likely, in the end, concluded that she was too neurotic for him, just as Kevin was too neurotic for *her*.

Kevin and his "Bad Girl" note. Had he actually seen her and Joe last Friday night, or had he kept watch on her apartment, noting the time she came home and thereby arriving at his own deduction? She envisioned reporting Kevin to the police, imagined their derisively knowing smiles when they learned of her alias and two telephone numbers.

Had Joe called, they could have made plans for Sunday, plans that would be a remedy for the night before. Saturday, her father was taking her to dinner to celebrate her birthday. She would just as soon attend a public hanging.

At Seventy-fourth Street she climbed the steps to the front door, turned, and scouted the street. Nothing. With one dread out of the way, she faced another in the vestibule: her mailbox. But here, too, was relief. Only a bill.

Mrs. Fleming's door was open, and the voice called out to Fay before she could escape up the stairs. She offered up a frantic prayer that Kevin had not made a second call on the landlady.

It was only an invitation to come down for tea or brandy after Fay had had her dinner.

The living room telephone began to ring as she was unlocking her door. It was Marsha.

"Well, do I get to meet the new beau this weekend?"

"Uh, no. Something's come up."

"Like what?"

"My father's taking me out for my birthday Saturday

night, and Joe . . . Joe's family is coming to town. We'll have to wait."

"This isn't a stall?"

"No."

"I might be gone all next week. Anyway, your birthday present is with UPS. I think," she said suggestively, "*Joe* will like it."

After dinner and her bath Fay tried to read, but her thoughts kept running to Joe and Kevin. Joe brought on an embarrassment she had never before known; Kevin made her go to the window twice and look out at the street.

At ten minutes to nine she pulled tight the belt of her robe, readying herself for the visit downstairs, when the telephone rang. The sound of her father's voice cleared away Joe and Kevin in an instant.

"I'm about to make a reservation for Saturday," he said in his formal, almost declamatory manner. "We're going to Côte Basque."

"That'll be nice."

"I wondered if you wanted to bring someone with you."

"No, no one."

"You're sure?"

"Yes."

Pause.

"Would you like to come here for a drink first?"

"Actually, it would be more convenient for me to meet you there."

Her breathing nearly stopped when the phone in the bedroom rang. The door was open, and the sound seemed amplified threefold.

"What's that?" her father asked.

The answering machine took over.

"It's my . . . business phone."

"Business?"

Don't explain, she told herself. You needn't. "I'm just

on my way out. I'll see you at eight on Saturday. Say hello to Claire and Sheila."

She stood for a moment with her arms wrapped around her chest, wondering if he believed the lie, then chastising herself for caring *what* he believed. She began to relax when she thought about *his* lie. He was not "about" to make the reservation; he had already made it. His favorite table at Côte Basque was a popular one, and he'd never wait until a Thursday night to reserve for Saturday. No, the call was a ruse to worm his way into her privacy.

She crossed the room and stood before the oak-framed oval mirror. The spit and image of her mother, except that her face was fuller in the cheeks. Twenty-nine. Her mother's twenty-ninth year had offered up despair and death. She talked about her mother only in Maxson's office, and four or five months ago she had begun to think more frequently about her age, about the night she was four years old and heard the receding howl that didn't prevent her from going back to sleep. The memory, two Sundays ago, had impelled her to walk past the building on Sixty-sixth Street, to chart the tenth floor and locate the balcony from which her mother had launched her escape.

In the bedroom she rewound the tape on the machine. There were two calls, one from Sam in the afternoon, the other from a few minutes ago: "Hi, Ann, it's Andrew. I'm at Kennedy Airport, back from Barbados and on my way to London. Only popped in for two meetings today. Be back in a week or so. I'm dying to see you."

She called Sam at home and said she would love to meet him next Wednesday when he came to New York. "I want to take you to dinner," she ventured. She had always had excuses *not* to dine with him, and his surprise was measured by the length of the pause. "Has something happened with your situation?" he said.

"I'll tell you about it when I see you."

She hung up and, thinking of Joe's retreat from her, muttered, "From the frying pan into the fire."

She looked forward to tomorrow's session with Maxson. No matter how deeply or painfully they probed, it would be an oasis between the Joe-less past two days and the dread chore of seeing her father on Saturday night.

She went downstairs, ready for that brandy and Mrs. Fleming's usual (she hoped) uncomplicated chatter.

"Don't you think," Dr. Maxson said, "you might dispel the vagueness and uncertainty of the situation by calling him?"

"There's nothing vague about *him* not calling *me*. I regret it, but I don't blame him."

"Are you afraid of what he might say?"

"Yes. Last night when I was with Mrs. Fleming it occurred to me that maybe Kevin got to Joe and said the same things he said to her. His note said 'Friday Night,' and if he *was* following us he might have approached Joe after I went off in the cab. If I called him, what could I say? I couldn't lie to him, not when I've made my mind up to start telling the truth."

"When you were with Mrs. Fleming last night did she make any reference to Kevin?"

"None. But I have the distinct feeling she's not forgetting anything." Pause. "I'm seeing Sam next Wednesday night. I'm scared as hell, but I'm going to jump right in and tell him everything."

"Assuming that Kevin might have followed you and then spoken to Joe, are you prepared for his doing the same with Sam?"

"It won't make any difference. I'm going to lay everything on the line at dinner before we go back to his hotel— if he still wants me to go back with him. It's going to be hard, but no harder than waiting the next five days till I see him." She moved on to the more immediate concern of seeing her father tomorrow night. "At least Claire and Sheila will be there to serve as buffers."

"Against what?"

"Any attempt at so-called intimacy. I know he wants to pry into my life, and he's groping for a way to do it."

"Have you considered breaking the tension by confronting him first?"

Fay's laugh sounded, in the sanctuary of the room, like a shattering of glass. "You don't confront Curt Colby. *He* does the confronting. I know he wants some kind of resolution between us, but there can't be any! What's the point of working myself up to telling him what I think of him when he already knows? Words won't change anything. Maybe I sound hard, but I can't give him what he never gave me. I was four years old with a dead mother, and he took himself away from me. I had to learn that he'd never be there again, and I learned it fast! I watched Lenore and Fiona, I know what happens to people who turn themselves over to him. He chews them up and, oh, he chews so quietly—" She was crying now. "I hate this! He doesn't deserve tears."

"The tears are for yourself, Fay," Dr. Maxson said softly, and waited for them to subside.

"You'd think after all these years..."

"Yes?"

"That I'd have better control."

"Our purpose is to get you out of this false control so that you can gain true control. And 'all these years' haven't diminished your sense of loss and abandonment; they've increased it. I think we're making excellent progress."

This report card from Maxson produced in Fay a swell of childlike pride and, at the same time, keen regret. How differently her life would have turned out had this woman been her parent. With that cool beauty and dignity she was probably not the touching, embracing type; she would caress with words and smiles. The lack of effusion would be the flip side of her father's—it would prove the quiet depth of love rather than the absence of love.

"Excellent progress." She let the praise settle in, and her chest expanded like a smile. "I would like to move up to two sessions a week."

"I think that's a good idea."

"I want to keep Friday. Maybe if you had an opening on Tuesdays."

She did, at seven P.M.

"We'll begin the week after next. In fact, I won't be able to see you next Friday either. I'm going out of town."

"Oh?" Fay sat up. "A vacation?"

"Of sorts."

Of sorts. How nice it sounded, pleasanter than "sort of." Fay rose from the couch. She turned to face Dr. Maxson, and treated herself to a reappraisal of the woman's clothing. Today it was a pale yellow belted dress that set off her chestnut hair; the alligator shoes and single strand of brown beads were the color of her eyes. Fay had never seen her in slacks and wondered if she even owned a pair.

"You have very good taste," Fay said impulsively.

"Thank you."

"Did you learn it from your mother?"

Dr. Maxson laughed lightly. "Perhaps not; there wasn't the leisure to develop it. But I recall the good taste of the food she put on the table." Then: "See you a week from Tuesday."

"Yes."

"In the meantime we'll hope for the best with Sam."

10

*W*E'LL JUST WAIT AND SEE WHAT HAPPENS. O'BRIEN'S words to Beckhorn had been casual, a throwaway remark, but the past two nights' sleep came grudgingly. Both mornings O'Brien had woken up groggy and heavy, and although he recalled no dreams he felt as if he had been working in his sleep. He knew very well that the report about Joe Blakis was conjuring up in him the distant and the not-so-distant past, culminating in that instant when O'Brien's life swung so violently out of control that he crossed the line every decent cop was aware of and feared—the line that separated law-enforcer from law-breaker, public protector from public menace.

On this night, Friday, he sat with the lights dimmed, a beer beside him, his shoeless feet propped up on the edge of the wicker magazine basket. No need to worry about sleep and the lack of it—Beckhorn was working alone tomorrow in exchange for Sunday off. The apartment was hospital clean, someone from the service having been there that afternoon and left it redolent of ammonia and Windex; the two clean odors hung in the air like planted evidence. The building was quiet, the bickering (and, O'Brien suspected, drug-using) couple next door gone skiing in Canada. Lacking present diversion, and with no next-day responsibilities to ponder, he now gave reign to the thoughts he had been keeping at bay.

Tunnabricks. It was the nickname Lee Irwin, another detective with the sixth precinct, had given him after Irwin and his wife spent their first evening with him and Joy. "I think," Irwin said the next morning, "cool-hand Earl has fallen like a ton of bricks." And for a month of mornings after that, Irwin's greeting was "Hey, Tunnabricks." Irwin had a frame of reference, for he had seen O'Brien with numerous women, only two of whom were serious candidates for matrimony—Joy being the second.

When O'Brien was in the third grade at Our Lady of Perpetual Help in Bay Ridge, Brooklyn, his mother became a policeman's widow, her new status bestowed by a black gunman who also shot but only wounded the drugstore owner and who was never captured. The funeral was heavily attended, the church packed with family, friends, fellow workers, and public officials, the sidewalk peppered with reporters and scantily dressed onlookers stopping off on their way to the beach. Over the treetops across the street, the August sun stationed itself as the stern overseer of the proceedings, radiating a brutal heat that insured the proper suffering of all but the deceased. In the limousine O'Brien's twelve-year-old sister vomited out the window and rode the rest of the trip to the cemetery with her head down between her knees. Their mother sat rigid, unweeping and seemingly unbreathing, less animated than the statues in the church. O'Brien stared at his polished black shoes and drew the unreasonable but firm conclusion that his legs weren't so long as they had been two days before.

Within a month his sister's stomach settled down and his

legs went back to normal. And their mother came furiously to life. Father Fons visited the house several times to comfort, but ended up as a sounding board for Betty O'Brien's newly acquired views of herself and the world. "Any woman who loves a cop more than her dog is an idiot. And if she marries him she deserves everything she gets."

"Betty, he was a good man, a good husband, a good father. You had him for thirteen years. Most women never have as much as you did."

"Hell. I'd settle for less to have him alive."

"Betty . . ."

"I say hell."

Six months later the priest reappeared, now less indulgent and placating: Betty was going neither to mass nor to confession. Besides her own soul, he warned that her children were endangered by her behavior. "Oh, I pray," she answered hotly. "I pray every night that that man is caught. When he is, *then* I'll come to mass. As for the children, the only reason I'm keeping them at Our Lady is to make sure they never have to go to school with *them*."

Father Fons's raised eyebrows asked his question.

From the dining room table where he was doing his homework, Earl looked through the archway to the kitchen. He watched his mother dip her head like a bull before the attack, then saw her spit the words: "Niggers. Cop-killing niggers." Father Fons scraped his chair back, came to the archway, and told O'Brien to go outside for a while. Before the boy made his exit he heard his mother say, "The Lord giveth so He *can* taketh away."

Betty O'Brien rejected the rigors of charity and forgiveness for the comfort of sherry. But only in the evenings and on Sundays. Six days a week she worked in a neighborhood dry cleaner's, at a pressing machine and behind the counter. The fame of her husband's death endured—helped along by the police's inability to find his killer despite the standing offer of a hefty reward—and that fame became hers as well.

The customers, most of them longtime friends of the family, overlooked her loss of faith and applauded her industriousness, her devotion to her children.

That devotion, however, was not without its expectation of a return. When O'Brien's sister was seventeen she brought home a boy whose olive complexion made her mother's turn red. The boy's name was Dan LoCicero, and after he left there was a row in the living room, with Betty slamming shut the windows so the neighbors wouldn't hear as she railed against this betrayal. "Why—tell me *why* you can't find a *white* boy!"

"Mama, he's white. And he's Catholic."

"You call that white? And his hair, it's just like *theirs*. Have you run your fingers through it, miss? What about his name? Dan does *not* go with LoCicero. Daniel, is it? You don't give your child that name unless you're trying to pass for something you're not."

"Daniel's Hebrew, from the Old Testament," offered the boy. "And *my* name doesn't go with 'O'Brien.'"

"Your name will be mud if you don't stay out of this!"

Three years later O'Brien's sister dropped out of Brooklyn College to marry Dan—Dan Noonan. Betty glowed at the wedding. She hadn't been to church in nearly a decade, but this brief return was not traumatic, for her daughter and Dan had wisely elected to be married in *his* parish.

When O'Brien himself decided to leave Brooklyn College at the end of his sophomore year, he knew he would also have to leave his mother's house. In announcing his decision he faced her as if she were a firing squad: "I've been accepted at the police academy." The silence was long, her face a blank. "I'm prepared to move out."

"You are? I don't see your bags packed."

And as he packed them he heard the rocker start up on the porch. The motion halted when he came out the front door.

"I'll come back for the rest in the morning."

"No you won't. Send me an address I can mail them to."

His eyes raked her face in an attempt to find something there to pity. But what he saw was satisfaction, and he knew he was giving her something she wanted: at long last, the opportunity to punish the dead through the living. "Your *father*," she muttered.

"My father would be ashamed of you." He walked down the steps for the last time.

During his training at the academy he tried to analyze his choice, the motives for it. A tribute to his father? Not really. He was well aware that it was possible he loved the memory of the man more than the man himself; and he knew that death had come before disillusionment and bitterness could stake a claim and pull the corners down on that huge Irish smile. Nor had the man lived long enough to try to direct his son's vocational preference.

When, after a year, his mother refused to see him or even speak to him on the telephone, he went to Father Fons, who reassured him in his decision but was more concerned about his absence from mass. Soon afterward O'Brien learned that his ballistics instructor was the son and grandson of policemen, and one day over coffee O'Brien told the man his story. Tipping back in his chair, the instructor nodded with a matter-of-fact familiarity in which sympathy played no part at all. "Listen, my *father* didn't speak to me for almost *three* years. My mother just sighed and said, 'Don't get fat.'" With that, O'Brien stopped his search for approval.

And oh, he'd travel a long way down the road before he learned how much of Betty O'Brien's emotional baggage traveled with him. . . .

Living in Manhattan, he discovered that "city" girls were more reluctant than their Brooklyn sisters to become "involved" with a cop; however, more than a few were happy enough to sleep with him. And so while his married fellow workers ogled miniskirts and cooked up fleeting pedestrian fantasies, O'Brien lived the reality of easy sex.

His success with women was steady, and he never examined it. It was once explained to him by an NYU graduate student from Kansas who was hoping to become a playwright. She was forever analyzing: the hippie movement, radical politics, herself and O'Brien. Women were attracted to him, she said, because of his "incongruities"—a broad boyish face affixed to a long lanky body, lazy eyes and a lazy smile in counterpoint to a brisk step and a sharp wit, a cynic on the sofa and a romantic in bed. "And," she concluded, "the fact that you're Irish Catholic and *still* a good lover." Yet O'Brien didn't overcredit himself in the animal magnetism department; the new freedom spawned by the mid-sixties allowed just about anyone who wanted it a steady diet of nonmarital sex. And he was not one for counting calories.

In 1967 his mother died of cirrhosis, a condition possibly resulting from her replacement of sherry with cheap whiskey. Until the end she held out against him—but not against the church. A new young priest at Our Lady of Perpetual Help performed the last rites in her room at Victory Memorial eleven hours before she succumbed. O'Brien's sister told him that Betty had gone into delirium after hearing about the riots in Harlem, Detroit, and Watts, muttering incessantly, "They're going to get Earl, they're finally going to get Earl." He could not have known what these words would come to mean to him.

Two months later he met Ellen, a Polish Lutheran from the Bronx who taught English at City College. He was as ready for her as he would have been for a tidal wave sweeping in from the Atlantic. She chain-smoked Lucky Strikes, loved dirty jokes, despised cooking and housework; she went to church every Sunday, worked on Thursdays as a hospital volunteer, budgeted one-fifth of her salary for charity. After a six-week courtship she gave up her virginity. There was, of course, the "hitch": she wouldn't consider marrying O'Brien so long as he remained a cop. Her reasoning was founded upon immutable beliefs, given tongue in dire predictions. "You think drugs and riots and all this social discontent is a passing phase? Don't bet on it. When the dewy-eyeds find out they can't change things overnight, all that junior high optimism is going to have to deal with all those spoiled brats—not to mention *their* enemies— when they turn nasty. And I won't be along for the ride. I'll have better things to do."

He had dreams of her along for the ride: attending his funeral; shot down in the street along with him; and, the most horrible, being accidentally struck by his club because she was caught in a melee he was trying to quell. Violent though they were, the dreams never woke him, but in the morning he would feel a generalized anger and recall his mother's face the day he left her house.

As, due to extraordinary initiative, his star rose in the department, his chances for any future with Ellen declined daily. Gradually there were arguments where none had existed, arguments about his remaining "on the job" whenever he was off duty. And then one night as they were on their way to her apartment after having dinner out, they passed a deli in which a man was holding two employees and a customer at gunpoint. O'Brien pushed Ellen on ahead, instructing her to hide in the entryway next door, and waited for the gunman to hit the street. There was the "Halt, I'm a police officer" and then the thief's laughter and his spray of bullets; O'Brien felled him with a single shot in the hip. Ellen went home in a taxi and pretended to be asleep when O'Brien phoned her after the booking. The next night she said they were through, and with fury in her voice but tears in her eyes she added, "He laughed at you, and I could've seen you killed. I'll never forget that laugh."

There were other laughs, other crimes, far worse, when he became a detective. For nine years he was moored to the job, and the women who climbed aboard his life stayed for only brief visits. Neither happy nor miserable, he was as content as he thought he would ever get to be. There were plenty of dinners at the homes of his married friends, and the state of their relationships on any given evening would either advance or diminish his contentment.

Lee Irwin, a black detective, and his wife, Iris, were as close to being the perfect couple as O'Brien had ever seen. They had a large apartment on Eighty-eighth Street right off West End Avenue, which Iris had furnished in Early American. "*Black* Early American," Irwin teased her, "was some orange crates, a rickety old chifforobe, and some sacks for picking cotton." She retorted, "You're telling me America was growing oranges back then? *How*," she addressed O'Brien, "does he ever find clues to solve a case?"

Irwin was, in fact, a fine detective. He had a string of successes in vice cases dealing with sex, owing in part to his exceptional good looks; Iris's mother, a raucously good-natured woman, called him the Hollywood Nigger. Iris herself looked as if she had stepped out of the 1930s or '40s blues circuit: a long reedlike body; slick, straight (perhaps straightened) hair that was worn in a bun with combs or a flower for ornament; her clothes were always in solid colors, most often whites, yellows, greens. She taught in a public elementary school so that their young daughter could attend a private one.

Sometimes at their dinner table, O'Brien would envision the ghost of his mother looking on, gnashing her teeth while they laughed, joked, talked politics; and, with vengeful satisfaction, he imagined her howling each time little Lena called him Uncle Earl.

He had lost Ellen in the line of duty; in 1977 he met Joy in the line of duty. He was returning to his apartment with a bag of groceries, watching the sway of her skirt some twenty yards ahead, when two boys leapt from a doorway, knocked her to the sidewalk, and tried to snatch her purse. She held on to it until one of the boys kicked her in the stomach. O'Brien released the bag to pursue them; the one he caught pulled a knife but dropped it as O'Brien broke his arm.

On the heels of a divorce in Chicago, she was new in the city and working for an interior decorating firm. For six months she was his constant companion, and an eager pupil as he schooled her in restaurants, theaters, the subway system, architectural landmarks. Finally she gave up her expensive tiny studio and moved into his rent-controlled one-bedroom apartment with its rarest of assets: an eat-in kitchen. At last it was used for more than perking coffee, scrambling eggs, heating up frozen food. Seeing her love and talent on display at the stove, he bought her a Cuisinart. It remained behind, gathering dust, after the divorce.

Unlike Ellen, Joy was not yet "settled into" her profession, at least not at the station she hoped to achieve, and so she worked hard toward becoming an independent decorator. Perhaps hoping that her blond beauty would be an asset in her advancement, she was studiedly fastidious in her grooming: manicures, pedicures, facials, hair cutting and waving, eyebrow plucking—all was done as naturally, ritualistically, as O'Brien washed his hands or brushed his teeth. O'Brien readily accepted her desire for a lifelong career without the interruption of child-rearing, and they were married in May of 1978 in a civil ceremony with only Lee and Iris Irwin in attendance.

Over the two years that followed, she grew less interested in his stories about his work, more interested in her own stories about her clients, their abundance of money and lack of taste. But he saw that as only natural because her career was still fresh to her; and he enjoyed watching her flower. Besides, she was always good company among their friends—an excellent and indefatigable bridge player, a willing advisor to those who wanted to spruce up their drab furnishings and decor. His sex with her was never heated fireworks. It was more quietly exciting, something deliciously murky and secret-holding, and most of their sessions were prolonged by an ebbing, flowing, ebbing, rhythm that often reminded him of a line of poetry from high school English: "The moon was a ghostly galleon tossed upon cloudly seas." He would learn, in October 1980, just how cloudy those seas were.

Texas was extraditing to New York a heroin dealer suspected of murder, and O'Brien flew to Houston to bring him back. Captain Steiger told him to spend three days down there to "unwind." Joy hadn't wanted to go, but she echoed the captain's advice, affirming that O'Brien had been looking haggard for weeks. He checked into a motel and tried to enjoy the sun and the pool, but after a single day he found himself restless and depressed by the tall buildings that seemed out of place in their setting of cactus and wide-open sky. He picked up his human parcel and flew home.

Joy would be surprised by his quick return, then amused by his big-city-hometown attachment. He would take her to dinner at the Coach House on Waverly Place and order the outrageously expensive rack of lamb.

As he turned the key in the door of his apartment he heard the radio playing Muzak. He smiled and thought: does she usually play that stuff if she's home in the afternoon? A little surprise in return for his big one.

Then the full opening of the door revealed, on the chair next to the radio, trousers and a shirt and jacket that were not his, and surely weren't hers—and at this moment he didn't want to admit that he had seen the jacket before, and the tote bag too.

The voices in the bedroom were soft but urgent. And recitational, as though they were acting out a script. He set down his own bag, rounded the corner to the kitchen, and noiselessly crossed the floor that Joy had had covered with industrial carpeting. The door to his bedroom was ajar about five inches, the space making clearly visible the bed and the shaded window. Joy was lying in profile with her hair splayed out on the pillow in so elegant a fashion that it had to have been painstakingly arranged; she wore a pale blue silk brassiere, and below it layers upon layers of white crinolines, the likes of which O'Brien hadn't seen since they puffed out prom dresses in the fifties. Standing at the foot of the bed, also in profile, was Lee Irwin—shirtless, shoeless, clad only in a pair of uncharacteristically soiled overalls.

"Do you want to see more?" Joy said in a voice husky yet coquettish. And more than vaguely Southern in its drawl. What in God's name *was* this?

"Yes, ma'am, but are you sure no one's home? If your daddy caught a field nigger in his house, in his little girl's room . . ."

"No one's here," she purred. "Do you want to see more?"

"Yes, *ma'am*."

She hiked up the crinolines to mid-thigh, bent her legs, and opened them. "I know you've been watching me every time I go by in the carriage, my handsome field hand, and one day you licked your lips. Look, look up inside my skirts. What color do you see?"

"I see white, and way up there I see yellow. Looks like cornsilk."

She opened her legs wider and slipped her hands between them. "Now what color do you see?"

"I see pink, oooo, pretty pink." He stuck his tongue out as far as he could and moved it from side to side.

Irwin dropped to his knees, flicked his tongue over the pearl-shaped pads of her toes, then started working his way upward, over one ankle and the inside of her leg until his head and neck were lost under the crinolines. Joy went from whimpering to moaning to bucking; and Irwin's hands climbed her ribs, tore her brassiere, and worked her nipples with his thumbs.

O'Brien did not move or call out; indeed, he scarcely breathed. Something unnamable inside him was determined to watch until the conclusion.

Irwin yanked off the crinolines, tossed them aside, and stood up to unhook his overalls. They fell around his feet and he stepped out of them. He walked slowly forward alongside the bed, hands behind his back, his banana-shaped erection bobbing up and down.

"Feel it. Feel how hard my black dick gets for your white pussy."

She stroked it, then took the head into her mouth and descended more than halfway down him, hollowing her cheeks. The air whistled through Irwin's teeth as he drew a sharp breath; then he turned his face to the ceiling, moaning, "Oh, yeah . . . oh, *yeah*."

There followed a quick blur of movement and they were coupled below the waist, Irwin pumping furiously, perhaps brutally, while Joy beseeched, "Don't stop, don't come."

O'Brien did not check his watch, but he thought it took them more than ten minutes to climax. Joy cued Irwin of her approach with that noise in her throat, the one O'Brien knew so well—it was like distant thunder.

"I love it, I love it, I love it," Irwin gasped.

"Yes, yes, YES!"

"Y-E-E-E-S-S-SSS!"

He rolled away, and they lay still to regain their breath. "Next time," Irwin said, "I'll play a salesman who comes to your door."

Joy laughed. "Stop. I can't think of that right now."

"I'll bring what I want you to wear. It'll be a surprise."

Next time, thought O'Brien. Next time. How many next times had there been? Slowly, he swung open the door.

They froze, like children awaiting the parental strap.

"Get up," O'Brien ordered Irwin.

But it was Joy who stood, acting as a blockade. "Earl," she said hastily, her eyes huge, "come with me into the living room. Let him get dressed."

He looked at the shiny rivulet working its way down the inside of her leg. "*You* go into the living room. Alone."

"No." She remained, defying him, protective of Irwin.
"I won't let you do anything foolish. For Christ's sake, let
him get dressed and then ... we'll ... talk."

"I have eyes. And ears. Scarlett O'Hara screws Stepin
Fetchit."

Her face registered the information. "You were there all
along." A look of nausea moved in. "Jesus, Earl," she
whispered in disgust.

But he was not about to let the tables be turned. "All
right, Lee," he said with the kind of softness that telegraphs
menace. "Get up and get dressed." He stepped aside and
Irwin slunk past him. In the living room he stood against
the front door and watched the man put his clothes on.

Joy began her explanation in haste: "What you saw doesn't
mean anything; it's just—biological."

"Yeah," echoed Irwin. "That's all it is." But he would
not look O'Brien in the eye.

As Irwin slipped into his second shoe, O'Brien lunged
and Joy screamed. Irwin backed away, holding up his arms
to fend off the fists. "I'm not going to fight you, man, I'm
not going to fight you!"

Joy gripped O'Brien's shoulders and yanked hard enough
to give Irwin a chance for the door. O'Brien caught up with
him halfway down the stairs, and once again his friend
yelled, "I'm not going to fight you." Three doors to other
apartments cracked open to reveal wary faces, and when
the two men reached the sidewalk, windows were raised
and passers-by halted to watch the spectacle. Irwin was true
to his declared resolve, and when he fell to the ground,
covering his face and huddling his body to protect his stomach, O'Brien pulled him up, again, to continue the beating.
As he looked into the bloodied black face he recalled his
mother's prediction as his sister had repeated it to him:
They're going to get Earl, they're finally going to get Earl.

After Irwin's nose was broken, his lip split, and two teeth

chipped, a squad car arrived and its two occupants pried O'Brien off his prey.

There was a departmental hearing at which Irwin was exonerated for not having struck back. O'Brien was suspended. He filed for divorce and Joy moved in with a girlfriend. He was reinstated with the force six months after his suspension, then he resigned and took the state exam for his license as a private detective.

Tunnabricks...

He yawned, rubbed his eyes, and opened another beer. Joe Blakis and his doorman, especially the doorman, swirled in his thoughts with newspaper headlines from October 1980.

COP BEATS PARTNER ON STREET

COP BEATER SUSPENDED FROM DUTY

COP BEATING POSSIBLY RACIAL

The *Post* and *Daily News* had their field day, although the *News* charitably pointed out that he had no previous record of brutality. Now, suppose by some fluke he were to be traced and identified by the doorman. There would be suspicion and questioning and publicity; a public rehashing of his past offense would do his present business no good. Not once so far had any client of his got him involved with the police.

He knew better than to lay much weight to the supposition that Blakis's death was a random killing. It was possible but highly improbable, especially when he recalled Curt Colby's bloodless exterior—a facade that hinted at a smoldering rage inside. He had seen the type too many times: the proper (and often prosperous) citizen who was a madman at home.

He wanted no involvement, but not wanting it didn't dissolve his preoccupation with the murder. A single knife wound in the heart—accidental accuracy by an amateur, but more likely the precision of a skilled premeditator.

No point in rushing into anything. There was time yet to ponder, consider—or so he told himself.

11

FAY BELIEVED SHE HAD HANDLED HERSELF ADMIRABLY
at her birthday dinner, thanks to the predictability of her
father's behavior. The pattern was as she'd expected, albeit
more marked. Despite his verbal remoteness, she felt his
intense surveillance, his watching her every gesture, cap-
turing every syllable she uttered.

And there was something else: a turnabout. It was always
he who kept an eye on Sheila's drinks, but on this occasion
Sheila and Claire exchanged a quick glance of—apprehension? knowingness?—when he ordered a second Rob Roy,
straight up. And Fay surmised that the glance also meant
he had tipped the bottle earlier at home—he who confined
himself to wine with dinner, an occasional single brandy
afterward. And there was an edge to the manner of both
women as they chattered a shade too shrilly, each starting
up when the other left off to insure against any sagging
silence. This was not the cool and collected Claire Fay knew.

In the ladies' room, the woman was visibly startled by Fay's directness: "What do *you* think of the way he's acting?"

Claire's lipstick halted, then in one stroke finished its job. "Acting?"

"His preoccupation. His drinking."

"I imagine his work is distracting him. Matheny's novel hasn't been selling well at all. As for the drinking, he's just celebrating your birthday."

The look Fay gave her aunt said she didn't believe this for an instant, but Claire merely dropped her lipstick into her purse and said, "Ready?"

Riding home in a taxi, relieved to have the evening over with, she turned her thoughts to Wednesday, and Sam, and hoped that would be a pleasanter evening.

On Sunday her confidence in Sam's understanding and acceptance began to increase, and on Monday four people at Mayhew commented on how wonderful she looked. Nancy Greene, in straight from the hairdresser's to claim her husband for a special luncheon at the Plaza, pronounced Fay "positively glowing." Even Jim DeLuca, that master of the elegant understatement, said she looked "special" today.

But she imagined the reactions were she to tell these people that, at long last, she was about to start dating the men she had been sleeping with.

Her "glow" continued until Tuesday at five-thirty.

Mayhew was on the eighth floor of the Gregson Building, and because Fay liked elevators no more than heights, she invariably left only once the five o'clock crush was over. Jim DeLuca got onto the elevator with her. They were alone together, but not for long. When the doors opened at the fourth floor, they framed Kevin Ivory. He entered, looked at Fay, and smirked; then he glanced at DeLuca and smirked again. As the car reached the lobby, Kevin stepped aside with an elaborate courtesy to let them exit first, and from the corner of her eye she saw his leering grin and glittering eyes.

"Some creep I once made the mistake of going out with," she explained to DeLuca as they hurried across the terrazzo toward the revolving door. Outside, he turned left, she right. She waited half a minute, and when Ivory failed to appear she rounded the corner to the building's other entrance. He was nowhere in sight.

She was too shaken to sit still in a taxi and so began to walk, sporadically glancing over her shoulder. Kevin had got onto the elevator at the fourth floor, which housed only two firms: G.G. Fahringer & Company, CPAs, and Lloyd Burnham Associates, a literary agency. Kevin *could* have been visiting his tax man, or trying to peddle the poems and short stories he often claimed he was writing. . . .

That evening, she picked up the telephone twice, dialed, but hung up before the connection could be made. Calling him might encourage him, give him the reaction he wanted. By the time she went to bed at eleven-thirty she had gone to the front windows a dozen times to look up and down the street.

The specter of Kevin remained all the next day, right up to her arrival at the lobby of the Hotel Hanson.

As usual, Sam was waiting for her in the discreetly lighted cocktail lounge, and as she entered it her eyes scanned the room for a blond head. The only one belonged to a middle-aged woman. Eight couples in the lounge, six at tables and two at the bar. Two patrons sat alone, Sam at their customary booth.

Sam stood and pulled the table away from the booth to admit her. "I want you to know," he said, "I've been on cloud nine for five days."

"I can't match that. I've only been on cloud eight." There was, she said, a great deal for them to talk about—could they go to dinner right away? Certainly. Nearby was an Armenian restaurant where he was a regular and always assured of a good table.

They chose one in a corner, and with their first drink she

began her confession, omitting only Joe and his withdrawal from her. Sam's eyes remained warm, his face open, and so she told all: her fears about intimacy, the fictitious husband and daughters, therapy with Maxson, the trouble with Kevin, and finally her inability to promise she would not see Andrew while she continued to see *him*. "Except for my work, I don't know exactly where I'm going," she concluded. "All I can say is I'm making progress," and she felt a surge of pride as she echoed Dr. Maxson's affirmation.

Sam's smile was small but not ungenerous. "I'm glad you are. And if I have to share you, so be it. We can't hide from the fact that I'm older than you are. By seventeen years. In fact, I'm already a grandfather. How old is Andrew?"

"Sam, your age and Andrew's have nothing to do with it. It's just that for the time being I'd like to see you both, get to know you. In the conventional way."

He nodded his assent. "Do you think we might work our way up to a weekend at my little farm?"

"I would like to. Very much." Emboldened by the two drinks she'd had, she now looked him in the eye and said, "For starters, I'd like to spend this whole night with you."

His smile broadened. "I can at least assure you that I don't snore."

"Well, *I* do," she teased.

"Nice. A little night music."

Back in his room he called room service and ordered a bottle of Dom Pérignon and four bottles of domestic champagne.

"Sam, what are you *doing*?"

"The Dom Pérignon is for us." One eyebrow lifted to form a wicked arch. "The domestic is for our bath."

She sat on the lid of the toilet with her glass of champagne and watched him uncork the four bottles and pour them into the tub half full of water. "You *are* a wanton under those Brooks Brothers threads," she said.

"My ancestors were grape-growers."

"In Greece?"

"Italy."

"But you're Greek."

He nodded. "They migrated. Come on, hop in."

As she eased herself into the bubbly water she realized how much there was to learn about this man, who had married, had children, been widowed; who wanted eventually to retire to life on a small-scale farm.

They made love for over an hour, in the tub and on the bed, and again just before dawn; when his travel alarm sounded, she awakened to find that her arm was draped across his chest. This unconscious gesture, performed in her sleep, she considered progress.

Downstairs in the coffee shop they ate a large breakfast, and afterward he walked her out to the sidewalk. He would, he said, definitely come to the city next week—not on business but just to see her. He would call her on the weekend to confirm. Then he cradled her face in his hands and kissed her lightly under her right eye. "Have a wonderful day," he whispered.

"I don't think I could have any other kind."

She walked up the street in the direction of Mayhew, saying to herself, "I've been kissed in public." Like couples she had seen from her office window. And not on the mouth, which would have appeared vulgar, especially in front of a hotel. Under her eye, tenderly, while he held her face as if it were a precious jewel.

She was brimming with emotions that manifested themselves in a boundless energy, and despite her high-heeled shoes she walked at a clip that was close to sprinting. If only Maxson weren't gone! Tomorrow, she could have detailed her evening with Sam, the exhilaration outweighing the tears of her previous session.

Her chest seemed to be expanding to the point of bursting, and she wanted to shout, let out a wild whoop. Instead, she began to hum.

Sam Telias, smiling, arms folded, stood on the sidewalk and watched her until she disappeared up the avenue. Then he turned and entered the lobby, charted by the pair of eyes across the street that had witnessed his farewell to Fay.

A few minutes past three o'clock the next afternoon, Marsha called Fay at her office and asked if they could have dinner together. "I'd love to. When did you get back?"

"This morning. And I have to fly out again first thing tomorrow. But I wanted to see you first."

Fay detected a fleck of anger in Marsha's note of seriousness. What had she possibly done to upset her friend? She had sent a thank-you note right after UPS delivered Marsha's gift to her, an orange satin nightgown.

At ten minutes to six Fay sat down across from her in a small French restaurant on West Fifty-first Street. A waiter glided up as if on wheels and took their drink orders. Marsha's face wore a veiled look, and Fay attributed it to insufficient enthusiasm in the thank-you note.

"The nightgown is just gorgeous. I love the color so much that I've been looking for it in a blouse or a sweater. So far, no luck."

"Did you show it to Joe Blakis?"

"No." Her insides seemed to shift: it sounded vaguely unnatural for Marsha to say the whole name.

"Did he give you a gift?"

"No, I—we went out to dinner. But it wasn't very pleasant. There was an argument and—"

"When was this?"

"Uh, Sunday."

"Just this past Sunday?"

"Yes. Anyway, after the argument we decided to take a breather from each other."

Marsha's face went rigid. "A breather, huh? Try a *non*-breather. He's been dead for almost two weeks."

There were several seconds of disbelief, but Marsha's eyes were like two stakes driving home the truth. "Dead?" she whispered. "He—you *can't* be right about that, Marsha. How—"

"I was passing the library today, and couldn't resist popping into the Art and Architecture room just to get a look at him. The two men at the desk looked too old to be him, so I asked if he was around. Right away they wanted to know who I was. I said I was a friend of a friend and thought I'd say hello. That's when they told me: two weeks ago this Saturday he was murdered."

"Murdered!"

"Stabbed on the street three doors from his apartment building."

Fay whimpered but could form no words.

"The police assume it was a mugging, but they're obviously still investigating. One of the men said my 'friend' should call a Lieutenant Abdella, and he gave me the number."

For a while neither of them spoke, and Marsha reached across the table for Fay's hand. The grip unleashed the tears, and she turned her face to the wall. "I thought . . . thought he ditched me. He was supposed to call me last Wednesday, but he was *dead*, he was dead." She imagined a funeral at which she should have been present, far in the background, to offer a prayer and silent thanks for all the hours of escape, of serene happiness, he had given her. A gentleman, a gentle man, murdered, dead and disposed of by that afternoon she had expected his call.

Marsha waited until she'd wiped her eyes with the napkin, then spoke again. "He was murdered on Saturday night. You and I had brunch the next day, but you didn't know anything about it. You didn't until I just told you. Why didn't the police ever contact you? Why did you lie about having a date with him this past week? What exactly is *going on* in your life?"

Marsha's entreaty, the shock of Joe's death, Maxson's being out of town and out of reach—these thrust her into a full-scale revelation of her setup with Joe, Sam, Andrew. She omitted Kevin only because, for the time being, she didn't want to think about him.

Marsha looked flabbergasted. "All this time you've been seeing three men and I imagined you pining away with nobody."

"My . . . promiscuity has not been for thrills. If it were, it would probably be healthier." She now thought of what Marsha had said about the police. They had left no messages on her answering machine. Certainly they would have searched his apartment. Could he have concealed her number so well that it eluded their detection? Or had he simply memorized it, never written it down at all? "Do you think I ought to go see this Lieutenant—what's his name?"

"Abdella. I wouldn't. If Joe was the victim of a mugging—which he probably was—what's the point in revealing your private life? You know reporters hang around police stations waiting for stories."

A shiver ran through Fay, one she was ashamed of: in seconds, her grief had been forced to shrink to make room for self-concern. Carlos, Joe's doorman, knew her as Ann Decker, and the police would demand to know what *that* was all about. She imagined her colleagues at Mayhew reading the newspaper accounts of her nocturnal life.

She and Marsha shared a taxi across town and up Madison.

"Try to relax this weekend," said Marsha. "Get out and do something. I'll call you Monday from Chicago." She paused and, lowering her voice, added, "I know you've got Maxson and Sam and Andrew. But remember, I'm always available when you need me. No more of this big independence act, okay?"

"Okay."

The taxi stopped to let Fay out at Seventy-fourth, then continued on with Marsha.

She opened her mailbox and withdrew the contents, an advertising circular from a department store wrapped around a few business-size envelopes. Her tread on the stairway was light, for she wanted no contact with Mrs. Fleming tonight.

She dropped the mail into a chair, made a cup of tea, and laced it with brandy; it was tepid by the time she trusted her hand to lift it unshaking to her lips. The two images she could not shake away were the freckles on Joe's shoulders, the fish darting about in his aquarium.

When the tea was finished, she unfolded the circular and was confronted by the white envelope with the familiar block printing. Permitting herself no hesitation, she tore it open.

WEDNESDAY NIGHT—ALL NIGHT.
BAD GIRL.

Wednesday night and Sam.

The scream in her lungs did not find her voice, but her fist came down hard twice on the arm of the chair as she saw Kevin grinning at her in the elevator.

In bed she lay staring at the ceiling, repeating silently over and over her murderous wish: that the mugger's knife had found Kevin instead of Joe.

12

CLAIRE COLBY POWELL MADE IT HER BUSINESS TO MIND no one else's, and this policy most emphatically embraced her brother's wives. And so when Sheila began showing signs that there was more than the usual trouble in paradise, Claire extended not the subtlest invitation to confidence. Yet, a week ago, the night they had dined with Fay, Claire's two-second lapse into spontaneity unlocked a door she realized Sheila might now open; when Claire had exchanged a glance with Sheila at Curt's ordering a second drink, she saw something resembling supplication in her sister-in-law's eyes. There had been glimmerings of it daily ever since, and Claire found herself dipping into an arsenal of tactics for avoiding time alone with Sheila.

But on Saturday morning when her brother announced at breakfast that he was taking his Audi for a spin in the country, Claire knew, from the readiness of Sheila's "I think it would do you good," that the moment had come. After his departure, she'd waited in her room no more than ten minutes when the knock came.

"I need to talk to you," she said so meekly, tremulously, that Claire felt like a headmistress—Mother Superior—an unqualified one. "About Curt."

Claire nodded and Sheila sat down. In the past, Lenore and Fiona had come to her with their fears about the impending dissolution of their marriages, seeking antidotes with, she believed, the assumption that she had some kind of power over her brother. She, of course, had none: his generosity toward her over the years had been calculated precisely for the purpose of maintaining his autonomy. And she, better than anyone, understood his need for what he *thought* was autonomy.

But now, before Sheila continued, she had the feeling that fear of divorce was not the issue. With the two previous wives she had witnessed the signposts to Curt's waning interest—and, quite clearly, he was not yet tired of this one. His current change of behavior was rooted in something else entirely.

"You know," said Sheila, "that I don't poke my nose into Curt's and your relationship, and I'm not about to start now. Part of my bargain in this marriage is not to pry into the past. And I'm not asking you to reveal any secrets the two of you might have. But you *do* have a past together, and certainly more clues than I as to what's troubling him lately." She waited. And Claire waited. "You're aware of his staying out late some nights, but did you know there are other nights he *goes out* late, gets up after he's been in bed for hours?"

Claire concealed her alarm but lighted a cigarette.

"He says he just walks, but often I can detect he's had a few. A number of times I've looked into his office and seen him staring *at* a manuscript, but not reading it. And he doesn't talk about his work anymore—his first love. If his work goes, Claire, he'll crumble. You know that."

"I don't think it will go. Do you . . . suspect another woman?"

"Not in the least. And I don't think *you* do, either. I think you suspect what I suspect—that the trouble with him has something to do with Fay."

Right on the mark. "What in particular?"

"I was hoping *you* would tell *me*."

Claire dragged on the cigarette. "Well, then, what do you feel this 'something' is?"

"A search for resolution," said Sheila. "Exactly what kind I don't know. I know she gives him no inroad, but I can well imagine she has her reasons. Good ones."

"Yes, she does."

"If there was some way we could . . . help."

"There isn't. He must help himself."

"And if he's incapable?"

For an answer, Claire merely shut her eyes.

Sheila rose and started for the door. Her concern, Claire felt, was as genuine as could be. "Sheila, I'd like to ask you something pretty bald."

"Yes?"

"Naturally, you needn't answer. Why do you love Curt? I mean, what qualities in him?"

"He lets me live my own life, which is not a terribly productive one, but he doesn't seem to mind. He allows me to spend as much money as I like, and I spend a great deal of it—partly because I think he *enjoys* my spending. He asks my opinions about his writers and dismisses about three quarters of them, but still he asks. He has impeccable manners, a mind much keener, I know, than mine. And he's a terrific bridge player. Most important, once in his life he had a grand passion—Rosemary—which is why, I think, he doesn't talk about her to me. Most men never know such feeling."

"I wouldn't romanticize it. Rosemary killed a great deal in him."

"Fire consumes," said Sheila.

"You've adjusted well to his lack of affection."

"I wouldn't call it a lack. His display of it is just . . . unorthodox."

She knows him, thought Claire. She does know him.

"And," Sheila added, "if I may be indelicate . . ."

"Be."

"It's sexual."

Claire laughed at the warning. "I was married once."

"He's an animal in bed. And not the domestic variety."

"I see."

Sheila's pause indicated that the conversation was over if Claire wanted it to be. But Claire spoke up. "I'm sure I can trust to your discretion if I were to tell you something I don't want repeated to Curt."

"You can."

"He—was not a good father."

"I've suspected that. And I'm sorry for Fay. Even if we were both younger, I would never have a child with him. Some people aren't meant to be parents."

"You're right about Rosemary having been his grand passion. But not *just* his."

"She had a lover?"

"Several, ultimately." Claire offered her a cigarette, and the two of them lit up. "Curt had a brief indiscretion with a woman Rosemary was jealous of, and when she found out she went wild—Curt's wasn't a one-sided grand passion. She had plenty of admirers at her disposal, and she used some of them for revenge. But when she became pregnant she and Curt made a pact to let bygones be bygones. Then, after Fay was born, she became pathologically suspicious. There would be fights, a hiatus, and more fights. She began to drink, threatened to leave him and take Fay with her. But she never threatened suicide, and so when she *did* it he was thoroughly unhinged for a while. Instead of clinging to Fay he rejected her—passively, as if . . . as if to sever all connections with Rosemary. He immediately enrolled her in nursery school. He welcomed invitations I made for Fay to spend a night or a weekend with my husband and me. When he married Lenore, he more or less turned Fay over to her. Until Fay was old enough to be sent off to boarding school." She paused, took a long drag from her cigarette. "For all those years of coldness he cannot demand exoneration from her. If and when she's prepared to give it, it will have to be strictly voluntary on her part."

"Yes," Sheila said. "The shame is that it seems to be a no-win situation for both of them." She stood, asking nothing more. "Thank you for telling me."

"I didn't want to color your feelings for him."

"The only coloring is that I feel sorrier for him. *Because* of what he did to Fay."

Left alone, Claire remained sitting, heady with relief at having been able to tell part of the truth. There was another truth too, a complete one: she liked that woman.

Beckhorn was quick to point out that O'Brien had "walked through" the case they had just finished, involving the bakery owner and his embezzling employees. Beckhorn offered his observation out of concern, not complaint.

"Blakis, huh?" he said, sitting on the other side of the desk from O'Brien. O'Brien nodded and sighed. "Do you want to do something about it or let it keep eating at you?"

"I don't know yet."

An hour later O'Brien met with a prospective client, a young woman who suspected that her lover had given his wealthy wife a fatal injection of barbiturates, though the police were calling it a self-administered overdose. Shades of the Von Bulow affair, and one that could end up in court with O'Brien himself testifying. He was not in the mood, and referred her to another agency.

He spent the rest of the morning staring into space, chain-smoking, refusing telephone calls, and ordering up early lunch from the coffee shop downstairs. Another name besides Blakis's kept nagging at him, kept growing in weight and volume. Still he held back, restrained by the inertia of indecision.

As if the pastrami sandwich and vanilla malted had persuasive powers, the inertia dissolved when his stomach was full. From the top desk drawer he pulled out a telephone number from the Colby case, one he had never had cause to use. He dialed "1" and then the area code that would take his curiosity—and suspicions—long distance.

The company switchboard rang the extension belonging to the name he asked for.

"Mr. Telias's line." The woman's voice was raw and faint, a lugubrious signal over the wire.

"Is Sam in?"

Pause. "Who's calling?" Said without the usual appendage "please."

"Bob Harper. I'm an old friend of his from college." If Telias got on the phone, O'Brien would quickly establish that he had mistakenly reached the wrong man.

"I'm sorry, Mr. Harper"—the voice softened—"but Mr. Telias is dead."

"Oh, no! Was it recent?"

"Saturday. The funeral was yesterday."

"Had he been ill?"

"No." The hitch in her voice might have been a sob. "He was murdered."

"God almighty..." O'Brien moaned appropriately. "Who did it?"

"They don't know that yet. Someone... someone went out to his house and shot him in the heart."

O'Brien paused. "Is there a fund or a charity I can make a contribution to in his name?"

The woman now broke down completely, her grief probably sharpened by irony. "The Heart Foundation. Sam once had a heart attack."

"Thank you," O'Brien murmured. "I'm very sorry."

The second the receiver hit the cradle he called out: "Les—get me the Hartford papers from Saturday through today."

Beckhorn fairly ran in from the secretary's office.

"The Colby business?"

"You got it."

By four-fifteen O'Brien had what he wanted. There was nothing in Saturday's edition or Sunday's, and Monday's front-page coverage gave him the reason. Sam Telias, an insurance executive, was found dead just before midnight on Saturday, the victim of a single bullet from a .32-caliber. Friends who lived twelve miles from Telias's weekend farm had expected him for a dinner party at eight-thirty. When several telephone calls went unanswered the couple drove over after the party. The body was found just inside the unlocked front door; there were no lights on, no signs of a struggle, no apparent burglary. Speculation put the time of death at early afternoon. It had taken the authorities all day Sunday to locate and notify his immediate family.

Beckhorn read all this standing over O'Brien's shoulder, then popped two antacids into his mouth and sat down. "Well, what now?"

"I think," he said at last, "it's time for me to call on the mysterious Miss Colby."

O'Brien, however, missed her when the Gregson Building, which housed Mayhew Advertising, emptied its human contents between five and six o'clock. Fay was ten blocks north, making a presentation to a client.

She grabbed a quick supper in a pseudo-café that charged the earth for a hamburger by calling it something else. She ate little, but drank two glasses of wine in an attempt to calm herself for the first Tuesday-night session with Dr. Maxson. There was plenty to tell—good, terrible, and horrible. The horrible included her suspicion, following Marsha's news, that Kevin could possibly be responsible for more than just sending notes. She needed to find out from Maxson if her imagination was running away with her— and, if not, exactly what action to take.

At seven o'clock she began with Marsha's story.

"I can't go near that building. If Carlos the doorman ever spotted me—he knows me as Ann Decker, and if the police questioned me they'd want to know why I used that name, and why I visited Joe there. I'd look pretty suspicious."

"Yes. This doorman has probably been instructed to be on the lookout for you, so you'd be wise to stay away. But if the police do find you, is there anyone who could verify your whereabouts at the time Joe died?"

"Mrs. Fleming. I was home all evening. But, God, her encounter with Kevin was bad enough. If she knew I was involved with still another man, and using the alias Kevin told her about and I denied..."

"Don't worry about that unless the time comes. Now, about those notes..."

Fay affirmed her belief that they were from Kevin, then told about the "chance" meeting with him in the elevator.

"About that second 'Bad Girl' note, Fay: did you spot Kevin Wednesday night?"

"No, and I looked for him as soon as I entered the cocktail lounge."

"The note said 'all night.' Did you see him in the morning anywhere?"

"No. If he kept watch, then he's truly demented. But he might have bribed a bellboy or the desk clerk—Sam and I did leave together in the morning. I just can't believe he would be crazy enough to do something to Joe. But in case he *is*, I have to protect Sam. I have to warn him—and that will be the end of us. If Joe was killed by a mugger, then Kevin still wins, and I'll have to give up Andrew too."

"When you warn Sam you must be prepared for the possibility that he'll want to go to the police. It would be a natural reaction."

Fay now revealed her night with Sam, including the detail of waking up in the morning with her arm across his chest. Then she closed her eyes and was quiet for a while. "I don't know what to do," she almost whispered.

"I know the difficulty for you in this, but whatever decision you make must be yours alone."

Fay was thoroughly distraught by the end of the session, and the long taxi ride home was shortened by her preoccupation. What must she do about Sam? What might she do about Kevin?

Emerging from the taxi, she didn't notice the tall man leaning against the wrought-iron fence two buildings away. He started toward her before she'd even closed the car door.

The taxi drove off.

"Miss Colby?"

She nodded and took two steps back.

"I'd like to talk to you. My name is Earl O'Brien. I'm a private investigator."

"Talk about what?"

"Joe Blakis and Sam Telias."

"Who do you work for?"

"Right now, for myself."

"You're lying," she said with a vehemence that surprised him. "You tell your 'employer' to stop harassing me or I'll go to the police."

"Wouldn't a meeting with the police be a bit tricky for *you*? Since you're connected with two murders."

The world stood still. "Two! Not—Sam," she said, shaking her head.

"His funeral was yesterday."

Her eyes rolled back just before the lids closed, and he

caught her in mid-fall. Her slack mouth, icy hands, the absolute dead weight in his arms: this was no act. He was pleased that, to him at least, she was no longer a suspect.

He sat her down next to him on the steps of the brownstone, pulled her head onto his shoulder, and kept one arm around her; his free hand gripped both of hers and rubbed them vigorously. He knew he should be gently slapping her cheeks to bring her around, but for one prolonged moment his professional ethics flew out the window as he nuzzled his face against her satiny black hair and brushed his lips lightly over her temple. He realized now that, for weeks, this was what he had longed to do—this and more. Breathing deeply, he took in the scent of her, so different from the synthetic suggestiveness of the perfume and the stale-smoke muskiness that clung to the women he picked up in bars. Right now would be the closest he would ever get to her, and he wanted it to last.

When she stirred and groaned, he quickly pulled his face away. But *she* did not pull away from him, not from his enveloping arm or the hand that held hers. "Where...I thought I fell," she murmured.

"I caught you."

"I thought...I hate falling."

"Most people do."

"You're—what's your name again?"

"Earl O'Brien. We have to talk, Miss Colby. Do you think you can stand?"

In a sudden panic she swung her head around to look at Mrs. Fleming's windows. "Yes, but we can't talk here. There's a restaurant nearby where we can get a drink. I think," she said, rising unsteadily, "I could use a brandy."

When they reached the place, two blocks away, he wondered if it was the same one where Beckhorn had witnessed her tête-à-tête with Kevin Ivory. All the tables were taken, so they ordered their drinks at the crowded bar and waited in silence; it seemed that she could not stand and talk at the same time.

At last they were shown to a cramped corner, exactly what both of them preferred. O'Brien ordered a second round and said to her, "I'm sorry I had to break it to you that way about Sam Telias. But seeing it from my side—well, I had to be sure you weren't involved."

"Involved?" Her face reddened, and tears blurred her eyes but didn't fall. "What *is* this thing against me? You know, don't you? You *have* to know—you've been working for Kevin, following me, watching me."

"I swear to you, I have never worked for him, although I do know some things about him. For instance, a few weeks ago he slapped you on the street."

"If not Kevin, then *who* hired you to watch me?"

"I'll tell you, but not yet. You're going to have to trust me—just as I'll have to trust you. I have my own reasons for not wanting to go to the police, but I *will* go if you don't cooperate with me. I'm going to ask you some very blunt questions, and I want the truth to every one of them."

"I don't lie."

"But maybe 'Ann Decker' does." He watched her close her eyes and turn away. "I'm sorry, but my questions can't be soft. Two men are dead."

"Ask what you want."

"What was the full extent of your association with Blakis and Telias?"

"It was—romantic."

"You mean sexual."

"Yes, that too."

"Did they pay you?"

Her eyes flashed and her jaw tightened.

"Forget the indignation, Miss Colby. We don't have time for it."

"No, they did *not* pay me."

"You used an alias with Blakis's doorman. Did you also use it with Blakis and Telias?"

"Yes."

"For what reason?"

"To . . . maintain my privacy."

"You claim these relations were 'romantic,' yet you wouldn't divulge your real name."

"I did divulge it, finally."

"Why not at the beginning?"

"It's complicated."

"Try me."

"It's difficult for me to . . . trust people."

"Men, in particular?"

"Yes." She began shredding the cocktail napkin.

"Why didn't you trust these men?"

"Nothing specific. Look, I told you it's complicated. It's all mixed up with not trusting myself. I was afraid they would disappoint me or that I myself wouldn't be capable of living up to a real relationship."

A real relationship, thought O'Brien. What a sweeping and hazy term. He wondered what it meant to her.

"My alias was my out if anything should go wrong."

"What went wrong with Kevin Ivory?"

"I tried to break it off with him. Our last night together he went through my purse and found out my real name. He's been tormenting me ever since, sending me notes." She told him of the first one, in the Palmer penmanship, then of the other two that affirmed he had been spying on her.

"I would like to see those notes. Tonight."

"It will be awkward getting past my landlady. Her apartment's on the first floor, and she often keeps her door open so she can hear me come in. I never have visitors, so . . ." She stopped, looked embarrassed.

"You mean she keeps tabs on you?"

"Not exactly that. We're quite friendly, but sometimes she can be overly motherly."

"We'll think of something to tell her. Besides looking at the notes, there are some things I have to say, in a place where we'd be absolutely alone. But before we go—" He asked if she was involved in drugs, either taking them or dealing in them. Neither, she said. What about Blakis and Telias? Blakis, she suspected, smoked a little pot, but he was never incoherent or "spaced out." Telias smoked nothing at all, and he rarely had more than two drinks whenever she was with him. Anticipating his next question, she added that she was positive neither Kevin nor Andrew was involved with drugs.

"Andrew? Is that who you see on Fridays on Fifth Avenue?"

"Fri—? No. I see my analyst."

"Then who is Andrew?"

Embarrassment again. "Another man I've been seeing. I'm surprised you didn't know, since you've been spying on me." Suddenly, a look of shock came to her face. "Here I've been answering your questions and you haven't shown me any identification, and proof that—"

Stopping her words with a gesture, he withdrew his wallet and flipped it open in front of her. "And in case you think I'm a dangerous type to let into your apartment, I can call the waitress over and tell her to remember specifically serving us."

"That won't be necessary." She sipped her brandy. "You're very smooth, Mr. O'Brien."

"Honesty *is* smooth."

"Not always. For some it can be awkward."

"You're right, of course. One more awkward question: are there any other men you haven't mentioned?"

"No."

When they returned to the brownstone, Mrs. Fleming's door was indeed open, but O'Brien had prepared Fay for the woman's curiosity. "Mrs. Fleming, this is Mr. O'Brien. He's a private detective who's investigating a money matter at the agency."

O'Brien smiled and nodded. "Let me assure you your tenant is not a suspect."

"Well, I should think not."

"This is all confidential," Fay confided. "We're not to say anything to anyone."

"Then we certainly won't," replied Mrs. Fleming in a tone that revealed her delight in being included.

Inside Fay's apartment O'Brien surveyed the living room. Aside from its beauty he was struck by its order, an order that said only one person could live here. The *disorder* of his apartment made the same statement.

She produced the notes, but stood so close to him, awaiting his reaction, that her trusting and beseeching eyes seemed to raise the hairs on the back of his hands. He walked away, over to the lamp, pretending to need more light. "What makes you think the second two notes came from the same person who wrote the first?"

She was, of course, stunned by the very idea that there might be another note sender. "But who else would—?" She recounted her episode with Kevin in the elevator.

"Sounds like a very heavy coincidence. Even if he'd tracked you to the building, he had no way of knowing you would be on *that* elevator, at that moment."

"You're saying Kevin isn't responsible for those last two notes?"

"I'm not saying that at all. There *is* the condescending term 'girl' in all three, suggesting you're not a mature woman, or not as clever as the writer. Miss Colby, did—"

"Call me Fay. I never feel much like 'Miss Colby.'"

Gladly, he thought, but merely nodded. "Did the brandy steady you?"

"Yes," she murmured with the inflection of a question.

"Good. Would you please sit down. What I have to tell

you now isn't as bad as what I had to tell you earlier, but still it won't be easy for you."

Of the two or three possible reactions he had expected he saw only a hint of one—disbelief. But then that dissolved into a blankness. Perhaps the impact from the first blow of the evening had left her too numb to absorb the second. She stared at her knees and said nothing.

"I'm telling you the truth," he said. "I can describe—"

"I believe you," she said flatly.

He waited until it seemed she would sit there, silent, the rest of the night. "Can you give me some possible reasons why he hired me?"

"Only a general one: to try to control me."

"Control you? In what way?"

"Any way he can."

"Why would he want to?"

"His means of survival is to have everyone around him under his thumb. His present wife is his fourth; my mother was the first. She killed herself when I was four—jumped from the balcony of our apartment."

Something clicked. "On East Sixty-sixth Street?"

"How do you know that?"

"A guess. The Sunday I followed you over to the West Side and back, you paused for a while in front of the building. It seemed to me you were staring at a specific apartment, though if I remember right they all have balconies."

"You're *very* observant."

"I'm paid to be."

"You're asking *me* for reasons. . . . What reason did my father give when he hired you?"

"He implied you were secretive and he just wanted to know how you lived. I gave him my findings: your visit to Blakis's apartment, the meeting with Telias at the Hotel Hanson, the incident on the street with Ivory. The only information I hadn't been able to supply was the identity of the person you were seeing at Two Fifth Avenue. Your father agreed with me that it would be too risky to try to bribe the doorman of such a prestigious building."

"If he knew I was seeing an analyst, his blood pressure would skyrocket. He doesn't believe in them—although *he* should have gone to one years ago."

"Are you saying he's disturbed?"

"Yes."

"Enough to commit murder?"

The color left her face. "You mean him and not Kevin?"

"We're only considering possibilities right now. Would you consider your father a possibility?"

The look on her face was one not of reasoning or calculation, but of sadness. "I've felt . . . for the past few months . . . that he's been different around me. Watchful and insistent."

"Insistent about what?"

"He always seems to be on the verge of *saying* something."

"Any idea what it might be?"

"No."

"Maybe if you asked him outright what's on his mind."

"That's next to impossible for me to do. We haven't exchanged an intimate word since my mother died."

O'Brien recalled Colby's cold formality and containment, the knot in his tie a perfectly symmetrical triangle; the picture stirred the memory of the emotional holdout his own mother maintained until her death. "I think," he said, "that for tonight we've talked enough."

"Do you *strongly* suspect my father?"

"I don't know. But I have to tell you that one day your father was anxious for me to continue the assignment, and then the next day terminated it. He must have dropped me and hired someone else, to cover his tracks. . . . Tell me, have you met with this 'Andrew' in the past two and a half weeks?"

"No. He's been in Barbados and now he's in Europe."

"When is he coming back?"

"He said in about ten days, so that should make it the end of this week."

O'Brien pondered. "Can we talk again tomorrow night?"

"Yes, of course."

"Shall we make it dinner? It would be more relaxing."

"All right."

Before he gave her his card he wrote his home telephone number on it, and she did the same with her card. "You call me," he said, "tomorrow at ten at my office, and we'll decide where and what time to meet. Before I go, there's two things I want to do. Turn off the lights."

As she did, she experienced a tremor of renewed mistrust. It passed, however, when he went to the side of the window and looked out at the street in both directions. "All right," he said, "turn them on." Next, he went to the telephone, motioning her to join him. "What's Kevin Ivory's number?"

"I threw it out and have managed to forget it. But he's listed in the directory."

While O'Brien punched the numbers he instructed her: "I'll hold the receiver at your ear. If he answers, don't say a word. Just nod."

When she nodded, he pulled the receiver away and spoke into it. "I'm sorry. I must have the wrong number."

"What's this all about?" she asked when he'd hung up.

"One, there doesn't seem to be anyone out on the street watching us. Two, Ivory's still alive."

"Still alive!"

"If he's the killer, then your friend Andrew is safe as long as you stay away from him. If your fa—if Ivory's not the killer, then he himself might very well be in danger. Do you know where he works?"

"At home. He's a free-lance writer and a would-be poet."

"I'll pay him a call tomorrow. I'll need to take the notes. Don't say anything to anyone about knowing me—not even your friend with the blond hair."

"Marsha?"

"If that's her name." He tucked the notes into the inside pocket of his jacket.

"Mr. O'Brien—"

"Earl."

"Uh, I appreciate what you're doing for me, but would you mind telling me why *you* haven't gone to the police?"

"I have every intention of telling you. Tomorrow night."

In the hallway she stood at the top of the stairs and watched him descend. Mrs. Fleming appeared at her open door. "Good night, Mr. O'Brien."

"Good night, Mrs. Fleming. We may meet again."

As soon as he was out the door, the woman aimed her beaming face up the stairs at Fay. "He's very attractive, in an offbeat way."

"I suppose he is."

"A nice voice, too. Is he married?"

"I didn't ask."

Mrs. Fleming cocked her head to one side. "If she wants to, a woman can find that out without having to ask."

13

THE SECOND HIS EYES OPENED AT THE SOUND OF HIS morning alarm, O'Brien began his wait for her ten o'clock call. The night before, he had allowed himself two drinks before going to bed, and in sipping them slowly he had spent much less time in mulling over the newly learned information than in recalling the scent of her hair, the feel of her skin against his lips. He was in dangerous territory— proven by his failure to ask a crucial question—and yet he looked forward to having the day over with and cozying into dinner with her.

Perhaps his nonchalance was too forced when he entered the office, for Les Beckhorn surveyed him carefully—slyly, it seemed. Beckhorn's expression resurrected the unwanted memory of the knowing grin with which Lee Irwin had always delivered "Tunnabricks."

Beckhorn waited until the coffee containers were uncapped and the doughnuts bitten into. "So how's life and death treating the fair Miss Colby?"

"Not so well. She knew about Blakis but not Telias."

"Oh?" Beckhorn said too innocently.

"Right," O'Brien answered too firmly. "I'm going to try to see Kevin Ivory today."

"Then she's definitely hired us?"

"Not exactly."

Beckhorn's silence was as pointed as any quip would be.

"You'll still be getting paid," said O'Brien.

"Good. Rising prices have not overlooked Maalox."

O'Brien assigned his assistant an overnight trip to Hartford and got him out of the office before the call came.

"Earl?" Her voice saying his name made his grip tighten on the receiver.

"Hello, Fay." He asked how she had slept and if she had had any calls. Then he got to the important question he had neglected the night before. "Did Ivory ever threaten *your* life, even indirectly?"

"No."

"That night he slapped you on the street, did he threaten bodily harm?"

"No." She lowered her voice. "He called me a sick bitch. He said I'd been using him and now it was his turn to use me, that he wasn't going to be dropped." She told him about Ivory's conversation with Mrs. Fleming about her "stable." "That's why I was so apprehensive about last night—I mean about her seeing you come up to my apartment. I didn't want her to think—"

"I understand."

They set the time and place for dinner. Her last words before good-bye were "Be careful."

At eleven-fifty he buzzed Kevin Ivory's apartment on Perry Street and identified himself as the police. At the open door and under Ivory's sleep-puffed eyes he displayed his identification. "You can see that I'm *not* the police, but for your own good you'd better talk to me before I go to them."

"What the hell is this about?"

"Murder. And you."

Ivory's anger became astonishment, then fear. O'Brien already had a firm hunch but, as always before an interrogation, kept his mind open and judgment suspended. In the living room he took note of the two dirty glasses and empty wine bottle. Through the cut-out square in the kitchen wall he watched the man tip an aspirin bottle into his palm and suddenly look across the room at him.

"Who do you work for?"

"That's not important."

"What's this about murder? Who's dead?"

"We'll get to that. The first thing I want to know is where you were last Saturday *and* two weeks ago Saturday."

Ivory swallowed the aspirin, returned to the living room, and sat down. "I could call a lawyer right now."

"If you do, tell him to meet you at the Sixth Precinct."

There followed a long pause during which Ivory tried to outstare O'Brien. "Last Saturday I took pictures in Central Park and on the West Side. Then I had dinner out and went to a movie."

"Any proof of that?"

"Yeah. In there," he said, nodding toward the closed bedroom door. He got up, opened it, and leaned in. "Tina? . . . Tina?"

A low moan preceded a petulant "Whaaat?"

"Wrap the sheet around you and come out here a minute."

A pretty but pouty girl appeared in the doorway and looked at O'Brien.

"Tell this guy where you were last Saturday."

"What for? Who's he?"

"Never mind. Just tell him."

She rolled her eyes, pushed her hair away from her cheek. "Saturday, Saturday," she muttered in the obvious attempt to pull memory through a hangover. "In the park and then Riverside Drive."

"And that night."

"At the movies." She yawned.

"Who with, day and night?"

"You," she answered, as if Ivory were an idiot.

"Where was I two weeks ago Saturday?"

"Jesus, Kevin, I really need twenty questions right now!"

"Just answer."

"You were in Chicago."

"When did I go and when did I come back?"

Exasperated, she snapped, "You went Friday afternoon and you came back Sunday afternoon."

Ivory glanced at O'Brien. "Anything else?"

"No."

"Go back to bed."

"Thanks. And will you tell that bitch who walks her dog at six A.M. to keep its yapping mouth shut in the hallway." She closed the door behind her.

"I suppose," said O'Brien, "you flew to Chicago."

"Yes."

"And you have the plane ticket receipt."

"Yes."

"I'd like to see it."

"Christ!" He went into the bedroom, and O'Brien heard a girl snarl, "What the hell is going on!"

"Just shut up and go back to sleep."

"You're making it real easy."

O'Brien inspected the receipt. It had Ivory's name on it, a one-forty P.M. Friday departure from La Guardia, a twelve-thirty P.M. Sunday departure from O'Hare. The ticket had been paid for with MasterCard.

O'Brien produced the first of the three notes. "You wrote this, didn't you?"

Ivory's face reddened at the evidence, then promptly shifted to a look of horror. "Murder, you said. Not Fay!"

O'Brien kept silent and watched the openmouthed man go slack on the sofa. "Oh, Jesus, oh, God." Then came the fear. "You don't think *I*—you're not trying to accuse *me*, are you?"

"You'd make an excellent prime suspect, even though it's not Miss Colby who's been murdered."

"Well! *Who has* been?"

"In a minute. Tell me about the other two notes you sent to her."

"What other notes?"

O'Brien merely waited.

"I don't know what you're talking about. I only wrote—" He stopped, sensing the danger. "What are you trying to pull?" He jumped up. "You're not pinning anything on me!"

"You've got a nasty temper, Ivory. Don't try to use it on me or I'll have your ass in jail by the end of the day. Sit down."

He did.

"Now tell me about the other two notes."

"There aren't any other notes!" he practically screeched. "Who the fuck is dead?"

O'Brien let him squirm for a full minute, then stood up. "I think that's all I need to know for the time being." He returned the note to the pocket that contained the other two and started for the door.

"You can't do this! You can't come in here and make accusations without telling me who's dead."

"I'd suggest you and your girlfriend keep your mouths shut about this visit."

"This is harassment!"

"Yeah. Sort of what you did to Fay Colby."

"Fuck you. I'll call the cops."

"Do that. I've got the note. I've got witnesses that saw you slap Miss Colby on the street. I've got a landlady who listened to a tirade from you."

Ivory sputtered. "But you said Fay's not dead."

"Doesn't matter. The evidence I've got connects you to the person who *is*."

"Look, are you after money? Is that what you want?"

"You couldn't pay me enough. You just keep quiet about our little talk. I may be back, and I may not. Depending." O'Brien opened the door, then paused. "A bit of advice. For your own well-being, don't make a habit of dispensing wild accusations to your girlfriends' landladies. Besides, it's not nice."

They met at six-thirty in Chelsea, near his apartment. He noticed at once the circles under her eyes, the result of a poorly slept night, yet she smiled warmly the moment she saw him. The incongruity of dulled eyes and bright mouth was winning, and underscored what he had suspected during the time he'd followed her: despite the many signs of a "successful" life, hers had never been an easy lot.

She ordered white wine—"It's all I can handle right now"—but he opted for a double vodka martini—"It's what I need." His declaration turned her smile into a tight line of apprehension in preparation for his report. To minimize the tension he added: "After Kevin Ivory, I had a day of tying up loose ends at the office. And how was yours?"

"Pins and needles."

They sipped, and he lighted a cigarette; this, he knew, was the limit to which he could stall the information.

"Mr. Ivory showed me a piece of his temper."

"He didn't hit you, did he?"

The macho sector of his pride reared up and wanted to say, "Do you think I'd let him?" but he answered with a simple no. "Fay, I don't think he's our man."

Her eyes dropped to his fingers that held the cigarette, and then they wandered over the tabletop as if searching an escape from the obvious alternative to Kevin. O'Brien recounted in detail the meeting with Ivory, emphasizing the plane ticket receipt and the man's immediate assumption that it was Fay herself who had been murdered. In concluding his summary, he attempted a positive touch by assuring her that Ivory was squirming, gagging on his own medicine, but this in no way consoled her. "So now," he said, "the guy is going to need protection. Just in case."

"You mean the police?"

"Not yet. For the time being I can arrange with my assistants for a round-the-clock watch. But it's *you* who might be able to set up the most effective protective measure."

"Me?"

"By letting your father know you're through with Ivory."

The direct reference made her left hand tighten into a fist. After a long silence and two lifts of the wineglass, she said huskily, "And what about Joe and Sam?"

"It will be hard on you, I know, but you're going to have to help me look for evidence. Someone, no matter who it is, has to pay for those lives."

"I *want* someone to pay—no matter who it is. I also want you to understand something, Earl. Even though I don't love my father, I hope he . . . isn't the one."

"I'm sure you do. *Is* there anyone else you think could be responsible?"

"No."

"Andrew?"

She shook her head. "He's like Joe and Sam were, gentle as—"

"Was Kevin Ivory gentle too?"

"In his own way, at the beginning."

"Andrew, I take it, still thinks you're Ann Decker?"

"Yes."

"You said he was in Barbados when Joe was killed."

"Yes."

"What kind of work does he do?"

"He owns an art gallery in Soho. And one in San Francisco."

"His last name?"

"Thompson. Do you have to talk to him?"

"Yes. I'll be discreet and reveal as little as possible."

"And my father?"

"You and I will work that out together. I want to ask you something now, and you must think it over very, very carefully before you answer. If we talked to your aunt or your stepmother could they be trusted to say nothing to your father?"

"Not Sheila," she answered immediately. "Claire . . . Claire I'm sure would honor a vow of silence."

"Which one is Claire?"

"Sorry—my aunt. Will we have to tell her . . . everything about my involvements?"

"I don't see any need to be graphic. The term 'dating' should suffice."

Her smile of gratitude was childlike. "So now tell me *your* reasons for not going to the police."

He tapped his glass. "I'll need another one of these while I do. It's a long story."

"My favorite kind. And it's still early."

When he got to the part about finding Joy and Lee Irwin in bed, Fay winced; she winced again at his being suspended from the force. At the end, her face looked like an exposed nerve that would spasm if touched.

"When you beat up criminals," he said, "some of the guys you work with are outraged and some quietly applaud you—if you're smart enough not to be brought up on charges. But when you beat up a fellow officer, that's another story. Since I resigned, I like to stay out of police stations."

"Of course," she murmured.

"Now as applies to this case, I have to confess to something that makes me look paranoic—but it's something I do consider a possibility, albeit far out. There's an outside chance that when your father hired me to follow you, he chose me *because* of my record of—'brutality.'"

"How would he know—"

"It was in the papers when I was suspended and then again when I was reinstated and resigned. With pictures of me both times. I waited a year and a half before starting my agency, but even so I've had two people come to my office and recognize me. One took me on anyway—probably with the hope that I would beat the sh—beat up the husband who was cheating on her. The other one got up and walked out. But not before he told me I had no right to be in the business."

"But why would my father choose you specifically?"

"To set me up as a suspect if or when the police do connect Blakis and Telias."

"But what motive would *you* have?"

"Motives can be invented by suggestion. Look, I'm not saying I'd be indicted or even booked on suspicion, but I *would* get publicity I don't need. I like to work, and, even more, I like to eat." He lighted another cigarette. "And your father's lucky. You see, *I* have no alibi for the time period of both deaths. I was home alone. I didn't even talk on the phone. Which is why I'm steering clear of Blakis's doorman."

"So am I."

"Since we're on the subject of possibilities, don't forget that you would make a pretty good suspect yourself."

"But the notes—"

"Simple. You sent them to yourself."

"But the night Joe was . . . I was home. Mrs. Fleming can substantiate that."

"So you hired a hit man."

"Earl!"

"I'm only preparing you for what could be said."

For half a minute she looked dazedly into a far distance.

Then her eyes snapped back into focus and sought out a waiter. She ordered another glass of wine.

"Fay, what's your gut feeling about the possibility of your father being the one?"

She sipped twice, was about to speak, then sipped again. "He's so cold that in his presence you can be absolutely numbed. His cruelties are quiet ones, and they're beautifully calculated. But to kill someone—I don't know. Frankly, I don't think I or anyone else means that much to him."

"You meant enough for him to hire me."

She considered this in silence. Then: "You know, my analyst has dug up a lot from my memory." The silent move of his eyebrow made her ask, "You don't approve of therapy?"

"It's not for me, but I'm not against it."

"Well, it's been good for me. Anyway, I've come to remember things I had put aside or buried. There were some strange circumstances at the time of my mother's death. The next morning—the morning after my mother jumped—I noticed the edge of a bandage slightly visible above Claire's collar. It was a very high collar. I asked her about it and she said she had hurt herself when she fainted. Today she still carries a very thin scar just below the spot where a man would show an Adam's apple. How could she have got that from fainting? Another thing: my father didn't allow me to go to the funeral. Claire explained to me that he was concerned for me; he thought I'd find it too upsetting. But it was precisely the evening after the funeral that he sat staring at me at the dinner table, then threw down his napkin and left the apartment. He left me alone with the new maid until early the next morning. After breakfast he took me out and enrolled me in a nursery school."

The muted pain in her eyes made O'Brien recall the front-porch farewell to his mother, and he questioned the value of exhuming these traumas for clinical inspection. Then an important difference occurred to him: his mother's banishing him had happened when he was an adult; Fay's emotional abandonment had taken place at an age of utter dependency and powerlessness.

"The change in him was so radical I thought it would pass. Maybe seeing him that way, and being preoccupied with it, lessened the grief I felt for my mother. I know that memory is selective, and looking back now I can pinpoint the one incident, the one gesture, that symbolized his *committed* withdrawal from me. The nursery school required a medical examination. It was all painless until the end, when the nurse had to draw blood—"

"Draw blood? What for?"

"It was part of the exam. I wanted my father with me, but he refused to come into the room, so the doctor had to come in and do the procedure himself—he was our family doctor and the nurse was a stranger to me. We sat there for hours waiting for the results—"

"Why did you have to wait for them?"

"I guess he was anxious to get me into that nursery school. I went the very next day. Anyway, he went into the doctor's office to hear the report, and when we left we walked for a long time. It was at a quick pace, though not one I couldn't keep up with, but at one point I reached . . . reached for his hand, and when I touched it he pulled back like a snake had bitten him. Then he offered it, but as I held it I could feel the limpness; I could feel his discomfort. So I let go."

Her eyes were moist but not exactly teary, and O'Brien discovered he was holding his breath. As he was searching for something consoling to say, he was saved from failure by her next statement: "Let's order before this wine really gets to me. Since you're a regular here, what do you recommend?"

Halfway into his salad he said, "I want to ask you a favor, Fay, a big one. I'd appreciate it if you would not discuss this with your friends *or* your analyst."

"But—"

"For the time being."

"But I already told her about Joe and the notes, and when I thought Sam might be in danger she went along with me in my decision to warn him."

"You never know when an analyst can be forced to testify. With all the best and friendliest intentions in the world they can be extremely damaging, by saying too *much* or too *little*. I've seen it happen. Just wait awhile, until we're sure of our footing."

"I see her twice a week. Just last night I said I was going to warn Sam, so on Friday she's certain to ask how it went."

"Say you warned him."

"Earl, I can't lie to her."

"Right now, your best protection is to know nothing about Telias's death. Talk about other things. All right?"

"All right."

After dinner, she enthusiastically accepted his suggestion that they walk around for a while. It was ages, she said, since she had been in Chelsea. They talked about the city, the changes it had undergone in recent years, its slim chances of ever being a reasonably safe place again. When she asked for his views on the criminal justice system he answered that they were too complicated and depressing to repeat. "By my own code, I should've gone to jail for what I did to Lee Irwin. And, of course, I'm glad I didn't." They rounded a corner onto Sixteenth Street and he pointed. "That's the building I live in."

"Very solid-looking."

He laughed. "Discreet of you to seize on its one virtue. Actually, it *is* solid, although you wouldn't guess it by looking at the plaster in my apartment." What had been unconscious minutes ago was now fully surfaced. "Would you like to come up for a nightcap?"

"Sure" came so quickly that the tingle in his nerves was delayed until he unlocked the vestibule door.

"It's not the palace your place is."

"New York rents being what they are, no one has to apologize for where he lives."

Nevertheless, in the living room he apologized for the clutter.

"Clutter is only clutter," she said. "It's not dirt."

When they rounded the corner into the kitchen, she turned to him with a smirk. "No palace, huh? An eat-in kitchen, which anyone would give his right arm—well, a few fingers at least—to have."

"Well stocked too. Brandy?"

"White wine, if you have it."

"I do."

They settled into the living room and he hoped he was successfully concealing the full depth of his pleasure. After twenty minutes of light and smooth conversation he shifted to painful business. "Fay, as much as I dislike Kevin Ivory I have to think of his safety. As I said, he may be the next candidate, so we have to work fast. Do you talk to your father often, I mean on the telephone?"

"No. Once a week. If that."

"What about your aunt?"

"*At least* once a week, but usually during the day when I know he'll be at work."

"Have you talked to her this week?"

"No."

"Good. Would it be out of the ordinary for you to confide that you've split up with a boyfriend?"

"I've never discussed my relationships with her. For obvious reasons."

"If you were to find some way to confide in her—without calling it a confidence—do you think she would discuss it with your father?"

"I don't know. Probably."

"Then we'll take the chance. I hope you're a good actress. Very casually, I want you to get around to the fact that you've split up with a man you've been seeing. Mention

Kevin's name but not his *last* name—that's too blatantly informative, and your father could end up suspicious."

Five minutes later Fay was on the phone with Claire. "I just had to call," she began, "because I saw a dress in Saks today that's absolutely made-to-order for you. . . ."

O'Brien sat listening, fascinated by and proud of her performance. The second she hung up he applauded loudly. But she returned his praise with a blank stare and her face went white. "I don't know why," she said barely audibly, "but all of a sudden I feel—" Her head began to sway.

He jumped up and guided her into a supine position on the sofa. "Hold on, I'll get a cold cloth." He applied it to her forehead. "Last night and today have taken their toll. I'm sorry for clapping. It was a crass thing to do."

"It wasn't crass." She opened her eyes to convince him, and closed them again. When her breathing felt almost normal again she said, "How could you keep this apartment after what happened here?"

"Because it's big and it's cheap and life goes on. I *did* give the bed to the Salvation Army."

She finally was able to stand, but her legs were far from steady.

"Stay here tonight. I'll take the sofa."

"I couldn't. I—"

"You can. The morning menu in these posh digs features Turkish coffee, croissants, and fresh-squeezed orange juice."

Her laugh—her spirit—was stronger than the rest of her. "Well, that settles it."

His double bed was a far cry from her king-sized one, but the mattress was the same quality extra-firm. Here she was, nodding off to sleep in a bed belonging to a man she had never slept with. But within minutes the strangeness of it evaporated and she felt amazingly snug and safe.

While she was drifting away, glad that the bed was not

the same one his wife and friend had cavorted on, O'Brien sat in the living room. Drumming his fingers on the arm of the chair, he considered the unlikelihood that any school would require a blood test on a four-year-old.

14

O'BRIEN PRODUCED THE BREAKFAST HE HAD PROM-
ised, and Fay partook heartily. He ate half as much, his
eyes enjoying more pleasure than his palate: she had
obviously slept well, and he was delighted that a night in
his bed had erased the day-before circles from under her
eyes.

"Earl," she said as he poured her second cup of coffee,
"I think it's time we talked about money."

"Money?"

"Your fee."

"That can wait. We don't want any distractions now."
To support this excuse he got down to business. "Now,
you're sure Andrew Thompson will call you as soon as he
returns?"

"Yes, I'm sure," she answered, feeling embarrassed and
not knowing entirely why.

"We'll just have to wait till he gets here. But your aunt
... Fay, are you absolutely certain she can be trusted? I
mean, if you and I talk with her and reveal all we know, is

there even the slightest chance her allegiance would still be to your father?"

"I don't think so, not when she knows . . . murder is involved."

"Because if she were to compromise us we'd both be in danger."

Fay stopped chewing and swallowed. She pushed the croissant away and pulled the coffee cup toward her. "I can't be a hundred percent sure about anything when it comes to—my family. It's far from normal."

"Mine wasn't *Father Knows Best* either."

"Yet my instinct tells me Claire can be trusted."

"Then I'm willing to bank on your instinct."

"What exactly do you want to find out from her?"

"First, if she knows where your father was at the time of both murders. We'll go from there."

"Suppose he has—what do you call it?—'airtight' alibis?"

He hesitated, reluctant to dim the radiance a good night's sleep had done much to restore. "They could be valid and he could still be guilty. Again, Fay—there's such a thing as hired killers. I want you to be aware of all the possibilities before they present themselves."

"And the possibility that he's innocent—what then?"

He could not hammer her with his certainty about Colby. For evasion, he sighed and said, "Then we're back to square one. Now, about your aunt. When we talk to her I'd prefer not to use my office, and her coming here to a stranger's apartment might be equally intimidating. I suppose it would be awkward getting around Mrs. Fleming?"

"Tomorrow night would be good. She plays bingo."

"For sure?"

"Every Friday, without fail. She leaves at seven-thirty. Just to be safe, we could make it eight o'clock. I'll call Claire this morning." She saw O'Brien open his mouth, and she correctly anticipated him. "Of course I'll tell her to keep it secret."

"Suppose your stepmother answers or happens to be in the same room?"

"No chance of either. Claire has her own phone in her room, with a separate number." Precisely this arrangement had given Fay the idea for the second line in her apartment.

At the front door they agreed to talk at seven o'clock. He wanted to suggest dinner again, but managed to refrain.

"Thanks for everything, Earl. I'm much steadier this morning. The only thing is, I feel guilty for having slept so well while Joe and Sam—"

"Your losing sleep won't bring them back. Regrets and grief should be reserved for the waking hours."

She nodded. He stood at the open doorway and watched her until she disappeared into the elevator.

During his first half hour in the office he phoned six nursery schools in Manhattan, and with each person who answered, he launched his search in the same manner: "I wonder if you might help me. I'm enrolling my daughter in a nursery school that requires her to have a physical. Is that standard procedure?"

Yes, each child must receive certain shots before admittance to class.

"This school also requires her to have a blood test. Is that also standard?"

Certainly not, sir, never heard of such a thing. Not unless you alluded to some kind of blood ailment in the family. May I ask the name of this school?

He spent the remainder of the morning wondering what Colby's sister would be like and if she could indeed be trusted—and considering the possibility that once the case was concluded Fay might fly into the arms of Andrew Thompson.

Les Beckhorn appeared at two-thirty, immediately upon his return from Hartford.

"Let's hear it," said O'Brien.

"It's not much, but it's all I could get, keeping a low profile." Beckhorn sat and chewed two Maalox tablets as casually, automatically, as O'Brien would fire up a cigarette.

"In report-card terms, this guy was an honor student. From everyone I talked to, it was hosannas in the highest: he was 'so considerate,' 'so generous,' 'so hardworking and disciplined.' He loved his little weekend farm and had planned to retire on it. I used the cover that he and I had met and become friendly here in New York because we stayed at the same hotel. His friends, the couple that found the body, were especially nice to me. They're retired, and during the week, one or the other would drive over to Telias's to feed his chickens. The woman broke down twice and said if it had been robbery she could at least understand it—he has no enemies. His daughter and her husband have posted a modest reward for information leading to arrest."

"No wife?"

"Widower. I'll tell you, Earl, I think I'm getting old. It's harder and harder to shrug it off when nice people . . . I hated lying to that couple. When I said I was a friend of Telias's, right away they were treating me like family. Yet they'll go to their graves thinking my name is Leonard Wallace."

O'Brien replied quietly, "There's another way of looking at it, Les. You gave them the opportunity to talk about their friend. When people are grieving they need to talk." Before Beckhorn could agree or take exception, O'Brien moved swiftly on. "Would Edith kill me if I put you on a twelve-hour shift for the next few days?"

"She won't get the chance—*I* will."

"It may not even be for days, depending on information I get tomorrow night. Kevin Ivory has to be watched around the clock. You take whatever twelve hours you want; Hoag will take the other twelve."

"Hoag's gonna love me. And where'll *you* be? In Florida?"

"No, I'm going to try to dismantle a time bomb named Curt Colby."

At one minute to seven his telephone rang. Fay told him all was set for eight o'clock the next night; her aunt had promised to tell no one.

"Earl, Andrew's back. I had a message on my machine."

His heart dipped. "Is he usually at his gallery during the day?"

"Yes, I think he opens around eleven. He also lives upstairs, on the second and third floors. There's a separate entrance next to the gallery." She gave him the address.

"What does he know about Ann Decker? What personal circumstances did you present?"

"He thinks I'm separated from my husband and that I have children. What . . . are you going to tell him?"

"As little as possible. When I was working for your father, Fay, you never led me to Andrew, and you haven't seen him since. So I'm fairly certain he's in no danger. I just want to feel him out, see if he qualifies as a low-level suspect."

"He won't. He's a nice man, Earl, and very . . . mellow. Almost phlegmatic."

"Still waters run deep."

"Not in a placid pond, they don't."

He laughed. "All right, I'll see for myself."

The next morning he was irritated by self-admission: he wanted to dislike Andrew Thompson as much as he disliked Kevin Ivory. But when he entered the gallery in Soho at eleven-forty and saw and heard Thompson talking with a French couple, O'Brien's wish was frustrated. Dressed in chinos, crew neck sweater, and penny loafers, his hair clipped as short and evenly as grass on a golf green and his face clean-shaven, Thompson looked more like the proprietor of a small-town malt shop than the owner of this business located in one of the most pretentious neighborhoods in the world. About thirty-five, of medium height and build, he had a plain, pleasant face that would not distinguish itself in any crowd. Arms folded, standing with the couple before a nasty-looking piece of modern sculpture, he spoke in fluent French.

O'Brien felt intrusive, so he moved off to a far corner and pretended to survey a spotlighted object entitled "Angel with Melting Wings." If this were a glimpse of heaven, he thought, then the horrors of hell were best not imagined, much less depicted.

He heard the approach of the penny loafers and turned to see a winning—and modest winner's—smile trained on him.

"Hello," said Thompson. "Are you familiar with Mrs. Knudsen's work?"

"No. And if you'll pardon my saying so, it doesn't look like she wants anyone to get familiar with it."

Thompson laughed, and spoke in a conspiratorial tone. "I agree, but her stuff never gets a middle-of-the-road reaction. A decorator was in here last week and bought three pieces for his clients. The way he drooled over them, I thought I'd have to mop the floor."

O'Brien was quickly realizing why Fay liked this man. "Mr. Thompson, I'm here to talk to you about Ann Decker."

"Ann? Is there anything wrong? Is she all right?"

"She's fine."

"Are you—her husband?"

"No, just a friend. Listen, if you want to take care of those people over there I can wait."

"No, no, they're just looking. What about Ann?"

The concern in the man's voice and eyes was a clear indicator of his attitude toward Fay. Swiftly and decisively,

O'Brien worked at squelching his jealous imagining of her and Thompson in bed together.

"She wanted me to explain why she can't see you for a while."

"Then she's told you about us?"

"She had to. You see, she's pretty sure she's being followed, and of course she suspects her estranged husband is behind it. Until she gets the situation straightened out— well, she doesn't want you involved in any way."

There was a pause before Thompson asked, "You and Ann are only friends?"

"Only friends."

"Why didn't she call me? She could've told me this over the phone."

"She felt awkward and thought it best you be told in person. She'll be in touch as soon as she gets to the bottom of this."

"Mr.—"

"Wallace. Leonard Wallace."

"You say you're a friend of Ann's. Are you a friend of her husband's too?" And Thompson looked O'Brien straight in the eye.

This guy's no dope, thought O'Brien, knowing precisely Thompson's suspicion. "I'm not a friend of her husband's. Now I'll let you get back to your customers."

"Just a minute." Apology was already in his voice. "You must understand my position, with something like this coming out of the blue."

"I do understand. Another thing," he said, taking a small spiral pad and a pen from his pocket. "I'm going to give you phone numbers where I can be reached day and evening. If you find, or even suspect, you're being followed, don't hesitate to call."

"Is her husband—dangerous?"

"No, he's just being a pest. My own feeling is that he's

having her followed in hopes of finding something he could use in a custody action if they do divorce."

"Yes, I see."

The evening number O'Brien wrote down was his apartment phone; the day number was the direct line to his office that bypassed the secretary.

Thompson walked with him to the door. "Mr. Wallace, I want you to know I *am* glad Ann has such a helpful friend."

"Thanks. Tell me, do you think you'll unload that 'Angel with Melting Wings'?"

Thompson grinned. "Oh, yes. Reassuring, isn't it, that if there's no ugliness in your life you can go out and buy it."

O'Brien walked up Wooster Street with a feeling of relief that Andrew Thompson had not been included in the reports to Curt Colby. And the jealousy he had experienced just minutes ago was now transformed into an increased respect for Fay. With the exception of Kevin Ivory, her taste in men was superlative.

While O'Brien settled onto a stool at a lunch counter, Fay, a few blocks north and west, entered Olivia Maxson's office in a state of considerable but—she hoped—concealed anxiety. She would do as O'Brien had instructed, but it wasn't going to be easy.

Dr. Maxson was even more attractive than usual today. Or was Fay imagining a difference, exalting the figure she had to lie to? But no, the jade combs that held the rich chestnut hair away from the cheeks but not the ears, the string of jade beads, the cantaloupe-colored sweater coupled with forest-green skirt and matching shoes—all of these showcased her patrician face and complexion, and the younger-than-her-years figure. A class act, thought Fay, and one she would love to be seen with in public. Having watched Maxson walk only the distance between desk and analyst's chair, still she knew that the woman's posture contributed importantly to the total head-turning image.

"You look fantastic," Fay said, a little more exuberantly than she had intended.

Dr. Maxson's smile was small but sunny. "Thank you. It's a bit much for the office, but I'm going to a concert tonight and won't have time to change."

"The jade is beautiful. Just perfect for your skin and hair. You bought well."

"As a matter of fact, I didn't buy. They were a gift."

"From an admirer?"

Maxson's eyes closed, and reopened with languid amusement. "Yes, from an admirer. Now, are we going to continue in this vein or get down to business?"

"Let's continue," Fay said eagerly. "Why don't we talk about you for a change? We've never done that, and I *am* curious. It would be fun."

"You're in the mood for fun today?"

"Yes. The vacation might do me some good."

"All right. This is very expensive fun, so we'll limit it to ten minutes."

"Oh, no, let's not limit it."

"Fay, I like my work, and I like it even more when I know I'm doing it well. Frittering away your money is not doing it well. Ten minutes."

Fay dived in at once. "What concert are you going to?"

"Mozart at St. Bartholomew's."

"Who are you go—oh, if I ask anything you don't want to answer, just say so."

"I will. You were about to ask who I'm going with?"

"Yes."

"I'm going alone. Mozart is my favorite, so when I go to hear him I prefer to listen undistracted."

"How did you get interested in classical music?"

"Through friends. In college."

"I was always intimidated by it. I thought you had to be practically a genius to appreciate it."

Dr. Maxson laughed. "Not at all, judging from the conversations that take place in the lobbies."

"What are your other interests?"

"Not terribly active ones. Reading, haunting museums."

"Who are your favorite painters?"

"They're too numerous to list."

"Do you like Vermeer?"

"Very much."

Fay was delighted, since Vermeer had long ago become her favorite.

"I like his idealism," Dr. Maxson continued, "because it's not a naive idealism. There *are* times in your life when, perhaps just for a second, you glimpse an example of that startlingly perfect light he was able to create."

"Which of his is your favorite?"

"I suppose *The Letter*: the ambiguity of the maid's smile, the quiet alarm in the mistress's face. Such a contrast makes you wonder what the letter could possibly contain, makes you wonder whether or not the maid has read it. But then, the element of nearly opposite reactions *would* appeal to anyone in my profession."

Here, thought Fay, their tastes diverged. *The Letter* was, for her, an unsettling painting precisely because of the particular subjective qualities Maxson found fascinating. She herself preferred *The Instruction of the Virgin*, whose figures were a child kneeling before a benevolent, maternal woman. Its aspect was soothing, as it contained no ambiguity at all. Fay could not stop her mind from racing toward analysis: was Maxson's favorite a more mature work by the artist? And was her own preference defined by her deprivations, her lifelong desire for security, so that her taste was formed largely from wish-fulfillment? Suddenly, the value of her choice was diminished. And she told Maxson so.

"There *is* an accounting for taste," replied Maxson, "but

only up to a point. My choice is by no means superior to yours—after all, both paintings are accepted masterpieces. In choosing among great works of art it's not the merit of the art that's operative but rather one's personal taste. For example, *Lear* and *Hamlet* are both beautiful plays, but *Lear* captures me more. I don't apologize for my taste. Nor need you for yours."

The tone of finality in Maxson's voice implied to Fay that she was ready to turn to serious business. Fay hurried on to another subject.

"Are you athletic?"

"Not in the least. I find perspiring very uncomfortable."

"How do you stay so fit?"

"I walk, and when it's too hot for that I swim."

"Did you . . . have a happy childhood?"

"Reasonably."

"Were you as confident then as you are now?"

"Hardly. A child has no vocation except *being* a child. I was very anxious to get childhood over with so I could begin a career."

"Did you always know what you wanted to be?"

"Yes, except that from month to month it was always something different. Until high school. I decided then that in college I would have a dual major in English and theater. It was hard work, but enjoyable. I learned the value of a good diet and vitamins, which allowed me to get by with five hours' sleep a night."

"But how did you come to be an analyst?"

"I wanted some autonomy. You can't have that in the theater, even if you're a playwright. And I knew that being a college professor would sharply limit the power I wanted over my life. You can't create a position, you go where there's one available, and more often than not you end up stuck somewhere unsuitable because you want tenure."

"So you went back to school and started over?"

"Yes. Our fun is finished; it's been ten minutes."

"Really?"

"Really."

Fay felt her spine stiffen, as if to keep her afloat on the waters of wordlessness: she could not initiate the lie; she could give it only in response to a question. But Maxson waited. And waited. The silence was deadly—a live intruder, an enemy to both women. It destroyed trust and suffocated honesty. Reluctantly, Fay got up and went to the couch, then Maxson took her position behind it.

Still no words. Finally, Maxson did speak, and attempted levity. "Are you going to nap, Fay?"

"No."

"Then let's move along to Sam. Did you decide to warn him?"

"Yes."

Silence again, and Fay prayed to Earl for help.

"And his reaction?"

"He was—well, bewildered at first, and then rightfully apprehensive about the possibility of a connection between . . . him and Joe.

"Did you mention the notes?"

"No, I just couldn't."

"What decision did the two of you arrive at?"

"I said I thought it best that we not see each other for a while. The police might clear up Joe's death; it might have nothing to do with the note at all." She began to cry, noiselessly, for she realized that what she was saying was more than deceit with Maxson; it was an insult to Sam, this denial that he was dead and buried with a hole in his heart. He deserved a forthright expression of grief and outrage.

The tears subsided, but the trembling and guilt did not. "Dr. Maxson, I'd like to call it quits for today."

"I think it would be best if we continued."

"I can't. I'm sorry. It's going to be a tough afternoon at work and I need to—compose myself." Another lie. It was this evening's meeting with Claire that would require composure.

"Until Tuesday, then."

Fay wanted to flee without looking at the woman, but after wiping her eyes and cheeks she turned and said, "Enjoy your concert tonight."

"Thank you. And I hope your tough afternoon goes smoothly."

After the door closed, Olivia Maxson sat down behind her desk to mull over the abortive session. Beyond her professional concern over this setback lay a deeper regret that her favorite patient was caught in some mysterious turmoil that had prompted, first, evasions, and then not-so-subtle lies. Of course, the present situation in Fay's life was traumatic, but why this sudden dishonesty?

She swiveled the chair around, looked out the window, and wondered if that father of Fay's had had a hand in any of this.

15

CLAIRE POWELL WAS DUE AT EIGHT, AND O'BRIEN wanted to arrive at Fay's before her. Across the street and halfway down the block, he watched the building until Mrs. Fleming, on schedule, departed for bingo at seven-thirty. Three minutes later he was climbing the stairs toward the door Fay held open for him.

Her face was ashen, her eyes listless, and he wondered if she had either taken a pill or was coming down with a virus.

During that day she had advanced her skills in interpreting silences, so she quickly answered his unspoken question: "It wasn't an easy session with Dr. Maxson. I came home early from the office and tried to nap, but all I've been able to do is pace."

"You said nothing to her about Sam?"

"I said I warned him. She knew I was lying."

"She challenged you on it?"

"She wouldn't have to. She knows me better than anyone else, and I've never lied to her before."

"Fay, once this is over with and you can level with her, she'll understand why you did what you did."

"I know that. But suppose it's *never* over with. Suppose my father isn't the—isn't guilty. And you say Kevin has solid alibis. Suppose the notes just stop coming and no one else gets hurt. Then what do we do?"

She was, he knew, approaching hysteria, and there was no time now to coddle it. Gripping her shoulders, he said, "Look, you go to Dr. Maxson to find out truths about yourself—right?"

She nodded.

"No matter how painful those truths are?"

"Yes."

"And if you keep trying to avoid them, what happens? They get more and more difficult to face, don't they?"

"Yes."

"I'm not a shrink and I've never been to one, but my work is similar to a shrink's—putting together clues, sometimes clues that first appear insignificant, until I arrive at a fairly full picture of a person. Then from that picture I try to deduce motive. You say Dr. Maxson has helped you a lot. Isn't it because she's good at what she does?"

"Of course."

"And intelligent?"

"Very."

"And because you have the feeling she genuinely likes you?"

"Yes."

"And because you *want* to be helped, no matter how hard it is for you emotionally?"

"Yes, yes, but—"

"All right. *I'm* good at what I do, *I'm* intelligent, *I* genuinely like you, and I know you want my help. But I have to warn you that tonight might be rough. If your aunt's evasive, I can't go easy on her. If you prefer, you can wait in the bedroom while I question her."

"No. I want to be with her."

His hands left her shoulders, traveled down her arms, and lightly enclosed her wrists. "Just do this for me. Forgive me now, ahead of time, for the things I have to say to her. Please. It's important to me."

"Earl, I—"

"Please."

She closed her eyes and nodded.

Any second now the bell might sound. Yet there was still much to say, and considering what she had been through this week and what he would put her through tonight, he had to speak slowly. He wanted her to absorb it all. "Fay, we can think we know ourselves inside out—our faults and our strengths—but there can still be moments when we're a mystery to ourselves. That episode I told you about with Joy and Lee—"

"That would make a lot of people snap. A wife and a best friend carrying on."

"Yes, but that's not my point. The point is that I always prided myself for escaping my mother's flaming prejudice—but *would* I have flipped out the way I did if Lee were white? You see? I'll never know."

"No, you won't. But it's a common phenomenon for white men to attribute black men with—greater prowess."

"A polite euphemism. But in that department, probably I'm equal to him, so I can't use physical jealousy as an excuse. If that sounds like bragging, Fay, forgive me; I'm trying to make another point or two. One of them is that I still have no excuse for beating Lee Irwin up, and no explanation for standing there like a Peeping Tom watching them go through the whole thing. I could've interrupted them. I could've gone into the living room and waited until they were finished. But I stood there because some sick little part of my mind *wanted* to watch. Maybe is was an attack of masochism, maybe it was to reinforce righteous indignation, or maybe—despite who they were—it was a a thrill to watch black and white in bed."

"Maybe it was all three."

"Exactly."

Her face was brightened by a sly smile. "Are you *sure* you've never been in therapy?"

"Look, all this is to say that no matter how confident and brutal I may appear tonight, I'm not going to enjoy it. Please keep in mind that besides doing it for you and me, I'm also doing it for Blakis and Telias and possibly Andrew Thompson. On this occasion I *do* know what my motives are."

"God, you make it sound like you're going to draw and quarter her."

"Maybe, emotionally." And possibly you too, Fay, he thought to himself.

Both of them flinched at the sound of the bell. "One thing," said O'Brien as she moved off to the buzzer. "There's no need to show her that first note from Ivory. She could use it to deflect evidence from your father. When she gets up here and you introduce us, don't tell her specifically who I am. Leave that to me."

Fay opened the door, and she and Claire began their greetings while Claire was still ascending the staircase. O'Brien watched the aunt kiss her niece on the temple; then he assessed her at closer range, when she offered her hand in introduction. Just from her appearance, she was not the woman he expected. There was the strong resemblance to her brother, right down to the formal posture. But her eyes were not two discs of blue ice; they were darker, softer, and—he believed—more trusting.

She sat, accepted the offer of a gin and tonic, and looked around the room. "Fay, this is one of the most beautiful apartments I've ever been in. Do you have someone to clean it?"

"No, I do it myself. I find it's good therapy."

"Yes. There's nothing like a dustmop or a scouring pad to take your mind off things." This was said casually, good-naturedly, the first half to Fay and—with a turn of the head—the rest to O'Brien. Claire Powell had displayed not even the mildest surprise at finding a stranger present, and O'Brien wondered what her real thoughts were behind this relaxed facade.

Fay delivered the gin and tonic, and brandy and soda for herself and O'Brien. They all sipped at once, and Fay thought of an orchestra tuning up its instruments before the performance. Right now, she wished she were sitting next to Dr. Maxson, discovering Mozart.

"Claire, I asked you here tonight because Mr. O'Brien wants to talk with you."

Claire blinked and turned to O'Brien. "Oh. About what?"

"First, I'll tell you who I am. I'm the private investigator your brother hired to follow Fay." He saw the involuntary parting of her lips, the tightening of fingers around her glass. "You *were* aware that he hired me?"

"I . . . yes." She set the glass down.

"Claire!"

"Fay, he told me after the fact, and I told *him* to stop." She looked at O'Brien. "Did he or did he not terminate your services?"

"He did."

Claire's gaze shifted to Fay, then back to O'Brien. "This leads me to question your ethics, since I assume the client takes for granted your silence and discretion."

"He does. And he gets both, unless there are exceptional circumstances."

"What are these 'circumstances'?"

"In a minute. First, I have to say that I didn't find your brother a pleasant man."

"I have a distinct suspicion," Claire retorted, "that *I* am

going to feel the same about *you*." Then to Fay: "What kind
of trouble is he starting?"

"The trouble has already started," O'Brien answered.
"And not thanks to me."

"You were only employed by my brother and not for very
long, so you can't possibly know what kind of man he is."

"Mrs. Powell, I think perhaps *you* don't know entirely
what kind of man he is, what he's capable of." He paused
purposefully and narrowed his eyes. "Or maybe you do."

Slowly, Claire's face rotated toward Fay; visible in it,
besides anger, was confusion, and hurt that asked the silent
question "Why did you bring me here for this?" Fay clutched
the arms of her chair and said, "Earl, *please*." But the look
he gave her pleaded for her trust, reminded her of their
agreement. As she lowered her head, Claire made a motion
to stand.

"Don't get up," he warned, "unless you prefer to talk to
the police instead of me."

"The police?" She settled back, and he saw more than
alarm in her: this woman feared the police.

"First, can you recall your whereabouts last Saturday?"

"Yes," she answered in a tiny voice.

"Well?"

"I stayed home all day, until about four, when I went out
to shop for dinner."

"And your brother and sister-in-law?"

"Sheila left around one to play bridge. Curt went for a
drive in the country."

"At what time?"

"After breakfast."

"When did he return?"

"He was there when I got back from shopping."

"Did he say exactly where he had been?"

"West Jersey, Hunterdon County. He likes the old stone
houses there. For years he'd been toying with the idea of
buying one."

"Does he go for drives often?"

"Sporadically. It's his relaxation. Now will you please tell me what this is all about?"

"For the moment, rest assured that it's about something very serious. I'll explain fully once you've answered my questions. When your brother goes for these drives, is it always to Hunterdon County?"

"No, sometimes he goes to northern Westchester or to Connecticut."

"House-looking?"

"Yes. And . . ." She glanced at her niece. "Fay's mother's grave is near Greenwich. I suspect he sometimes visits it."

"After all these years?"

"After all these years" made Claire wonder how much Fay had told this man and why. "She was his first wife and a suicide. Of course, he still feels some guilt."

"Guilt?"

"Because he couldn't save her."

"He *wanted* to save her?"

"Yes." Her hands were sweating, but she dared not wipe them.

"More of that later. Now, Mrs. Powell, I must tax your memory. Can you remember where you were on Saturday night, three weeks ago from tomorrow night?" He gave her the date.

"Dates mean nothing to me. Whenever I write out a check I need to look at the calendar." She paused, fighting to squelch panic and bolster memory. "Three weeks . . . Oh, yes, I went to the Carnegie Hall Cinema. It's a revival house."

"I'm aware of that. What was playing?"

"*Philadelphia Story* and *Bringing Up Baby.* I stayed only for *Philadelphia Story.*"

"You've seen it before?"

"Yes, it's one of my favorites."

"Mine too. I've always liked the woman who plays the reporter. Ruth Roman."

"No, the reporter is Ruth Warrick."

"Ah, you're right." Now for the pounce from left field. "Mrs. Powell, why did your brother take Fay for a blood test right after her mother died?"

She blinked as if she had been slapped, but his stare was relentless, and it said, "Don't lie to me, sister, I'm looking right through you."

"How did you know—"

"Just answer the question."

"He—he took her for a physical for nursery school."

"I've checked with more than a dozen nursery schools," he said, lying about the number, "and not one of them requires a blood test. And your brother sat in that doctor's office all afternoon waiting for the results—it was that urgent to him. You'd better start giving me some straight answers or I'm going to pick up that phone and turn you and your brother over to the police."

"But what has a blood test got to do with anything? What," she pleaded, "is going on here!"

"You'll know soon enough. Now why the blood test?"

He watched her breathe deeply as she spread out her hands on the sofa cushion. "Mr. O'Brien, you don't know what you're asking of me. Fay—Fay has never known about this."

"She remembers the test."

"But Earl," said Fay, "what *are* you getting at?"

With her eyes trained on the wall opposite her, Claire said, "It was an attempt to learn once and for all if Fay was in fact his daughter."

O'Brien glanced at Fay, whose face was a total blank. "Go on."

"A few years into the marriage, Rosemary—Fay's mother—acquired several . . . admirers. She also became an alcoholic. She implied to Curt, whenever she was drunk, that Fay might not be his child. But the blood test proved nothing. Fay was type O, like Curt and Rosemary. And O is the most common type."

It was now time for O'Brien to switch tracks and return to the present. This was a tactic he had learned long ago: interrupt the line and the logic of the interrogation, hindering the subject's ability to anticipate questions and create lies.

"Back to the night you saw *Philadelphia Story*. What was the time of the showing?"

Claire looked around the room, trying to adjust to his refocusing. "It was—let's see. I remember it wasn't on the hour or the half-hour. Eight-ten, eight-forty, somewhere around there."

"Where were your brother and sister-in-law that night?"

"Sheila was in Baltimore. At her mother's. Curt was home."

"He was there when you left for the movie?"

"Yes."

"What time was that?"

"I don't know exactly. I did leave early because I thought there might be a long line at the theater."

"And was he there when you got home?"

"Yes, in his office. We had a brief talk about the movie before I went to my room."

"The time?"

"It must have been a little after eleven."

O'Brien and Fay exchanged glances of mutual recognition: Curt Colby had no alibi during the time slots of both murders.

"Mrs. Powell, I understand you have a scar on your neck. May I look at it?"

She stiffened like a soldier just before the salute. "If it's necessary."

She did not have to pull down the collar of her blouse; she simply tipped her head back. He leaned over her and looked at the hair's-width arc of white that ran from side to side.

"Ummhum," he said, but having finished inspecting it, he kept his face in front of hers, just five inches between their noses.

She could feel his breath; he could tell she was holding hers.

"You got this when you fainted?"

"Yes," she whispered.

"By falling on what?"

"The corner of a desk."

He paused long enough to force her to begin breathing again, then he quietly said. "You're lying. Through your teeth."

He straightened up but did not back away. Without turning, he looked over at Fay, who now appeared to be holding *her* breath. When his eyes returned to Claire Powell, she still had her head tipped back, her neck arched and throat exposed, as if compliantly poising herself for the executioner's blade.

Claire thought that if she did not shift her eyes away from his they would be driven into the back of her skull. Never had she seen such a condemning stare aimed at her— except, possibly, in her own reflection in the mirror.

"Do you care about your niece's welfare?"

"Yes" came out sounding strangled.

"Do you care about your brother's welfare more?"

"I care about them equally."

Now he began in rapid-fire earnest. "How did you get the scar?"

"I told you—"

"How did you get it?"

Only silence as she stared at him wildly.

"Did your brother give it to you?"

"No!"

"You got it the night Rosemary died, didn't you? Didn't you?"

"Yes."

"Tell me," he said, inclining so that his face was in front of hers again, "did your brother slash you *before* or *after* he threw his wife off that balcony?"

"Earl!"

O'Brien turned to Fay, scowled, and shook his head fiercely in reprimand.

"He didn't!" said Claire. "He didn't do either!"

"Then," he said softly, "did *you* throw her over?"

"No! She did it herself."

"You both saw her do it?"

"Yes."

"And neither of you stopped her?"

"We . . . no."

His head nodded slightly, slowly. "A fine pair."

Her lips trembled, then tightened, and her eyes suddenly looked like dead fish floating behind the tears. "You're right, Mr. O'Brien," she whispered. "A fine pair."

"Earl, let her go to the bathroom and wash her face."

"No. You can bring her a wet cloth and a towel."

"Christ, have a heart!"

His face harsh but his voice even, he said, "Have you forgotten the two men who lost *theirs*?"

She reddened, nodded acquiescence, and went off to the bathroom.

While Fay was out of the room, O'Brien kept his back turned to the softly sobbing aunt. She was, he suspected, a woman who did not cry easily or often, and he had struck a chord that made her behave out of character, a chord he hoped to continue playing on. By now he was convinced that the past—specifically the life and death of Fay's mother—held important clues to the present Curt Colby and the two murders. He knew how his own father's death had twisted his mother, how she in turn had left an imprint on

O'Brien himself, hidden until that afternoon he discovered Joy with Lee Irwin. In his earlier admission to Fay he had not mentioned his greatest fear about the incident: if he had not been pulled off and away from Irwin he might have beaten him until he was dead.

Fay returned. Claire held the cold wet cloth against her face, then folded it neatly and placed it on top of the towel lying next to her. Simultaneously, she and O'Brien lighted cigarettes.

"So," he continued, as if there had been no time lapse, "the two of you watched Rosemary throw herself over the balcony and made no attempt to stop her."

Claire's voice sounded nasal and fatigued. "She was drunk. We didn't think she was serious."

"Serious? Then she *told* you she was going to jump?"

"Yes."

Now it wasn't O'Brien's eyes Claire wanted to avoid. It was Fay's.

"They were having another one of their bitter arguments. She started insulting me, and when I thought she had gone too far I slapped her. That's when she—she picked up the letter opener from Curt's desk and slashed me."

"A *letter opener* left that kind of scar?"

"It was an antique dagger. Curt had bought it somewhere in Europe on one of their trips."

"What was the argument about?"

"Her drinking and her . . . men."

A chill and then a flush of shame passed through Fay.

"How many men?"

"Three, four."

"Your brother tolerated this situation?"

"Rosemary wasn't serious about any of them, and it's doubtful whether she even slept with them. She used them to try to make Curt jealous."

"If it's doubtful, then why did your brother take Fay for the blood test?"

"Mr. O'Brien, are you married?"

"I was."

"Then you know that marriages are not all black and white."

Excellent pun, he thought, if she only knew it.

"What one person will tolerate, another won't, and vice versa." She recounted the things she had told Sheila last Saturday: Curt's fleeting fling with another woman, Rosemary's discovery and desire for revenge, their resolutions for peace when she became pregnant, the reignition of her jealousy, her escalating alcoholism and "flirtations" with other men. "She had too much of everything. Too much beauty, too much attention, too many indulgences. Too *little* charity. She wanted to own people without being owned herself. The problem was she loved Curt too much and it overwhelmed her."

"You didn't like her, did you?"

"On the contrary. She had great charm. I just didn't like what she was becoming. It was not pleasant to watch."

Alcoholic, thought Fay. No wonder her father kept tabs on Sheila's bourbon.

"What," said O'Brien, "would you assume was her motive for suicide?"

"I think she was afraid she was going to lose Curt eventually. That night she told him again Fay wasn't his. That's when *I* spoke up and—"

"Were you living with your brother at the time?"

"No, I was married. My husband and I had been invited for dinner, but he refused to go, because he suspected there would be the usual argument. I could tell when Curt called he desperately wanted company, so I went alone."

"Go on."

"When Rosemary started up that 'she's-not-your-daughter' business I told her to shut up, we were tired of hearing it. She turned on me, saying I was married to half a man. My husband had a sperm deficiency, so we couldn't have children. Anyway, that's when I slapped her and she went for the letter opener. After she cut me, Curt slapped her. Hard. She walked out onto the balcony, turned around, and said through the door that she was going to jump. Curt was wiping my neck with his handkerchief and we . . . we just ignored her. Then we heard the scream and she was gone."

O'Brien remained silent, weighing what he had heard. It was a plausible story. And a slick one, too. He turned to Fay. "You slept through all this?"

"No, I heard the arguing but it was muffled. There were two rooms between mine and the living room. I must have been half asleep when I heard the scream—I thought it was someone on the street. I didn't know anything had happened until Claire told me the next morning."

"You slept through the night?"

"Yes."

"The police," said Claire, "were very considerate. When we told them Fay was asleep they conducted their business quietly."

"I take it there was an inquest."

"Yes."

"Was there any suggestion or suspicion of murder?"

"Not for long. Our friends—Rosemary's too—testified to her state of mind."

"Any witnesses to her leap?"

"No."

"Had she ever tried suicide before?"

"No."

"Ever threatened it?"

Pause. "No."

"What is your brother's *present* state of mind?"

"He's an extremely private man."

"That's not what I asked. What's his recent behavior been like?"

"He seems . . . agitated."

"And?"

"Just that."

"Claire," said Fay, "he's never been a drinker, but he's been drinking lately."

"Yes, I know." Claire looked at O'Brien. "I've answered your questions. I've revealed things Fay never knew and didn't *have* to know. I'm not saying anything more until you tell me exactly why I'm here and what is going on."

"You'll know soon enough, Mrs. Powell. As for those things Fay 'didn't have to know'—maybe if she *had* known them she wouldn't be spending time and money on an analyst. I have a few more questions, and you'll answer them if you *truly* care about her welfare."

"Don't insult me, Mr. O'Brien."

"Then cooperate, Mrs. Powell."

Their eyes locked until hers shifted to Fay. "Then," she said, "proceed and let's get this over with."

"Did your brother tell you he was *going* to hire me?"

"No. I've already told you. He mentioned it to me afterward and I told him to stop having Fay followed."

"'Mentioned' it to you? That's a pretty casual description for such an important revelation. Why did he 'mention' it to you?"

"Whatever this mystery is," she snapped, "and however it involves Fay, I hope you're genuinely concerned for her welfare. But even if you are, I can now heartily affirm I don't care much for you."

"Depending on what I find out, the feeling may be mutual. Now, how did he come to mention it to you?"

"He was concerned over the results of your findings."

"What results in particular?"

"That Fay was seeing a variety of men but only for short intervals, and that she was using an alias—her middle name and her mother's maiden name."

"In what way was he concerned about this?"

"Something like déjà vu. Rosemary's boyfriends were

toys, conveniences, and he was afraid Fay was duplicating her."

"According to Fay—and I believe her—he has never been warm or loving, has never had an intimate conversation with her since her mother's death. Why the sudden concern?"

"Fay just turned twenty-nine. Rosemary died two days after her twenty-ninth birthday."

"That's quite an outlandish and morbid connection to make."

"Yes, morbid it is. But add to it that Fay looks almost exactly like her mother, that Curt has never known for sure if Rosemary was lying or telling the truth about the paternity. Look at her," said Claire, and she did so herself. "Do you see the slightest resemblance to her father?"

"No, but that happens often enough. And some kids don't resemble *either* parent."

"True. I'm not excusing Curt for anything, but he *has* had to live with it all these years. My own opinion is that Rosemary was lying just to punish him."

"Fay, do you have a picture of your mother?"

"Just one, and it's not a close-up."

"Why just one?"

"My father won't part with any. I have this one only because I begged for it when I was in college."

"Can I see it?"

She went into the bedroom, and O'Brien continued the questioning. "What did he plan to do with the information I provided him?"

"I don't know. He just said he wanted to help Fay in some way. I think the reason he's been so agitated lately is that there *is* no way to make up for all those years of..."

"Of what?"

"Coldness. Emotional neglect."

"He's had three wives since Fay's mother. Why no more children?"

"I don't know. We've never discussed it."

"He would discuss hiring me, but he won't discuss having or not having children?"

"I don't pretend or presume to understand everything about him. He goes his way, I go mine, and if he chooses to discuss something private, I'm available. But I don't pry."

"You've lived with him for a long time, haven't you?"

"Since he divorced his second wife. I take care of running the house."

"And what does his present wife do?"

"Plays bridge, shops, reads."

"Convenient for her."

"I hope you don't intend that as a slur. She's a nice woman. Not having to work for a living doesn't preclude virtue."

Sharp, thought O'Brien, very sharp. Despite his necessary stance as a quasi-adversary he was beginning to like her, and found himself hoping she was in no way linked to the activities he suspected Colby of.

Fay returned with the picture. Although it was a black-and-white, the couple in it sported easily discernible glossy tans; they were sitting with arms folded on a table in a restaurant. Instantly he saw that Claire Powell had not exaggerated the resemblance: except for Fay's fairer skin and fuller cheeks, she could have been the twin of this woman. And Colby was every bit his wife's equal, for in terms of debonair good looks he could have given the young Cary Grant a run for his money.

"Your brother," he said to Claire, "kept *all* the pictures of her?"

"Yes, and an assortment of mementos."

"His whole private world is in that little office," said Fay. "Fiona—his third wife—used to call it Hernando's Hideaway."

"What little office?"

"Off the kitchen. It was originally intended as maids' quarters."

O'Brien thought for a minute, then said, "Mrs. Powell, do your brother and his wife have any plans for tomorrow?"

"In the evening. They're going to the ballet."

"Does he keep his office locked?"

"No. But if you're about to suggest—"

"I think once you've heard what I have to say, you'll be willing to let me have a look at it."

He took the two "Bad Girl" notes from his pocket, dropped them into her lap, and told his story.

BOOK THREE

Full Circle

16

SHE HAD ALWAYS DESPISED ANONYMOUS PHONE CALL-
ers—the obscene, the breathers, the prefacers who began
with "Guess who this is"—and then she imagined that as
children they had tortured insects and then frogs and finally
puppies, kittens, and children smaller than they. The anonymous notes in her lap, which she could bear to touch only
once, were not only horrifying when aligned with the facts
O'Brien provided; they were embarrassing for their childish
smugness.

She knew the conclusion the detective was heading for,
and she found her mind whispering, If only you had known
Curt before he met Rosemary....

"And so, Mrs. Powell, if he's not stopped at once, two
more men might join Blakis and Telias." In his account he
had named Kevin Ivory but referred to Andrew Thompson
only as "the fourth man."

Claire said to Fay, "That's why you called me the other

night—not about the dress you saw but to let me know you had broken up with this Kevin."

"Yes."

"Hoping I would tell your father?"

"Yes."

"And *did* you tell him?" said O'Brien.

"Yes, I did."

"Under what circumstances?"

"The next morning, at breakfast."

"What effect did this information have on him?"

"I don't know. He's not demonstrative. He simply asked if it had been because of an argument. I said I knew no details, and the subject was dropped."

"Did you actually mention the name Kevin?"

"No. I said Fay had stopped seeing a young man."

"Why did you say 'young'?"

"Because I assumed he would be."

"Why did you tell him at all?"

"Fay was very casual about it and gave no indication that it was confidential."

"What," he said, "was your motive for telling him?"

"My 'motive' was to pass on a piece of family information."

"What effect did you *hope* it would have on him?"

What, she wondered, *had* she hoped for? That Curt would later ask his daughter directly about the man, and be answered? That his recent agitation would culminate in an outright overture of reconciliation, an overture whose consequences he would accept once and for all? "I don't think I hoped for anything," she answered.

"You said Rosemary had three or four 'admirers.' Do you see the connection between that and the information I provided your brother?"

"I see the *coincidence*," she said evenly, although her throat felt like a muscle newly taut.

"Rosemary's admirers—what reactions did they have to her death?"

"I couldn't guess."

"None of them came to the funeral?"

"No."

O'Brien paused, paced, asked Fay for another brandy and soda. He'd noticed that Mrs. Powell hadn't touched her gin and tonic since she had set it down at the beginning of his questioning. "Will you let me see your brother's office tomorrow night?"

"Yes. But I want you to understand why: only because you *think* you'll get somewhere in helping Fay, *not* because I believe you'll find anything incriminating."

"You're not planning to warn him, are you?"

"If I warned him he would put a lock on the door."

"And you have no intention of inspecting the office on your own."

"No, I do not. I respect his privacy."

"And believe he's innocent."

Fay handed him the freshened drink. He took a long swallow, then sat on the sofa, two feet away from the woman. He spoke next with parental authority and softness. "You *do* believe he's innocent?"

"Yes."

"Even though he has no alibis for the time of each murder?"

"You don't know that yet," she said triumphantly. "Last Saturday when he went to Jersey he may have stopped at a restaurant or a gas station where someone might remember him. Frankly, Mr. O'Brien, I think there's something very strange about you. You don't just think Curt is guilty; you're *eager* for him to be guilty."

"I'm eager," he continued, unruffled, "to save two men's lives if there are designs on them. You said a minute ago you thought it a coincidence that Rosemary and Fay both had admirers, the same number. Do you honestly believe it's also a coincidence that these two murders took place very soon after I delivered the names and residences of the victims to your brother?"

"I—"

"Would you swear," he interrupted, "that Rosemary died exactly the way you told me she did?"

"Yes."

"Would you swear it in court?"

The involuntary fear in her eyes and the quickness of her reply reaffirmed his suspicions about her concealments regarding Rosemary Colby's death.

"Yes, I would," she said.

He watched her over the rim of his glass as he took another swallow. Then: "What time do you suggest I come tomorrow night?"

"Nine would be safe."

"I'm going with you, Earl," said Fay. "I'll wait down on the corner at Madison. You can pick me up there in a cab. Ten to nine."

"I want to see everything," O'Brien said. "Including those mementos."

"He keeps those in a locked cabinet."

"Then would you try to find a way to make sure it's *un*locked? Before there's another murder, before Fay has to go to the police and reveal her private life to them and to the reporters who snoop around precincts."

"I'll do my best."

When she rose he rose with her, offering to go downstairs and put her into a taxi. She preferred to leave alone. He hung back and let the two women say good night in the hallway.

It was a fragile exchange for both of them, each wary of her own words for fear they would be the wrong ones.

"I *am* sorry," said Claire, "you had to find out those things under these circumstances."

"I—I'm glad you told Mr. O'Brien the truth."

"You do trust him, don't you?"

"Yes, I do."

"And your father, do you believe he's responsible for . . ."

"I don't know. I honestly don't know."

Claire lowered her voice. "I've often wondered if you resent me for not having taken you in as a child."

"I don't resent you."

"Herbert wasn't like your father, but he wasn't an easy man, either. Yet . . . it might have been for the better."

"Don't think about that, Claire. We'll see you tomorrow at nine."

They parted without a kiss, without a touch, and Fay was back inside the apartment with the door shut before Claire reached the bottom of the stairs.

O'Brien watched her go into the kitchen without saying a word, listened to her refill ice cube trays and slide them into the freezer. She then started washing dishes, and he wished, against all odds, that she would ask him to stay the night on her sofa. After ten minutes he got up and went to the doorway of the kitchen.

"I'm sorry, Fay."

The fullness of her lips disappeared into a thin line as she nodded and rinsed a plate.

"You don't have to go with me tomorrow night."

"No, I want—I *have* to." She began to cry, but her hands did not stop their task.

He ached to go to her; instinct told him not to. "Am I forgiven?"

"You did what you had to," she said.

"I hope you believe that."

"I do." She raised one arm out of the dishwater and wiped her eyes against the sleeve, rolled to a point just above the crook of the arm. "It's just so much all at once."

"Yes, it is. Would you like me to stay awhile?"

"I'd rather be alone."

"Okay, but call if you feel like talking. Come on and lock the door after me."

"Just let yourself out. I'll lock the Medeco in a minute."

"Uh-uh. Those dishes can wait. Your safety can't."

She followed, and as he stepped into the hallway, she said, "Thank you, Earl."

"Chin up," he replied softly. "If I don't hear from you, I'll see you on the corner at ten to nine."

After he had gone, she switched off the kitchen light and went to the bathroom to fill the tub. Sitting on the edge of it, she watched the water from the spigot funneling down, down to crash into the miniature sea it was making.

He might not be your father.

She gave Claire that scar.

Earl can't hide what he thinks: that my father killed not only Joe and Sam but my mother as well.

In which case, Claire is lying.

The usual comfort she derived from the sound of running water was now a torment: in its hard rush she heard her mother's final scream. She swiveled on the tub's edge, opened her knees, and dropped her head between them to bring back her equilibrium. When the dizziness—but not the weakness—passed, she turned off the taps and went to the telephone.

"Six-one-two-one," said the voice that answered after a single ring.

"Yes, I'd like to leave a message for Dr. Olivia Maxson." She gave her name and telephone number and said that Dr. Maxson could return the call tonight, no matter how late, or anytime tomorrow. Then she got onto her king-size bed and lay dead center, her arms spread out at her sides. For several minutes she had the unreasonable, agonizing sensation that, in addition to sideways and down, one could fall upward too.

* * *

When the sound came she scurried off the bed and ran for the living room. She had not, of course, given the number of the "stable" phone in the bedroom; besides, right after O'Brien's news about Sam Telias, Fay had put the instrument out of commission by disconnecting it from the wall jack.

"I just received your message," said Dr. Maxson, and waited.

Fay evaluated the voice, but heard no irritation in it. Then she glanced at her watch. It was eleven-ten.

After a considerable pause Maxson said, "Fay, has something happened?"

"I don't know how to—" Now that the possibility of comfort was at hand she was tongue-tied before it. "I think I should tell—I wanted to tell you that I lied today. I *had* to lie. For certain reasons."

"Lied about what?"

"I never warned Sam. I couldn't, because he was already dead!"

"Dead? Murdered?"

"Yes, like Joe!"

"Oh, Fay, I'm so sorry."

Her trembling was so uncontrollable that her jaw could scarcely still itself to form words. "C-c-could I have a—an appointment tomorrow?

"I won't be here tomorrow. Can you tell me now what you want to say?"

"I don't know. I'm shaking, so cold."

"All right, I'll come there. Wrap yourself in a couple of blankets and sit in a soft comfortable place. Don't try to resist the shaking; just give in to it. Don't try to make tea or anything. Don't pick up anything. Just sit and stay warm until I get there. What's the address? I don't have my file handy."

Fay gave it to her, then went for the blankets and sat on the sofa until the buzzer rang twenty-five minutes later.

When she opened the door, the sight of Maxson produced several internal reactions, all of which led her to admit to herself that she felt envy: gladly would she have given up the rest of her youth and advance fifteen years if she could be this woman with the jade combs in her hair and the take-charge calm in her face.

At once, Maxson guided her back to the sofa. Then she took off her coat and asked, "Do you want something to drink?"

"Maybe a brandy." She nodded in the direction of the tea cart that held the liquor and glasses. "No ice. Make yourself whatever you want."

"Thank you but I'll pass." She set the brandy glass on the table next to Fay and asked for her hands. Feeling both sides of them she said, "They seem warm enough."

"I wasn't faking about being cold," Fay answered meekly.

"I wouldn't be here if I thought you were faking." She released the hands and sat in the chair that Fay had occupied during O'Brien's interrogation. "Do you want to talk now or wait until you've had your brandy?"

"Now is fine." She sipped the brandy. It went down like a torch to ignite her stomach. "I'm sorry to drag you up here. I—"

"Fay, I didn't come for apologies. The fact that Sam is dead would make even an idiot realize the seriousness of your situation." She folded her arms. "Tell me about it, but take your time. There's no need to rush."

She did not rush, but still had to backtrack now and then to supply information that would clarify a detail or deduc-tion. Her account covered everything from O'Brien's approaching her on Tuesday night up to his encounter with Claire four hours ago. And while she talked, she was amazed at how easily and thoroughly she could describe-assess-conclude on this man she had known less than a week.

Dr. Maxson listened without a single interruption, right through Fay's wrap-up remark: "That's why I lied about

Sam in our session today. I'm sorry. I guess I—well, Earl doesn't understand the analysis relationship. He's never been in therapy."

"Perhaps he doesn't need to be. In any case, the two of you were doing what you thought best. More important, what do *you* think about the likelihood of your father being responsible?"

"I don't know. A lot will depend on what—if anything— we find tomorrow night. But no matter what we do or don't find out, I lose either way. Joe and Sam are gone, and I don't want anyone else to die. And no one will if my father's . . . the one. But I don't want him to be the one, especially if Claire's telling the truth about his not knowing whether or not I'm his daughter. It doesn't necessarily forgive him, but it does help to explain."

"Yes, it does."

"On the other hand, if he's innocent and we can't find out who's doing this, then there could be more deaths. Oh . . . I can't *take* this. I can't be responsible for—for any more." The trembling returned in full force.

Without moving, Dr. Maxson said, "Breathe deeply and slowly. Don't say anything more until you're ready to."

They sat in silence, waiting until Fay was able to reach for her brandy.

"Fay, do you agree with Earl O'Brien about waiting to go to the police?"

"I—yes, I guess I do. Maybe even more so now, because, as Claire said, it seems that he *wants* my father to be guilty— I think he wants that because he suspects he also killed my mother. But I don't want either case to be true, I want Claire to be telling the truth."

"Of course. But if Mr. O'Brien finds evidence, or what he considers evidence, tomorrow, does he intend to confront your father?"

"I don't know."

"That could be dangerous, if your father really is guilty.

But then, Mr. O'Brien *is* a former policeman. . . . Is he absolutely convinced that Kevin couldn't be responsible?"

"He seems to be."

"And Andrew?"

"Andrew was in Barbados when Joe was killed, and he was in Europe when Sam was—" She could not say the word again.

Silence.

"What do you think?" said Fay.

"About which aspect?"

"Any of them, all of them."

"I think Mr. O'Brien has strong grounds for his suspicions, beginning with your father's having hired him to follow you. But I'm sure he knows better than I that courtrooms demand evidence. A morbid preoccupation such as your poor father has with your mother's death isn't the same as a murder weapon containing fingerprints. However, he might find something tomorrow night that will—" She saw Fay wince. "Please understand that *I* have no personal hopes or wishes one way or the other, nothing beyond the desire that the right person is apprehended. Soon. What concerns me most now is your state of mind after *tomorrow* night. You're going to have to be ready for anything."

"I know."

"Do you feel sturdy enough now to be alone?"

"Yes. I can't thank you enough for coming. You don't know what it's meant to me."

Dr. Maxson got up and put her coat on. "I'm glad you called. This is nothing to endure alone."

"Still, it was kind of you."

"Many people have helped me in my life. You return the favor by helping others. Incidentally, since Mr. O'Brien didn't want you to tell me about Sam, I'd suggest you don't tell him that we've talked. So far, he's done a fine job in helping you, so I don't think you should distract him from it through disagreement."

"You're right. I've never met anyone quite like him. He's an exceptional man in so many ways."

Dr. Maxson smiled as she put on her gloves. "I'm glad. There *are* a few of them around."

At the door Fay said, "By the way, how was the concert?"

"Good. By no means superb, but enjoyable. Good night, Fay, and good luck to you and Mr. O'Brien. If anything comes up I'll be back in my office Monday morning. Otherwise I'll see you Tuesday night."

"Yes. And thanks again."

Dr. Maxson started for the stairs. "Oh, I meant to say, your apartment's lovely. I knew it would be. Try some deep breathing to get to sleep. Good night."

Fay did the deep breathing on the sofa, in the dark. As she did she counted her blessings: Earl, Maxson, probably Claire. Yes, and Marsha. Now if only she would be given another blessing—the captured murderer who was not her father, someone like Kevin, for whom she could feel simple loathing.

17

WHEN SHE PICKED UP HER BROTHER'S KEY RING FROM its customary resting place—a clay dish on the small table in the vestibule—Claire Powell felt not only frightened and dishonorable but foolish as well. Such an act might be sensible and thrilling in the movies—as Ingrid Bergman had performed it in *Notorious*—but in real life, *her* life, it smacked of the ludicrous. Nonetheless, her fingers worked quickly and deftly at the task while Curt and Sheila were in their room, dressing to go out. There remained on the ring more than a dozen other keys, so the one she needed should not be missed unless Curt were to go to the memento cabinet later tonight.

That, Claire knew, was unlikely. For her brother the ballet was a tranquilizer, its gracefulness and precision a testament to the two commodities he respected most—beauty and order. Almost always, he came home from a performance and went directly to bed.

All day long her stomach had shifted, curled, rumbled

like an angry animal seeking escape, and she dared not disturb it with anything more than grapefruit and toast. At dinner she only sipped on wine, telling Curt and Sheila she had foolishly snacked late in the afternoon.

When they came downstairs she was in the living room pretending to read a magazine. She had warned herself to sit with her back to the vestibule, yet she chose the chair that provided a full view of it. And when Curt lifted the ring from the clay dish her eyes disobeyed and looked up to record the transfer to his pocket.

Finally they were gone and she reached under the skirt of the chair for the key. Such a small thing, weighing no more than a nickel and with just three teeth, one of them shaped like a truncated claw. It was an ugly object: appropriate, she thought, since it opened the lock on an ugly past.

At one minute past nine the buzzer sounded, and over the intercom Donald announced that Miss Colby and a gentleman were on their way up. This was thirty-four minutes after Curt Colby stood in the men's room in the New York State Theater and used the clippers on his key ring to remove a hangnail.

Claire did not want to be a party to O'Brien's search but remained as an overseer, like a stern but saddened librarian who must admit the ignorant and unappreciative to the archives.

Yet O'Brien handled the mementos delicately, respecting the items as the property of another. Looking up to see the quiet awe in Fay's eyes, he felt she'd have seen its twin in his own. He studied quickly, for it was the papers under them that O'Brien wanted to spend time with. Fay looked over his shoulder as he examined the last birthday card her mother had given her father: "The best present I could give you would be to leave, but I haven't the strength. Give yourself the present and leave *me*."

Then came the notes, none of them dated, so O'Brien had no clue as to their sequence. The shortest one said, "I apologize for the argument. Forgive me. I need you. Love, H." The other two were longer and more revealing.

Rosemary darling,
I know you are hiding from me because you are afraid of Curt. Believe me, I can protect you from him. I can protect you from anything. My father will transfer me to Los Angeles if I want to go. Come with me. Bring Fay. Call me. DON'T BE AFRAID.

All my love,
George

Rosemary,
My patience is wearing thin. Your cowardice is not only damaging to you but insulting to me—changing your phone number, instructing your doorman to refuse me admittance. I can handle Curt and, if necessary, Claire too. You know that Fay is ours, as much mine as she is yours. I'm the only one for you—you know it and can't go on hiding from it. Don't make me have to come after you.

Yours,
M.

Fay took them from O'Brien's hand and began to reread. From where he squatted on the floor next to her, he turned his head and aimed his glance at Claire, sitting on the daybed. "You've read these?"

"Twenty-five years ago," she said. "I remember them."

"Then you remember 'You know that Fay is ours, as much mine as she is yours'?"

"Yes."

"Yet last night you said you suspected that Rosemary never actually slept with these other men."

"Rosemary purposely kept that note—all three of them—

where Curt would find them. I also suspect she arranged to *have* them written."

"Really? Where are the envelopes they came in?"

"I don't know."

"How did they arrive? By mail? By messenger?"

"I have no idea."

He pulled one from Fay's hand "'... hiding from me because you are afraid of Curt.' And it ends with 'DON'T BE AFRAID' in printed capital letters." He took another note and quoted: 'I can handle Curt and, if necessary, Claire too.' Well, Mrs. Powell, your role grows larger by the second."

Her retort was quick but it lacked energy. "Do you think I'd have unlocked that cabinet if I intended to incriminate myself?"

"Maybe you've never read the notes."

Without even glancing at them she said, "One is signed 'All my love, George.' the other two 'Love, H.' and 'Yours, M.'"

There was a pause before O'Brien spoke again. "You just used the word 'incriminate.' Were you referring to the deaths of Blakis and Telias, or to Rosemary?"

No reply.

He stood, now looking down instead of up at her. "Rosemary *was* murdered, wasn't she?"

"She was not."

"Who is 'M.'?"

"I don't know. I never met the person. I never met any of them."

"Is that so? Then you wouldn't know whatever became of them."

"No."

"You wouldn't know if they were murdered too?"

Now her face and eyes flashed with her temper. "Too! Stop your accusations this minute! Whatever you suspect Curt of in these deaths you're free to pursue. But I will not have you, in front of Fay, accuse him of killing her mother. She killed herself. I was there and I saw it."

"You said last night you *didn't* see it; you said you had your back turned—"

"No . . . more . . . games." Her tone was hushed but livid. "I am finished answering your questions. Now put those things back in the box exactly the way you found them and then get out of here."

"I'm not quite done looking."

"Yes, you are," said the voice from the doorway.

O'Brien spun around, and saw the perfect knot of the tie before he saw the face.

"You're done looking," said Curt Colby, "but I invite you to remain until the police arrive."

His blue eyes flashed until they fell upon Fay; in them she witnessed the transformation from anger to sorrow, and her heart shriveled like a piece of rotting fruit. In the past, she had had fantasies of betraying this cold man and claiming her victory. But there was no victory now, only shame. She turned to Claire, who sat with head bent in an attitude of mournful prayer.

"You've called the police?" said O'Brien.

"I'm about to," returned Colby.

"Then you'll save me the trouble."

"Save you—? You must be demented."

"And this"—O'Brien reached for the box of mementos and held it before him as if weighing it—"is *not* demented?"

"You know nothing about it. And I'll thank you to put that down and not touch it again."

O'Brien dropped the box onto the desk; it landed with a clunk that underscored his disdain. "Now if you'll call the police. We may not be able to expose the truth about your wife's death, but I think we'll get somewhere with the current murders."

"Current—?" Colby's gaze sped to his sister. "Claire, what's going on here? Why did you take my key?"

"How did you know?" she whispered.

"When I got to the ballet I saw it was missing. And with the way you were acting all day, the rest wasn't hard to figure out—to a point. I thought perhaps you were going to throw the box out. I certainly didn't expect *this*."

"When murder is committed," O'Brien said, "even by the most clever people, there's usually something unexpected. In your case, Mr. Colby, it was my happening upon a tiny item in the *Daily News* that led to a hunch that led me to call Hartford."

"Claire, what is he talking about? What do my personal possessions have to do with anything *he's* involved in? Why did you—"

"Mr. O'Brien seems to think—"

"Let me handle this, Mrs. Powell."

"Of course," she answered with tired sarcasm. "You always run the show. There's no room for conversation, it's question-and-answer or nothing at all."

"That's my business."

"This office is not your business," Colby retorted. "Fay, on my way in, Donald told me you came here with a man. How do you know him?"

"I introduced myself," said O'Brien, "after I learned about the second murder."

"Will you drop the cliched shroud of vague dramatics and tell me what *we* have to do with any case of yours."

"Vagueness—and I don't mean mine—is very much to the point. When you hired me you were extremely—and purposely—vague about your motives. 'I just want to see how my daughter lives.' And when you got my results and they resembled the way her mother had lived, you decided to do something about the situation." O'Brien was satisfied with Colby's reaction: it appeared that every drop of blood in the man's body had rushed to his face. "But instead of eliminating her the way Rosemary was eliminated, you hit upon another tactic. Eliminate the men instead."

Never in her life had Fay seen raw panic in her father, but it was all too observable now as he turned upon her aunt. "What have you said?"

"Plenty," replied O'Brien. "In fact, quite enough."

"I told him how Rosemary jumped, how we—"

"Mrs. Powell—"

"Shut up! You can play the dictator at Fay's but you will not play it here! I'll say what I have to say *when* I want to say it."

"At Fay's?" Colby muttered in confusion. He looked at his daughter and pleaded, "Will you tell me what's happening? Why would you bring him here to pry into my personal belongings?"

"'Pry,'" said O'Brien. "Isn't that what you've done with Fay?"

"And with whose help?" Claire said acidly. "That's the total nature of your so-called profession, isn't it? Pry, snoop, presume."

Colby persisted. "Fay, tell me, please, since these two won't."

O'Brien opened his mouth, but before a single word could come, Fay spoke his name in a tone of warning. She then took the few necessary steps to bring herself face to face with her father. "You hired Earl to follow me." As he nodded affirmation she saw that his eyes wanted to escape hers although they remained steadfast. "Then you're familiar with the names Joe Blakis and Sam Telias?"

"Yes, I remember."

"And do you know what's happened to them?"

After a pause his chin slackened and his mouth dropped open. "Not what . . . he said about murder?"

She nodded, and found herself wanting desperately to believe in his apparent incredulousness.

"And you think," he whispered, "you both think that

I . . . ?" His eyes narrowed and blinked as another realization opened up like a time capsule. Slowly his head rotated toward his sister. "And you, Claire? You think I would kill someone?"

"No, Curt. I don't. But this man believes you have a motive, and no alibis for the time of the murders."

Colby looked past Fay at O'Brien. "I think it's about time you gave me some details so I can defend myself."

The night of Blakis's death—while Claire was at the movie and Sheila in Baltimore—Colby was at home the whole time, or so he claimed, and O'Brien now stared at the evidence in his hand. On the computer-typed phone bill were two long-distance calls, one dialed at 8:14 P.M. to Baltimore and lasting twenty-three minutes, the other dialed at 8:45 P.M., to Cheraw, South Carolina, for ninety-seven minutes. The first call was to his wife; the second was to one of his authors, whose revisions on a new novel were unsatisfactory. O'Brien did not mistake Fay's look of relief as she inspected the bill with him: she knew that Blakis was killed a few minutes after nine.

As for the previous Saturday, exactly a week ago, Colby produced evidence in the form of a credit card receipt for gasoline purchased in Palmyra, New Jersey. O'Brien asked if Colby had a New Jersey map, and when it was handed to him for inspection he saw it would have been virtually impossible to drive from this town near the Pennsylvania border to Hartford, Connecticut, and back to New York within the time bracket of Colby's absence. "Unless, of course," he said to Claire, "you were 'mistaken' about the time of departure and return."

"Your innuendos, Mr. O'Brien, are as subtle as adolescent jokes. I'm not 'lying' about the time period. Nor am I mistaken."

"Your wife," O'Brien said to Colby, "is at the ballet?"

"Yes."

"I think we should wait for her to come home and see if she agrees with Mrs. Powell about the time."

"Earl," said Fay. "Come with me a minute, alone." She led him down the small hallway to the kitchen. "What's with you?" she whispered shrilly. "You accepted *Kevin's* alibi that had no proof, just the word of his girlfriend."

"He had the plane ticket, Fay."

"For the time of Joe's death. But not Sam's. My father has *two* pieces of evidence—tangible evidence—in there. *And* Claire's word, yet you want to stay and put Sheila to the test!"

He could hear and see her furious breathing, and it nearly stopped his own.

"I'll tell you what: you can step out of this right now and protect your name and the reputation of your agency. My father, Claire, and I will handle this ourselves, and when the police do become involved we won't mention you at all. I promise you."

He felt a dizzying fear. Five nights and four days he had known her; but the prospect of her exiting from his life so soon, so abruptly was . . . terrifying. He reached for her arm, but she pulled back. "Fay," he said softly. "I . . . maybe I've tried to cover too much ground too fast. Look, we'll let things rest for tonight. Okay? Tomorrow we can sit down, go over what we have so far, and see if there are other possibilities to come up with."

She stared at his chest but didn't answer.

"Please, Fay, I do want to help. Besides," he added with a weak smile, "you can't unload me that easily. I bribed Blakis's doorman and I've talked to Kevin and Andrew. All of them would remember me, so you'd *have* to tell the police. Come on now, we'll call it a night and I'll drop you off at your apartment."

She nodded, but wouldn't look him in the face. They returned to Colby's office, said good-bye, and prepared to leave. But Colby asked Claire and Fay to wait in the living room while he spoke to O'Brien alone.

"I hope you're satisfied with . . . my proof."

"I'll be thinking it over," answered O'Brien.

"I'm no killer, but that's not what's important now. Do you think *Fay's* life is in danger?"

"I don't know. But if anything happens to her I'll go after whoever's responsible. With my bare hands." He turned to leave, then paused. "I think you and your sister are lying about your wife's death. Of course, that can't be prosecuted now. But someday you might have the guts to level with Fay. Dr. Maxson might be able to give help, when Fay has more of the truth."

"Who is Dr. Maxson?"

"Her shrink. The Fifth Avenue visits—remember? In fact, maybe you and your sister should call and arrange for appointments now. Maybe the two of you need the services more than Fay does."

As soon as O'Brien and Fay left, Claire returned to her brother's office and placed the key on his desk. "I had to let them in. You were Mr. O'Brien's one and only suspect, and I had to show we weren't afraid."

"Yes," he answered tonelessly, staring at the wall opposite him.

She went on to tell him about the night before in Fay's apartment. "He doubts my story about Rosemary, but I held my ground."

They exchanged a brief, knowing glance.

"Did you, even for a few seconds, suspect O'Brien was right about me?"

"I considered the possibility. The possibility that I didn't really know you. It was like the night Rosemary died, when for those few seconds I didn't know what the two of you were capable of."

He nodded slowly, his eyes glazing over with memory.

"I'm going to a hotel tonight," she said. "I want to be

away from here. I've had quite enough of the past for one weekend."

He sat staring all the while she packed a suitcase, and when she came downstairs from her room she let herself out without saying good-bye.

Soon afterward, Sheila arrived at the door of his office, her coat still on, and asked if his stomach felt any better. He said it did, but he wanted to sit up alone for a while. She kissed the top of his head, and he secured her hand to run it over his cheek before kissing it good night.

He wanted a drink but not by itself. Into a cup of tea he poured a generous shot of whiskey. He sat on the daybed and looked at the now locked cabinet whose contents had told Fay and O'Brien only part of the past.

Downtown, a few minutes later, Earl O'Brien's ringing telephone pulled him from his chair filled with the hope that Fay was calling to say she couldn't sleep and wanted him to come up.

"Mr. O'Brien?" The sound was a whisper raised to the tenth power—the words were hissed out emphatically, in bursts that put spaces between them. The sheer force of the delivery permitted no inflection, no tone of voice, to come through. "This concerns Fay Colby and victims. Are you alone?"

"Yes, I'm alone."

"I have important documents and information for you. Northeast corner Eleventh Avenue and Seventeenth Street five-thirty A.M. sharp. My representative won't wait later. Will be in light green Buick. You come alone."

"Alone?" His suspicion and sarcasm registered, for the voice returned with "My man will be alone. I take a grave chance giving you information—*your* only chance at it. Won't contact you again."

There was a click, and the line was empty.

18

COULD THE ELABORATELY DISGUISED VOICE BE ANY other than Colby's? At the revelation of the two murders he had acted surprised, and perhaps that too was a disguise. How convenient, the night of Blakis's death, to have two long-distance calls on record. And equally convenient was the gasoline receipt from a location that precluded a trip to the environs of Hartford. Fay's objection to O'Brien's acceptance of Kevin Ivory's alibis over her father's struck the center of his belief and past experience: the innocent often had tenuous alibis, while those of the guilty were overly pat. Ivory's girlfriend might be a carping nincompoop, but that morning he saw her she was certainly no liar.

He set his alarm in case he should doze off, a precaution against an unlikelihood, and returned to his chair to mull and piece and fit. Kevin Ivory was dislikable but no serious suspect. And Andrew Thompson? The world was filled with charming, intelligent killers who could fool practically anyone, but he was betting that Thompson knew Fay only as

225

Ann Decker and still remained unaware of the other men in her life.

During the next few hours his mind ran in circles, but always returned to the starting point: his ever-hardening belief that Colby and his sister took part in Rosemary's demise, that that event had some kind of connection—however weird—with the murders at hand. If only he could get some information about Rosemary's admirers, particularly the one whose note said, "You know that Fay is ours, as much mine as she is yours."

O'Brien considered the obvious possibility of his being set up for murder. If so, who was going to do the killing? Most likely a hit man, not Colby himself. But the telephone call—why would someone *anonymous* disguise his voice? Did Colby perversely enjoy doing the calling even though a hired man could have done it? This led O'Brien to another conjecture. Claire Powell had been so cooperative in providing access to Colby's office, *knowing* that the notes would be found, *knowing* that their contents were grimly revealing, if not downright damning. She heatedly defended Colby, but in the past O'Brien had seen that stratagem: protest too much the suspect's innocence and thereby increase the likelihood of his guilt. And she, not Colby, carried a physical scar from the night of Rosemary's death. Was she resentful of her brother's charity? Did she harbor a pathological hatred of him—and Fay? Had an idea been born, an opportunity recognized, when Colby shared with her the results of O'Brien's investigation?

Or was the phone call genuine, from someone who really did have something valuable to give? O'Brien doubted this. Why didn't the caller simply ask to come to his apartment instead of meeting just a few blocks away from it, and at an hour of the morning when the street lamps were still on? And why was there no mention of an exchange of money for the "documents and information"?

After lengthy deliberation O'Brien decided against rousing Les Beckhorn and Dan Hoag from their respective beds in New Jersey and Brooklyn. For he had no intention of coming in contact with the caller. If a light green Buick did show up, the number on the license plate would be sufficient; this could be obtained through binoculars from a safe distance.

At ten to five he showered. At ten after, he locked the door of his apartment and swiftly descended the stairs, his pistol tucked inside the holster strapped to his left side between rib cage and hip.

He took Sixteenth Street to Tenth Avenue and turned north. Rounding the corner he saw two figures huddled close together sharing a joint. One was clad in full leather, the other in denim with cowboy boots and hat, and as he passed them they appraised him with hungry eyes. Yes, he thought, the leather boys and the queens would be sprinkled all over this area, cruising or heading home after a night at the waterfront bars or the docks. At Seventeenth he crossed the avenue and quickly reviewed his plan: he would find a doorway or crawl under a parked vehicle and watch the spot through the binoculars he had in his pocket.

When he stepped up onto the curb on the other side of the avenue there was another leather boy in full regalia, squatting down to make sure his trouser bottoms were tucked snugly inside his boots. For a brief few seconds, O'Brien allowed himself to wonder how much money these guys spent on their image-making drag.

What he failed to notice was that this particular figure wore something quite out of character for someone in this social set: the motorcycle boots were re-soled in crepe.

He slowed his pace and squinted at the corner at the end of the block. No one. No one up and down either side of the street. Just as he began to speculate on possible hiding places the voice spoke from behind.

"O'Brien?"

His hand went for the gun, but the powerful booted foot

smashed into the small of his back with enough force to send him sprawling. He rolled over and tried to get up, but the boot caught his chin and returned him to the concrete, then pinned the wrist of the hand that had now reached the holster. During the split second he looked up at the face, which he could not discern in the shadows, he thought just two things.

Blakis, through the heart. Telias, through the heart.

He bucked away from the boot and began to roll like a self-propelled barrel over the curb and into the street, zigzagging. There was a shot, the cry of a bullet that struck the pavement just inches from his ear, and then his own scream, which, to him, sounded like a giant's. Another shot, a thumping pain in his hip. A second scream, and he continued to roll. A third shot and then sudden light and sudden sound: a car rounding the corner. The screech of brakes. The fourth shot, which found his body, followed by a fifth, which flattened the car's left front tire. Then, no more shots, only the sound of footsteps running toward him, a man bending over him, a woman hanging back and moaning, "Oh, Jesus. Oh, my God." The pain in his hip was duller than the one in the right side of his back.

"Theresa, stay with him while I go find a phone."

O'Brien listened to the man run away at full speed, listened to the woman take a few steps closer and stop. He strained to hear her breathing, perhaps to help his own.

St. Vincent's Hospital was the closest to the scene of the attack, but O'Brien, still clinging to consciousness when the ambulance arrived, told the driver to deliver him to Lenox Hill at Park and Seventy-seventh, where his own doctor was an affiliate. The reluctant man was appeased by the hospital card in O'Brien's wallet, but said, "Man, you been shot *twice*."

"Lenox." O'Brien insisted. "It's Sunday. There won't be

any traffic." When he worked for the Sixth Precinct he had spent plenty of time in St. Vincent's, with both victims and perpetrators, and right now there might be some former buddies present. Besides, it was the hospital to which he and Lee Irwin had been taken that violent afternoon, and he could still remember the exact spot where Irwin had coughed blood and a fragment of tooth onto the floor of the emergency room.

The ambulance sailed across Twenty-third Street and turned north on Park Avenue South. Perhaps because dizziness was rescuing him from pain O'Brien succumbed to a romantic comfort worthy of a schoolboy: at Lenox Hill he would be just a few blocks from Fay's apartment. Then it occurred to him he would be equidistant from her *and* her father. Fearing he might pass out soon, he made sure that the attendant wrote down Fay's name and phone number with the instructions that she was the one person he wanted called. He decided to save his strength, and so did not mention Les Beckhorn.

She got the call at twenty after seven, was dressed and out of the apartment in less than fifteen minutes, and alternately walked fast and sprinted toward the hospital. Anger kept worry in abeyance as she muttered to the unknown killer, "Whoever you are, you damned coward, I'll rip your heart out if Earl dies."

When she arrived she could not see him; he was being prepared for surgery. He had lost blood, the doctor said, and his pulse was low, but he appeared to be a strong man. The full extent of the injury could not be determined until they opened him up. These last three words sounded barbaric to Fay, and her sudden light-headedness was apparent to the doctor, who gripped her arm, then reassured her, telling her how lucky O'Brien was: had the bullet entered the left side it might have struck his heart. There was, he added, no point in her remaining, no telling when she would be able to see him. Later in the day she could telephone to find out his condition. Before she left, she asked where O'Brien had been when he was assaulted.

It was raining when she started walking north on Park. Not a downpour, not even an assertive sprinkle, just a sporadic drizzle that added irritation to her rage and fear.

The night doorman was still on duty, and he touched the brim of his hat as a way of greeting even before they were close enough to speak. Unlike old Donald, whom she liked (and had fantasized a few times as the perfect father), this man was far too obsequious for her comfort. But she forced a smile as a preface to her question.

"Looks like a nasty day, doesn't it, Miss Colby?" he said, holding the door open for her.

"That it does. This weather is the absolute worst for my father's back."

"Lucky he got home before this started."

He had answered the question before she could ask it. Careful, she told herself, keep it casual. "Did he go out early?"

"A little before five. The street's quiet then. It's a good time to walk."

"Yes, it is. Did he have a long walk?"

"I'd say so. About an hour and a half."

For a natural punctuation she concluded, "Well, I just hope he didn't overdo it."

"I doubt that," he replied with polite confidentiality. "He came back in a taxi."

It took great control for her not to run to the elevator. As she waited for it to descend and open its door, she listened to her unwitting informant announce her arrival over the intercom.

"Fay, what a surprise," said Sheila, who was standing in the doorway when she got off the elevator.

"Hello, Sheila." In the vestibule Sheila reached to take her coat, but Fay simply draped it over the straight-back chair. "Where is he?" The blunt harshness made her step-mother pause before answering, "Upstairs."

"Will you please get him."

"He's trying to sleep. He didn't have a good night."

"I suppose he didn't, since his mission wasn't accomplished. At least, not yet. Tell him I'm here and I want to see him. Now."

Sheila stared like a puzzled servant and started for the stairs.

"Tell Claire to come down too."

"She's not here. She spent the night at a hotel."

"Why?"

Sheila shrugged. "Your father said she just wanted to be alone."

"I see."

Fay waited in the living room, arms crossed, huddled into a corner of the sofa. Less than twelve hours ago she had defended her father's "proof" to Earl. Earl, whose intuition defied that proof. And so, he had somehow been lured to a lonely spot to be shot down and left for dead. . . .

Her father came down in his bathrobe, a wary Sheila close behind. Fay turned, and when she did, Colby stopped cold in his approach. They stared at each other, and Sheila's eyes darted back and forth between them. Finally, Fay advanced until she could see the pores in his skin. It was like her dream, his standing before her, ready to be pushed. But she did not push. She spat in his face.

He winced, and Sheila gasped.

Yet he did not move, except for a slight twitch at the corner of his mouth. She wanted him to slap her so she could slap him back. But he meted out the worst imaginable punishment: silence, and a squint that could be either anger or hurt. It seemed he was waiting for her to spit again, *inviting* her to do it.

She walked over to the sofa and braced herself against the back of it.

The silence was broken by the turning of the lock, the opening of the front door. The three of them looked at Claire.

"Well," said Fay, her voice too raw and shaken to live up to the sarcasm it would deliver. "The second viper arrives."

She knew she was approaching hysteria as she told them about O'Brien, yet she wasn't so self-absorbed as not to notice the seemingly genuine shock in her father's eyes. She had to move away to the window to keep from being roped in by him again. At her first pause Sheila spoke up urgently: "What is all this?"

"I'll explain in a while," Colby answered. "Fay, will you please sit down. I have something important to tell you. And it's the truth."

Seeing the condition of her niece, the haggardness in her brother's face, Claire suggested coffee, and before departing for the kitchen she asked them to say nothing until she returned.

When Fay stirred cream into the Wedgwood cup and heard the stirrings of the other three spoons she was seared with shame. Here they sat with the trappings of Sunday morning gentility—silver coffeepot and tray, silver dish of croissants—while Earl was in a hospital being "opened up."

Without touching his coffee Colby gave an account of the anonymous phone call he had received late last night, instructing him to be at the corner of Eleventh Avenue and Fifteenth Street at five-thirty A.M., to wait for a green Buick to pull up. The caller promised information about the deaths of Joe Blakis and Sam Telias. "I went there and waited," said Colby, "but the car never showed. I heard gunshots a few blocks away, then a siren. A little before six I gave up and came home."

"Eleventh Avenue and Fifteenth Street," Fay said thickly. "Earl was shot on *Seventeenth* Street right off Tenth Avenue. What a thoroughly unlikely coincidence."

"Yes. Why should he be in that area at that time? Unless he received a call similar to mine. When the two of you left here last night, did he say anything about having an early-morning appointment?"

"No."

"I think . . ." He rubbed his forehead and then his eyes. "I think someone wanted us in that same vicinity at the same time."

"Of course," said Fay. "*You* did. Maybe someone did call Earl—you. No one had to call here, because it was you who set this up."

"There was a call," said Sheila. "I had just gone to bed when the phone rang. It stopped before I could reach for it."

"Of course you'll protect him. His wives always protect him in one way or another."

Sheila's hurt was undisguised. "Thank you for classifying me as just one more wife. Nonetheless, the phone *did* ring."

Fay turned to her aunt. "Were you at your hotel *all* night?"

"Yes, despite what you may be thinking."

"Well, *somebody's* lying!"

Fatigue apparent in his speech, Colby said, "Nobody here, Fay. When Earl O'Brien's able to talk, I'll bet he tells us he was summoned to that area by the same lure given to me."

"But why two blocks apart?"

"Because the attacker didn't want to be seen—but I think he wanted *me* to be seen in the area. And I was. Even by two cops in a squad car that cruised by. Of course, they gave me a good looking-over, since I wasn't appropriately dressed for the waterfront." He arched his back and stretched, and Fay heard one of his joints crack. "Last night O'Brien was sure I was guilty until I produced the phone bill and gas receipt. I believe that whoever called me knew of his suspicions but nothing about the evidence I showed him.

Have you discussed his suspicions with anyone? One of your boyfriends?"

"No!"

"But I imagine O'Brien has discussed them. With his assistants, for example."

"You don't believe—"

"I'm too tired to speculate. All I know is this—design circles around *you*. You are the target."

"Target" made her jump up. "I can't talk about it anymore. I'm going to the hospital to wait."

"All right," said her father. "But come back here afterward and spend the night."

"I'm in no frame of mind to spend the night *here*."

"Maybe not. But consider how foolishly dangerous it might be to stay in your apartment alone before O'Brien can tell us something."

"Has it occurred to you," she answered, "that he might not survive to say anything?"

"I will hope that's not the case."

Through pleading and, ultimately, insistence, Claire got Fay to let her accompany her niece to the hospital.

"Taxis, door-to-door, each way," Colby instructed. "I'd go with you but I haven't slept a wink. Nonetheless, call whenever you learn something about his condition."

The four of them stood in the vestibule while Fay and Claire got into their coats. Tremulously, Fay said, "If he dies I won't need my analyst anymore. She can close the book on me and call Bellevue for a straitjacket."

"She?" said Colby, surprised.

Claire shot him a look that said, "Wouldn't you have *expected* her to go to a woman instead of a man?"

As soon as the elevator door closed on them, Sheila Colby turned to her husband with an expression that said she was ready to be told the whole story.

"In a minute. Have some more coffee. I have to check something in the office."

The name O'Brien had dropped last night was now aligned with the gender Fay had supplied a minute ago. From the top of a file cabinet he took the telephone directory and slapped it onto his desk to flip through the pages. In the M's he found it: "Maxson Olivia PhD," followed by the lower Fifth Avenue address and the number.

Maxson Olivia. Olivia Maxson.

"Olivia Maxson," he said aloud, as if introducing her to someone. It was a name he had never confronted before. But the familiar rhythm. Maxson Olivia, the prominent "v" and the uncommon "x"...

Ludicrous, he told himself, this woman is an *analyst*, and he had never known a woman analyst in his life.

In the living room, he sat with Sheila and recounted all that had happened since he had left her alone at the ballet the night before, having escaped with his lie about the upset stomach. He told her about having hired O'Brien, about the murders and the notes sent to Fay.

"Oh, Curt," she said, squeezing his shoulder. "Oh, God." Pause. "But whoever is doing this to Fay, why would they want to put the blame on you?"

"I don't know. Maybe Earl O'Brien can help us find that out." He stood and arched his back. "I've got to try to get some sleep."

"Back hurt?"

"Ummm."

"Let's go upstairs. I'll massage it, and then you can have a hot bath before bed." Sheila let him sleep until Claire and Fay, with her overnight bag, returned. All four of them merely pecked at dinner while Claire gave the results of her afternoon with Fay at the hospital. They were not able to see the doctor or O'Brien, but a nurse assured them that the operation had "gone smoothly" and his being placed in intensive care was more precaution than necessity. They could learn more specifics from the doctor tomorrow at one o'clock.

Colby used the doctor to get around to the general subject of analysts, and specifically their working hours. Fay said that her analyst started every morning with a seven o'clock appointment.

Later, in his office, he called a limousine service and hired a car, one with tinted glass, for six A.M. sharp.

Riding down Fifth Avenue in the Lincoln the next morning, he felt his body being pulled in two directions, by fatigue and by a torrent of adrenaline.

The driver was instructed to park at the curb just behind the spot where taxis would discharge passengers bound for Olivia Maxson's building. She might arrive in a taxi, and he wanted a clear view of her—if she indeed *were* the "she" he would recognize.

She did not arrive in a taxi. She came on foot from around the corner, and before her face was close enough for reasonable scrutiny he knew her by her stride. His gaze traveled down her legs to her feet, and every footfall on the sidewalk seemed to strike at his lungs.

Closer, closer she came, and glanced at the Lincoln. He swung his head in the other direction, half expecting to hear her tap on the window.

When he dared to turn around she had disappeared into the building.

Upon his return home he found all three women still asleep. He rapped lightly on Claire's door, then opened it. Puffed eyes looked up questioningly from the pillow.

"Come downstairs right away, to my office. Don't bother to get dressed."

He stopped in the kitchen to start the coffee maker, and when he entered the office his sister was just seconds behind him. She closed the door and leaned against it with her hand pressed lightly against her neck. "Don't tell me," she whispered, "that Earl O'Brien is dead."

"No. Sit down." She did, not once taking her eyes from him.

"I just got back from seeing Fay's analyst."

"What about?"

"I didn't talk to her. *Seeing* her was quite enough." He opened the telephone directory and placed it in her lap, pointing to the name. "Does it ring a bell?"

She only stared. Perhaps, he thought, it didn't ring a bell; or perhaps she didn't want it to. "Keep it as it's listed," he instructed. "Turn the last name into her first name."

Something like a peep came from Claire's throat, and her eyes flared. "It can't be! It's not possible! She wasn't an analyst!"

"She is now. Fay's."

He left her to get the coffee, and as her eyes traveled back and forth over the name in her lap, she was struck by the realization that, for her and Curt, the past was no longer an odious dead weight they dragged along behind them: now it was a brick wall looming up ahead.

Colby returned with the coffee and said, "I'm going to talk to her."

"No!"

"I intend to find out how Fay came to choose her out of all the analysts in this city."

"What makes you think she'll even agree to see you?"

"I've already thought of a way."

Seeing his determination and fearing the consequences of his going alone, she said as firmly as she could manage, "I'm going with you."

"I don't think—"

"I'm going."

At breakfast, Claire asked Fay what time she was going to the hospital.

One o'clock, of course, to meet with the doctor. She would go from work, and perhaps take the rest of the day off.

Would she please, her father asked, spend another night here?

Yes. Despite her confused, ambivalent feelings about his possible involvement in the assault on Earl, she realized that while her adult self was watching him for a false move, the child side of her was hoping his concern was genuine.

After she left, Colby corraled his wife into his office.

"Sheila, I want you to call this number and ask for an appointment. For today. Say it's extremely urgent. Say your name is"—he fished for one—"Sue Potter."

"Curt, what's this all about?"

"You're calling Fay's analyst—"

"What!"

"For an appointment for me. Only I don't want her to know it's me. And you're to say nothing to Fay about this. Not a word."

"But why are you—"

"I'll explain it all later. There isn't time now."

He would have had Claire perform this piece of business, but there was a chance that, even after all these years, "Olivia Maxson" might recognize Claire's voice. He completed his instructions to Sheila and she dialed.

Immediately, she covered the mouthpiece and whispered, "Answering service."

"Leave your name—Sue Potter—and this number." The phone in Curt's office was unlisted.

Sheila did, adding the information Curt had coached her in: "Please tell her it's urgent and that I'm an acquaintance of Fay Colby's."

They waited only fifteen minutes before the call was returned. Colby leaned over so that his ear shared the receiver with Sheila's. The voice was as familiar as yesterday.

"You're an acquaintance of Fay Colby's?"

"Yes, I—used to work with her. She's spoken so highly of you. I'm calling you because, well, this is something new to me. I need someone whose credentials I can trust. It's very urgent. Would it be at all possible to see me today?"

"Today?"

"I know it's unforgivably short notice, but it would mean so much. More than you know. Frankly, I'm desperate."

Pause. Then: "Are you an acquaintance of Fay's from work?"

"Yes. At Mayhew."

"I see. Well . . . I do have an opening at three-fifteen." Colby nodded emphatically.

"I'll take it," said Sheila. "And thank you so much."

"See you then."

As soon as she hung up, Sheila asked for a full explanation.

"I'll tell you everything tonight. I promise. And remember, Fay is not to know anything about this." He raced out of the office and up the stairs to Claire's room. Sheila Colby hoped that his excitement, in the face of all this horrible business, meant that a solution was on the horizon.

The second Olivia Maxson returned the receiver to its cradle she was certain of two things: this woman was lying, but she herself was wise in having granted the appointment. More than a few times, Fay had said that no one but Marsha knew she saw an analyst. It wasn't necessary for Dr. Maxson to call Mayhew and ask Fay about one "Sue Potter." *This* call, coupled with her recollection of the figure in the limousine this morning—the man who had turned his face away as she approached the building—provided sufficient speculation as to whom and what to expect this afternoon.

"Curt, you're too eager for this," Claire warned in the taxi. She watched him staring through the plexiglass partition between the front and back seats of the taxi, staring through it and on through the windshield, the almost maniacal glitter in his eye seeming to add speed to the car. She shrank into the corner of her side of the seat, wishing there were a brake pedal at her foot.

The exclusiveness of a residence or a professional space in New York is not solely defined by the address or by the decorative trappings of a lobby: the quality of the security system can be a good indicator of rent costs.

The doorman had a list of Dr. Maxson's expected patients against which he checked Claire's announcement of "Sue Potter." With propitious suspicion he looked at her well-dressed companion. "My husband," Claire said coolly, "wants to wait for me while I have my session."

The doorman wrote the names, then gave Maxson's office-apartment number and their time of arrival on form slips which they carried with them and then surrendered to the elevator man. During the silent ride up, during the silent five-minute ordeal in the waiting room, Claire could not look at her brother.

The door to the office was opened and closed by a middle-aged woman who glided past with, it seemed, a firm determination not to acknowledge or be acknowledged. Staring at the door and waiting for it to open again, Claire could not rid herself of the lyrics sung by Judy Garland and her pals: "We're off to see the wizard . . ."

Was she purposely keeping them waiting? Or were they supposed to knock? Neither of them had ever been in an analyst's office, although, God knows, maybe if they had—

The door swung open. The smile she donned was professionally cordial, while the total lack of surprise in her eyes told them they were expected. "Hello, Claire. Hello, Curt."

The two stood up, and as they did Claire stole a glance at her brother. The glitter was gone from his eyes, the color from his face; he remained mute. Claire alone returned the greeting.

"Hello, Maxine."

19

"OF COURSE YOU KNOW IT'S 'OLIVIA' NOW," SAID Dr. Maxson as the three of them entered her office. She closed the door.

"When did that—come about?" said Colby.

"Oh, a long time go, just before I went back to college to change professions." She waved Claire to the chair in front of the desk and said to Colby. "You can pull that other chair over here to join us." Colby did, but positioned it farther from the desk than the one Claire occupied. Maxine's sameness, after all these years, nearly paralyzed him; her face looked a bit longer and thinner, but that might simply be an illusion created by the now shoulder-length hair. His throat began to shrink the way the pupil of the eye does before a glare.

"Now," Maxson said, "who was this Sue Potter on the phone this morning? Your wife, Curt?" Seeing him redden provided the answer. "She has a pleasant voice. I imagine she has a disposition to match—Fay has spoken fairly highly of her." She turned her head. "You're looking well, Claire. The white hair is very becoming." When Claire failed to answer, Maxson went to the point. "I assume you're here to discuss Fay."

Silence. Claire cast a sidelong glance at her brother, whose eyes seemed to be eating up bits of Maxson then shifting away to digest what they had devoured. This was precisely what she had feared during the taxi ride.

"Yes," said Claire, "we're here to discuss Fay."

"Then let's begin."

"How," Colby asked, "did you find her?"

"It was the other way around. I don't have to solicit to obtain patients. Word-of-mouth and professional referrals are more than sufficient. Surely if Fay told you she was my patient she told you that her friend Marsha recommended me."

"She only told us indirectly," said Colby. "I had to unscramble the name to realize it was you."

"And to confirm it this morning, downstairs in that limousine. When you saw me, why didn't you simply get out and ask for an appointment instead of using your wife to do it? But," she added significantly, "I suppose you wanted to consult with Claire first."

The truth rang with accusation, and Claire combated it with one of her own. "I can presume that *you* have never revealed to Fay you once knew us and Rosemary."

"No," Maxson countered. "But my purpose has been professional and to Fay's benefit. Having firsthand knowledge as I do of her mother's disturbances—disturbances that influenced Fay's crucial formative years—I have been able to put together pieces much more quickly than another therapist could. And in the substance of her progress, especially considering where she began, she is among my most exceptional patients."

"Progress from what?" said Claire.

"You should realize I am not at liberty to discuss that.

It's Fay's place to confide in you, not mine. Suffice it to say that she's working hard to clean up the mess created by her childhood."

In her head, Claire screamed at her brother: *Don't just sit there—say something! In her presence you're a frozen fool, just as you've always been. All these years have changed nothing. Nothing.* Then, aloud to Maxson: "This 'mess' created by her childhood—you claim to have had no part in it?"

"Claire, do be direct. Do you want to say I'm responsible for Rosemary?" No reply. "Well, do you?" Still, silence. "Because *if* you do, then you'll have to claim your own hefty share of responsibility."

At last, Colby spoke, but too softly to suit Claire. "I care now about Fay. And what happens to her."

"*Now,*" Maxson said evenly. "Like parents who put their children up for adoption and then twenty years later try to seek them out and cash in their consciences for the blood tie. But you, Curt, don't have the certainty of a blood tie, and you didn't even have the consideration to adopt her out to someone who would have loved her as you couldn't."

Now it was Claire who froze, condemned along with her brother. Like him, she had allowed Rosemary's death—and the revelations just before it—to distance her from the child; had followed her husband's heated advice to steer clear of "meddling" in *that* father-daughter relationship.

"She has much to overcome, and she has made an excellent start. Despite some recent misfortune."

"*Misfortune!*" snapped Colby. "You call two murders and an attempted third 'misfortune'?"

"My focus is on Fay, not the victims, or the society that permits murder to be commonplace. What's this attempted third? I know nothing about that."

"Don't you?"

"I won't play games with you. I'll wait for Fay to tell me."

"Fay won't tell you. Because she won't be coming here anymore. I'm prepared to tell her everything."

"You mean," said Maxson, "*your* version of everything." She leaned back in the chair and folded her arms. "It just kills you, doesn't it, that I should be the one who's helping her. So you must get even; you must try to malign me."

"I won't have her welfare resting in your hands!"

"Since it's so much better off in yours? Don't fool yourself, Curt. Your one and only concern is to get even with me—not to do Fay any good. Tell her anything you want, and then I will tell her my side of things."

"You won't get the chance."

"Fay is too intelligent to accept only one side of a story. Don't you know that? You're her father."

Maxson and Colby stared at each other in silence. Claire felt herself shriveling to the point where she had to blurt, "I think everything's been said. I think we can go now."

As Colby stood he reached into his jacket pocket, saying, "What's the fee?"

"No fee," Maxson answered lightly. "Do you really think I would take money from you?"

Nothing was spoken in the elevator because of the operator's presence, but as soon as they were outside the lobby Colby said, "I'll get you a taxi. I want to walk for a while."

"I'll walk with you."

"No. I need to be alone. I need to think." At once he turned toward the oncoming traffic and raised his arm.

As the yellow vehicle shifted lanes to reach them, Claire said, "You hate her either too much or not enough. Which is it?"

His only reply, as he opened the door for her was "If Sheila asks anything, just say I—I'll explain when I get there."

"How much are you going to tell Fay?"

He shook his head but did not answer.

He walked all the way home, carrying the burden of the task ahead, a burden that in no way could be relieved by self-pity. It had pleased Maxine Oliver to victimize him; but his own culpability could not be shed, reasoned away. He thought of all the novels he had edited, stories about men-in-search-of-identity. He himself didn't have to search: years ago Maxine had given him an identity, and now she was back like a disease that goes into remission but threatens to prove more virulent the second time around.

You hate her either too much or not enough. The riddle of his life that had reached out to taint other lives.

He found Sheila and Fay in the living room, sitting together on one sofa and speaking in hushed tones until they were interrupted.

Claire appeared from the kitchen as he was hanging up his coat. He glimpsed the stark apprehension in her face and turned away from it.

Fay, with eyes averted, gave him the hospital report she had already given to Claire and Sheila. The wound in the hip was only a graze, but the other bullet had had to be removed from his right lung. O'Brien, Fay concluded, might be taken out of intensive care sometime this evening.

Colby wanted nothing more than to ride the wave of this relief until after dinner, but he couldn't chance any lessening of the nerve he had built up during his walk home.

"Fay, despite all you've been through this past week, I'm afraid I have to heap a great deal more onto your shoulders. I assure you that everything I have to say is the truth. Claire, Sheila, I'd like you both to stay for this." Then to Fay: "When I finish, if you want nothing more to do with me I won't fault you a bit. All I ask is that you judge Claire softly—she was trapped in her concern for me, and I welcomed her into that trap."

Claire hung her head and fisted one hand into the other.

"I think we could all use a drink for this," he said, and Fay saw the seriousness of what was coming underscored by his generosity in pouring Sheila's bourbon. After distributing the glasses he remained standing, and Fay had neither the time nor the inclination to regard him as the imperious master with his three women in attendance.

"Fay, how did you come to choose Olivia Maxson for your analyst?"

She was confused by what she considered a casual and irrelevant question. "Marsha used to go to her, and she recommended her highly. She specializes in women's problems."

"As well she might . . . Claire and I went to see her this afternoon."

"Went to see her? What for!"

"We've known her a long time. Your mother knew her too. Back then her name was Maxine Oliver and she was in the theater, an actress. I believe she's *still* an actress. Friday night, when Earl O'Brien mentioned the name— Maxson—it stuck with me, and then yesterday when you said it was a woman you were seeing I thought—well, the name 'Olivia Maxson' was just too coincidental." Fay recalled Maxson having told her just last Friday that in college she had majored in English *and* theater. "But," she said, "if she knows you and Claire, why didn't she ever say so to me?"

"She had good reason not to." He swallowed the rest of his Scotch and poured another. "Thirty years ago she seduced me, and I was more than willing to let her do it. Several times. In . . . bed, she coaxed me into saying things that were highly complimentary to her, subtly denigrating to your mother. Sex talk. What I didn't know was that she had a tape recorder going, hidden somewhere near the bed. After our fourth encounter she played the tapes to your mother."

This is insane, she told herself. This can't be! And yet

she asked, "Are you saying she did this to try to take you away from my mother?"

He drew a deep breath. "No, Fay, she did it because she wanted to take your *mother* from *me*."

Her heart felt like a clapper beating a bell, but she could ring out no words, and so after a pause her father continued.

"In her own way, I suppose Maxine 'loved' your mother, although I would say it was nearer to obsession. Your mother, I learned, was sexually undecided or maybe truly bisexual. She wasn't the 'actress' Maxine was, and she seemed to enjoy me genuinely. And she loved me. Which is why Maxine secretly courted me, taped me, and presented the evidence for her case that 'all men are like this.' When she betrayed me I couldn't fathom what her game was. Only later did I realize she was trying to seduce your mother, and with the tapes she finally accomplished it.

"Maxine received an offer she couldn't refuse, a Broadway show that was going on the road. Soon after she left, your mother discovered she was pregnant, and she promised to break it off with Maxine. But she wavered in that decision, and her moods became highly erratic. She obviously answered Maxine's letters, because the day after you were born Maxine flew to New York and showed up at the hospital. I found her standing at the glass of the nursery. I expected her to be furious—as I was with her—but instead she was smiling, and when she saw me, there was this sly ... triumphant look. I didn't know what it meant, and I didn't find out until the night your mother died."

He began to fill his pipe, and his hands shook in the effort. Fay could not match up the woman she saw twice a week with the one her father was describing.

"She returned to the show in Chicago, but not for long. Soon she was back, and parts were hard to find, parts that paid anything. She had a hectic schedule, waitressing, auditioning, doing plays off-off-Broadway, but every spare moment was spent pursuing your mother. She wasn't in our circle of friends—she in fact didn't have many friends; she was a loner. Your mother and I had met her one night at a café in the Village. We struck up a conversation and talked for hours. She was incredibly well-read and charming. She invited us for brunch the next day. That was the beginning. But she would never see us with our other friends. She shunned groups, she said, because she preferred intimate conversation. The only ones who met her were Claire and Herb."

He paused to glance at the three of them: Fay and Sheila were watching him, but Claire was still looking at the floor.

"Your mother assured me the sexual thing was over with between them, that she was the only friend Maxine had and she couldn't just drop her, particularly since she was going through such a hard time with her career. I wouldn't allow her in the apartment while I was there, so your mother would often go to Maxine's place. After a while I found Rosemary was going other places as well. Seeing men, proving to me she could get anyone she wanted to pursue her. I left several times, usually for a week—she would call me up to apologize and reassure me there was nothing serious in her 'flirtations'—and then she would mention the tapes. And you, Fay. How much you wanted 'Daddy' to come home. So on it went until that night."

He relighted his pipe, added ice to his glass.

"Her drinking increased, finally to the point where she started at noon. One day I came home early and found her in a stupor, with the tapes going. I didn't know she had them; I didn't know she had a machine. Of course, Maxine had turned them over to her. You—you were in the corner playing with your dollhouse, or pretending to play, but you were listening." He paused, looked into his drink. "I got rid of them, then and there. The next day, I put an ad in the paper for a full-time babysitter. Your mother went to

A.A. for eight months, then quit. She tried analysis for six months and quit. We quickly returned to the treadmill. One night she would rage or sulk, telling me she'd never forgive what she had heard on the tapes and accusing me of having lunch-hour trysts with other women; then the next night it was all smooth again and we would play on the floor with you, putting together puzzles, teaching you how to read."

Fay had a dim but recurring memory of such a night, a rare occasion when her mother smiled. The three of them lay on their stomachs, semicircled around a puzzle, and when her father got up to go to the bathroom or the kitchen, her mother's smile faded and for a few moments she withdrew from playing. As Fay was trying to force a puzzle piece into the wrong place, her mother's attentiveness returned; her hand gently gripped Fay's wrist to guide the piece toward the correct assignment.

"There," her mother said, "now the rest will be easy." Then, in a curious, faraway tone she added, "If you're missing just one piece or you get it into the wrong slot, the whole thing is worthless."

Colby interrupted the memory. "Notes started arriving from men, and she would leave them for me to find. Sometimes when she was drunk she would threaten to run off with one of them. What I didn't know was that she was making the same threats to Maxine, that the affair had been in full gear all the while.

"Claire was here for dinner the night Maxine showed up. Your mother answered the intercom and told the doorman to admit her. When I objected she turned on me and said, 'I'm glad she's here because I've got some news for *both* of you.' Claire offered to leave, but your mother told her to stay because the news had to do with *you*, and Claire might be interested to know that in addition to having no children she might not have a niece, either. She made an insulting remark about Herb, and Claire slapped her and then the doorbell rang."

He looked at his sister, who had her head tilted back, eyes closed. "Claire, you don't have to stay for this if you don't want to."

"I've lived with it every day," she answered flatly. "Hearing it told is no worse."

He shifted his weight from one leg to the other and arched his back. "The 'news' your mother gave us was that you were neither mine nor Maxine's."

"Maxine's!" said Sheila.

"Yes. Maxine told me—and your mother corroborated it—that before going with the road show she had asked your mother to have a baby with her, one that would have both their blood. The method was simple: Maxine's brother did the honors."

"Oh my God." Sheila whispered.

Fay's lips tightened, then parted, and her mouth hung open. The wish she had harbored all these months: that Dr. Maxson had been her mother.

"But that night she said Maxine's brother had not impregnated her and neither had I. Only *she* knew who the father was, and both of us 'would-be fathers' could spend the rest of our lives guessing who it might be. She was going to leave and take you with her; she was going to take back her maiden name and give it to you too. Fay, when O'Brien told me you'd chosen to use that name in meeting men, I—" He bent his head and his hand moved up to cover his eyes. Then he raised his head and looked straight at her.

"Maxine and I just stood there while she laughed—and maybe because we didn't react at all she stopped laughing, came over, and spat in our faces. Mine first."

Spat. Exactly what *she* had done yesterday: had he used this to aid him in creating a fictionalization for this scenario of the past?

"Maxine picked her up—so easily, and your mother didn't resist. She laughed again. Maxine stood there holding her and said she was lying, that you *were* theirs, and your mother put her arms... put her arms around Maxine's neck and smiled and said, 'No, Max, I'm not lying. You may be able to pick me up the way a man can, but you can't give me a baby. And your brother didn't give me one either. Neither did Curt. So after Fay and I are gone, you and Curt can get together for another recording session.'"

Colby pulled a handkerchief from his pocket to wipe his forehead and hands. Then Fay watched him loosen the knot of his tie.

"For the first and the last time, ever," he continued, "I had a full minute of pity for Maxine. She looked into your mother's face and whispered, 'How I could have loved someone so vile...' Your mother said, 'You still do, Max. But I hate you. I hate you both. I thought Curt could never want anyone but me. I hate you, and I condemn you to each other.' Then Maxine carried her to the balcony, to the railing, and held her over it. I—Claire and I just stood where we were. Claire was a few feet behind me, and she said she didn't think Maxine was pretending. I didn't move. I thought Maxine wanted to frighten her—and *I* wanted her frightened. I wanted her to scream and beg even though it was Maxine she was begging. But that's not what she did. She let go of Maxine's neck and spread her arms wide and said, 'You wouldn't dare.' Then, just like that, she was gone."

He stopped, walked to the bar, and poured another drink. While listening to him Fay had tried to envision the scene, but all she could see were the jade combs in Dr. Maxson's chestnut hair, the look of concern when she had appeared at the apartment after Earl's interrogation of Claire last Friday night.

"I don't believe a word of it. I *know* her. You've got the wrong person. You've made a mistake."

"There's no mistake," said Claire without opening her eyes. And they remained closed as she continued. "Your

father collapsed right afterward. Fainted. He fell onto a
heavy pottery bowl on the floor. Maxine came running in
from the balcony, stepped over him, and started giving me
instructions. As if . . . as if she and I were two children who
had broken something and had to come up with a plausible
way to displace the blame. I said I was going to call the
police. She paused for just a few seconds, then picked up
the letter opener from your father's desk and slashed me.
She said that the next time it would be deeper—if I or Curt
implicated her in this. The police were to be told that Rosemary killed herself. And, she said, wasn't this perfect proof
of it: when Curt tried to stop Rosemary from jumping,
Rosemary pushed him, and when *I* tried to stop her she
slashed me. She looked down at Curt and said to me, 'You
see the way it is with men? They think they're something
special because they can get an erection and spear a woman,
but they can't stay on their feet when they're needed.' She
warned me again, told me exactly what to tell the police,
and said she was leaving by the fire stairs instead of the
elevator. At the door she turned and"—she hesitated for
almost a full minute—"so nonchalantly, she looked straight
at me and said, 'This isn't my first time, so you'd better
do exactly as I say. If not, neither of you will live long
enough to be sorry.' The look on her face, the complete
absence of panic . . . And so, the police bought the story,
helped along by the neighbors, who liked your father and
did not like your mother. Even the doorman, in his own
dumb way, cooperated. He had gone to the bathroom in the
basement, during which time the 'visitor' could have left
the building without his knowing it. At the inquest, Maxine
said exactly that: the doorman was nowhere in sight when
she exited. And she added that she hadn't stayed long in
the apartment because Rosemary was drunk and hysterical
and threatening suicide in a childish way. There we sat"—
she opened her eyes and rolled them toward Fay—"the three
of us being believed. Proving how easy it is to get away
with murder."

Fay saw Sheila reach out for her father's hand and gently tug him toward her until he sat on the arm of the sofa. Claire's eyes closed once again.

Anger escalated into fury as Fay watched her father receiving comfort while she and Claire remained stranded. But *what about* Claire? Turning herself over to her brother after her husband died, becoming his housekeeper-comforter-confidante in exchange for a room in an elegant apartment at a prestigious address. Was it possible that her allegiance had crossed a boundary beyond which she would even support his lies? Why had she said nothing about this 'Maxine' when Earl questioned her?

Sheila's hand rested supportively on her husband's knee; the sight of this suddenly made everything clear to Fay, monstrously clear. If you did not *serve* this man—as Claire and Sheila did—he discarded you. He had killed, or arranged to have killed, Joe and Sam. When he discovered Earl was a threat—more significantly, that Earl was important to *her*—he made a desperate move. And granting the possible coincidence of his having known Dr. Maxson years ago, his indictment of the woman was a loathsome and outlandish attempt—as lurid and diseased as anything in the novels he published—to sever the most important, the most helpful and healing, relationship she had ever had.

"You're both lying," she said in a voice made livid by its quietly contained rage. To her father: "You're sick beyond belief." Then to Claire: "And *you* are worse, for going along with him."

There was no reaction from her father, who had his back to her, and Claire did not even open her eyes. Only Sheila looked stricken.

The four of them remained still for nearly a minute. Then Colby rose, left the room, and returned with a piece of paper, which he dropped into Fay's lap. "Maxine wrote this," he said.

It was one of the notes she and Earl had found when

Claire had unlocked the cabinet for them. She scanned the typed message: 'My patience is wearing thin . . . I can handle Curt and, if necessary, Claire too . . . Fay is ours, as much mine as she is yours . . . Don't make me have to come after you. Yours, 'M.' The 'M' appeared in script.

She now examined the note in a new light. Her father was lucky in that the man who sent it just happened to have the same initial as "Maxine." Or better yet, her father had typed the message himself to incriminate the person he wanted incriminated. "Where," she asked, "is the envelope it came in?"

"I don't have it."

"I see." How convenient. "The envelope would have a postmark with a date. If this *did* come in an envelope."

"Fay—"

She interrupted Claire. "You lied to Earl Friday night. You said my mother slashed your neck before she jumped. You didn't have your brother there to coach you. Now your story changes after you've conferred with him. And Saturday night you up and go to a hotel and he"—she nodded in the direction of her father—"gets this 'mysterious' phone call soon after. A few hours later Earl is shot and left for dead, in a place he would never be at that time of the morning unless he were lured there." She struggled to keep Earl, Joe, Sam out of her thoughts, to keep grief subdued so as not to interfere with her feeling of control, her having, at last, the upper hand. "As soon as he's strong enough, Earl and I will decide what to do about you two and the police. In the meantime, you stay away from him. And Dr. Maxson. If you go near either one of them I'll go straight to the police, no matter *what* Earl says." She slipped the note into the pocket of her suit jacket and waited for one of them to try to stop her. But they neither moved nor spoke. "I think," she said to Claire, "my mother gave you that scar. I think the two of you . . . did something to make her jump."

"Oh, Fay, don't!" Sheila moaned.

Colby spoke up—slowly, in a failed attempt to steady the quaver in his voice. "We won't talk to O'Brien until *he* wants to talk to us. And there's no point in seeing Maxine again. But I want you to promise you won't see her either, until I've told O'Brien what I've told you."

"No. I have a session with her tomorrow evening, and there are some questions I want her to answer."

He came to her chair, leaned over with his hands on the arms of it. "Don't go," he said in a near whisper. "I know what she's like."

"And maybe vice versa?"

"Don't you understand? I think she's the one—the one who killed those men and tried to kill O'Brien."

Now he had gone the limit. As in her dreams, he was blocking her way, trapping her in this chair, pinning her to it with the most unbearable accusation. Roaring, "No!" she rose and rammed her hands against his chest; and as he backed away she pursued, jabbing at him until he was able to catch her wrists. He held them firmly, and her struggling ceased. After a short pause, she said, "Why didn't you send me with her? It would have been two birds with one throw."

He released her, but they remained facing each other.

"This is the last time I'll set foot in this—this sham of a home. We'll proceed with the assumption that I'm not your daughter. The only place I want to see you again is in court." And, she thought, there would be another legal matter for her to carry out: changing her last name to her mother's maiden name, Decker. It was a grim irony that her alias with Joe and Sam was perhaps her more rightful identity.

She walked home, down Park Avenue. At Seventy-seventh Street she glanced over at Lenox Hill Hospital and wondered if Earl had already been taken out of intensive care.

He had, she learned when she phoned from her apartment. He was now in a private room and, yes, he could accept her call.

"H'lo." The weakness in his voice alerted her to camouflage the anxiety in her own.

"Hello, Earl. It's Fay. How do you feel?"

"I'm not ready to run around the block yet, but the doctor assures me the morgue is nowhere in the picture."

"Did you see who shot you?"

"Some punk in leather."

"Not my father?"

"No. But possibly someone he hired."

"What were you doing in that area?"

He told her of the phone call, of the disguised voice that had promised information.

"Can I see you in the morning?"

"Better not. The doctor wouldn't let the cops up here tonight, so they're sure to come first thing tomorrow."

Suppose, she thought, Earl mentioned her father and he in turn pointed the dirty finger at Dr. Maxson and the police went to question her? It would be *too* humiliating. She herself had to talk to Maxson first. And warn her.

"Earl, I might have some useful information by tomorrow night. Maybe if, for the time being, you could be vague with the police, pretend you're groggy, until you and I have a chance to talk."

"What have you found out?"

"Nothing I can really prove right now. But tomorrow night I might know something more definite."

"Are you saying *you* now suspect your father?"

"Yes. And Claire too. I can't get there until eight. Is that too late?"

"Visiting hours are until eight-thirty. If I'm napping, will you wake me up with a cool hand on my cheek?"

She welcomed a flush of pleasure. "Two cool hands."

"I'm calling my assistant Les Beckhorn tonight. He'll be following you tomorrow, just as a precaution. He's five ten, roughly a hundred and forty pounds, brown and gray hair. Look over your shoulder and he won't be far behind."

"Earl, I . . . I'm so sorry this happened to you."

Pause. "I'm sorry you had to be *his* daughter. Keep your chin up. We'll work it all out."

20

A<small>T BREAKFAST THE NEXT MORNING</small> C<small>OLBY TOLD HIS</small> wife and sister his plan for the evening. He was going to hire a car, as he had the morning before, and keep watch on Maxine's building until Fay "safely" emerged from her appointment.

"Even if," said Sheila, "Maxine *is* guilty of what you suspect, certainly she wouldn't hurt Fay. Not in her own office."

"No, not in her office. But suppose she convinces Fay to go out someplace with her?"

"Why would Maxine—" Claire stopped, silently answering the question before she finished it.

"Fay will confront her. She took the note. She didn't throw it back into my face, she didn't tear it up, she took it. Who knows how Maxine will react when she sees it again after all these years. And although Fay may not believe her guilty of anything, she might have already decided to seek another analyst, since Maxine didn't level with her about having known us and Rosemary. That's the *last* thing Maxine would want—after all she's 'done' for Fay."

"Couldn't the police . . . do something?" Sheila said.

"Based on what proof? No, I'm afraid we have to wait until Earl O'Brien is willing to talk to us. Not today, since he just came out of intensive care last night. Maybe tomorrow. And," he added to his wife, "we might have to use you to convince him to see us."

Colby left for work, and Claire went up to her room to prepare for a full day out, one as distracting as she could make it: an hour at the Frick museum, some frivolous shopping, a long lunch, then an Astaire-Rogers double feature on the West Side. When she came downstairs Sheila was in the living room with the look of having been waiting.

"Give me a minute before you go."

Claire sat.

"I've been thinking. This Maxine must be a very complex woman."

"That's putting it mildly."

"I mean that she's capable of murder, yet, according to Fay, she seems to be very good at a profession that helps people." She waited for Claire to comment, but nothing came. "And the fact that she was able to seduce Curt when he was so much in love with Rosemary. Very early in the marriage too."

Claire saw at once what this woman wanted. "Sheila, as a young man Curt was exceptionally naive and highly receptive to flattery. This was obviously quite clear to Maxine, who was clever and cynical beyond her years. And more twisted than any of us knew, except possibly Rosemary. Maxine's intelligence, combined with her theatrical instincts, no doubt told her how to play the crucial scene with Curt. But he's no longer naive, as you well know. Don't romanticize the power Maxine and Rosemary had over him. They would never have it now. As human beings, Sheila, they couldn't hold a candle to you. Curt's well aware of that too."

Above her grateful smile Sheila's eyes lowered, and she resolved to let Claire go on her way without mentioning what she had witnessed last night. She had come out of the bathroom, into the bedroom, drying her hair, and found Curt sprawled on the bed drifting off to sleep. He was lying on his stomach, the fingers of one hand clutching the edge of the pillow while the thumb sporadically stroked the satin case. After a moment he began to murmur. She let the towel hang from her hand while she strained to hear the words. The murmuring stopped, but when it began again she stepped to the edge of the bed and knelt down. Tiny beads of saliva were clustered at one corner of his mouth as he begged, "Please . . . Maxine." A few seconds later he turned over onto his back, and she saw through the fine fabric of Curt's pajamas the outline of his full erection.

Fay was grateful for an activity-packed day that gave her mind little occasion to wander. And when she left her apartment in the morning, when she went to lunch, when she traveled twelve blocks to make a presentation to a client— she was aware of Les Beckhorn's presence. After work, as he followed her to a coffee shop where she would have only a sandwich, she turned and flashed him a smile that she hoped would communicate her appreciation. He not only did not smile, but actually scowled. Was it for professional reasons, to discourage a linking should anyone be watching? Or was he telling her he considered her partly responsible for Earl?

In the booth of the coffee shop she restudied the note, and the tug-of-war of belief started anew. The tug was not between her father and Dr. Maxson; it was between *Claire* and Maxson. She could easily believe her father capable of anything and Maxson incapable of the crimes he so eagerly assigned to her. But Claire clouded the entire picture. Why should she lie? Perhaps her brother had something with which to blackmail her? If so, what could it possibly be?

Since she had the time, she walked the entire distance from midtown to Dr. Maxson's office building on lower Fifth Avenue. Naturally she was aware of Beckhorn trailing her, but when she entered the lobby, greeting the doorman to whom she was now a familiar face, she did not see the chauffeured car parked across the street at one corner.

The two women sat facing Curt, who occupied the jump seat. Having considered the possibility that they might have to double-park a good distance from the building's entrance, Colby had brought along his binoculars. But another car had just been pulling out of this space as they were approaching it, and since it was legal, Colby opted for taking it despite the very close proximity to the building. His eyes scaled the floors until they found Maxson's office.

Shortly after they saw Fay enter, Claire said, "That man over there on the corner. He was walking behind Fay and now he's just standing there."

Colby squinted, then lifted the binoculars. "That's Beckhorn, O'Brien's assistant."

"But why . . . " Sheila began, and stopped.

"O'Brien has probably assigned him to protect Fay from me. Let's hope he doesn't wander over this way."

During the trip to the twelfth floor, the elevator operator chattered about the prediction of rain and the insufficient drainage at the city's street corners. She could not decide if his talking was a blessing or a curse before this coming encounter.

The waiting room was, as usual, empty, and the door to Maxson's office was wide open.

Entering, she locked her gaze to the woman's and said breezily, "It's going to rain."

"I know. Did you bring an umbrella?"

"I forgot."

With a hint of a smile Maxson said, "You forgot to close the door too."

"Oh." Fay turned and walked back to it, chastising herself. So stupid. Never before had she done that, not even on those days when she was her most self-absorbed.

She went not to the couch but to the chair in front of the desk. "I'd prefer to sit here for a while."

"All right." Maxson leaned back, away from the desk, and folded her arms.

Hoping to find courage in ritual, Fay looked at the woman's blouse. It was silk with raglan sleeves; the color was a dark rose that, in the folds, suggested purple. A beautiful and expensive garment, but Fay, thinking of Earl, imagined it as a large bruise.

She didn't know where to begin; she despised having to echo words and phrases her father had used. But there were questions to be answered. How to ask was the difficulty.

When more than a minute had passed, Maxson spoke up. "I would imagine you want to discuss your father's and aunt's visit here yesterday."

With partial relief, Fay nodded. And while Maxson talked she heard the inflection of matter-of-factness that comes easily to one who tells the simple truth.

"They wanted me to dismiss you as a patient because of our past association. I said that association is precisely the reason I've been able to help—*knew* I could help you from the beginning—faster and more thoroughly than another analyst could."

"But don't you think you should have told me from the start?"

"Absolutely not. It would have made our relationship

subjective, and I would have had to terminate it. You wouldn't have been able to make progress."

"But certainly *you* couldn't be entirely objective."

"You don't think I have been? Have I ever uttered a moral judgment against your father?"

No. of course she hadn't. "Wouldn't you ordinarily send a potential patient whose family you knew to someone else?"

"Ordinarily, yes. But as you now know, this was an extraordinary situation. As I said, I believed I could help you better than someone else. I still believe it. The one and only selfish motive lay in paying a debt to your mother."

"What debt?"

"Giving up and abandoning her when she needed a friendship most. Not taking her seriously when she threatened suicide."

"You were in the apartment the night she died?"

"I was. She killed herself soon after I left." Maxson closed her eyes, paused, then opened them. "After I told her she was hopeless. You see, Fay, I owe her something for having done that to her."

Fay breathed deeply, trying to take in courage as an antidote for embarrassment. "My father claims you seduced him—"

"What!"

"—that you used a tape recorder to give my mother evidence so she would . . . have an affair with you."

Maxson stared dumbly. "That's the most preposterous . . . Your mother and I were *friends*. The last months of her life I was her *only* friend. The others had been chased off by her drinking—and by the advances your father constantly made toward them. Your mother had let his countless indiscretions turn her into an alcoholic."

"What about my mother's men?"

Maxson shook her head. "They meant nothing. They were part of Rosemary's petty and pointless game of revenge in which she only harmed herself."

"You mean she never slept with them?"

"She told *me* she didn't. Apparently that's how she kept them dangling—with the promise."

There was a pause while Fay deliberated what to broach next. Then: "When you were in the apartment that night, did my mother say I wasn't my father's child?"

"No."

"Did she suggest it?"

"No."

"Did she allude to your brother?"

"My brother?" Maxson's face was clear confusion. "I don't understand."

"My father said you wanted a child with my mother so you arranged to have her sleep with your brother."

Maxson blinked. "That's too ludicrous to even be insulting."

"Then the night my mother died there was no discussion about who my father was?"

"No."

But there *was* the blood test, which Fay clearly remembered. And Claire had given the reason for it to O'Brien in her first version of what went on the night of Rosemary's death. Yet the subject of paternity could have come up after Maxson left the apartment.

"Why did you change your name?"

"When I was acting, I of course belonged to Actors Equity. There was another actress in Equity whose name was Maxine Olive. Because I was Maxine Oliv*er* there was constant confusion, so I made the change. It was easy," she added with a brief smile, "since I'd already been a longtime fan of Miss de Havilland's."

"Last Friday, when I was asking you questions about yourself during my session, you didn't say you had been *in* the theater. You were an actress for quite a while, weren't you?"

"Yes, a mediocre one. Which is why, out of sheer vanity, I did not go into the subject."

Fay now felt ridiculous playing the interrogator. Maxson was handing out calm truths; her father had served up feverish and outlandish lies. Still, Claire remained in the back of her mind, tugging, tugging. Fay recalled Earl's relentless interrogation, her aunt's resistance finally worn down to tearful admission. Why would Claire violate her brother's trust by stealing the key to the locked cabinet and then, after her visit here with him yesterday, side with him, defend him, corroborate his indictment of Maxson? Only for Claire, not for her father, would Fay perform the self-humiliating test on Maxson.

"Would you," she asked, "write a note for me? To my father?"

"A note? Saying what?"

"That I'm continuing therapy with you, that he's not to come to your office ever again or contact you in any way."

"Why don't you *tell* him exactly that?"

"Because I don't want to speak to him again. I'll mail the note with one of my own."

"All right." From the center drawer of desk she took out a sheet of stationery and a pen and began to write. "I'm very happy you've decided to continue with me, Fay. For reasons I stated earlier, I think we'll *both* benefit."

"I just don't understand Claire. Going along with my father's lies," she said, listening to the razor-point pen scratch against the textured paper, the noise of it reminding her of a nagging question she had forgotten to ask.

"Claire was always her brother's keeper. Too much so and at her own expense."

At her own expense. Expense. It underscored the very question Fay had neglected to ask. About the scar.

And she thought of Earl's method of questioning, like a machine switching unpredictably between fast-forward and rewind. And employing conjecture and innuendo to scout the truth.

"You went to the inquest they had for my mother, didn't you?"

"Yes."

Fay watched the pen continue on.

"Was there any speculation about murder?"

"Nothing spoken outright, although that suspicion is the reason for an inquest."

"Didn't they suspect Claire?"

"Claire? Why would they?"

"Given her appearance."

"Appearance? She looked fine, and she was in perfect control of herself. She told the people exactly what had happened to your mother."

Perfect control of herself. Which is exactly what Claire had *not* had when Earl questioned her. She had succumbed to tears when confessing that she and her brother had "let" Rosemary die.

"Why," said Fay, "did she *need* to be in perfect control?"

The pen halted for a second, then moved on.

"Because your father wasn't very coherent that night."

Maxine came running in from the balcony, stepped over him, and started giving me instructions.

"But Claire must have *looked* suspicious to the examiners."

"No, I don't think she did. She was telling the truth."

"I'm talking about her appearance."

"I don't know what you mean. I've told you, she looked fine."

"How soon after the death was the inquest held?"

"Two days, I think. I don't remember exactly."

But the gauze bandage around Claire's neck, so prominent when she awakened Fay with the horrible news the morning after, had remained for more than a week. Certainly, the bandage was memorable. If Claire's *first* accu-

sation were true—that Rosemary had inflicted the wound—
why should Maxson conveniently "forget" the telltale bandage she could not have failed to see at the inquest?

Consideration of this question was halted when Maxson
turned the paper around and slid it across the desk. "There.
Will this do?"

> Curt,
>   Fay is continuing therapy with me. Please do not come
> to my office again. My doorman will be instructed to call
> the police if you do. Fay's well-being is more important
> than our ancient dislike of each other.
>
>   Olivia

As soon as Fay finished reading, her eyes returned to
the "My" in the second line. It was devastatingly sufficient,
but she asked for more. "Would you sign your last name
too? That will make it less informal and add firmness."

Maxson did so, extending the proof.

Fay left the paper on the desk and, with fingers that felt
novocained, fished the note from her purse, giving the signed
'M.' a fleeting glance. She aligned the two pieces of paper
and pushed them across to Maxson. "Your 'M's," said Fay,
unable to look at the woman, as if it were she herself who
was guilty.

Closing her eyes, the letter remained, seemingly etched
onto the backs of her lids: $\mathcal{M}$. The idiosyncratic, insistent
third loop was uniform, and no other letters could be adjoined
to it. However, in Maxson's handwritten note to Colby all
other capital letters *were* joined to their adjacent small letters.

"I don't understand this," said Maxson, and Fay heard
the first unsureness in the voice that, for eleven months,
had been nothing less than sure.

"You wouldn't mention Claire's wound," Fay mumbled.
"What wound?"

Her eyes opened. "That's what I mean. It had to have been an issue at the inquest, but you wouldn't mention it. I believe it's called 'denial'—when one chooses not to acknowledge a guilty or a painful incident."

"Fay, this junior analyzing is leading you down the wrong path. I don't know what you're getting at."

"If you don't know what I'm getting at, how can you say I'm going down the wrong path? You *know* what I'm getting at. You wrote that note to my mother, you—"

"The note is an obvious forgery. Your father must have—"

"The *note* is a forgery? You mean the signature is. No, I don't think so. Look at the edges of the paper—they've yellowed with age. Twenty-five years ago there would have been no reason for my father to make this up. You wrote it, you cut Claire's neck as a warning, you made her and my father lie to the police."

"Your voice sounds so hard, Fay. Do you know how hard it sounds?" She actually winced; as people often do at a piercing siren, Fay thought. "May I have a chance to talk?"

"I want the truth; I want all of it. I want to know why you—" She stopped, for Maxson's face suddenly appeared weary, almost haggard.

"*I* want a cigarette." She opened the top left drawer of the desk and brought out a tiny ashtray, then rummaged around farther back in it.

"You said Claire was in 'perfect control' at the inquest. Those were your words. It was because you threatened her."

"If you'll allow me to get a cigarette." She stood and walked to the closet behind Fay.

Fay looked at the ashtray and said to herself, I never knew she smoked; she didn't smoke the night she was in my apartment.

In a flash the rope, thick as a cable, passed in front of her eyes and tightened around her body just below her breasts, pinning her arms to her sides. She let out a cry.

"Don't bother to scream," said Maxson as she secured the double knot behind the chair. "The paneling on these walls is soundproofing, and you've opened and closed that door often enough to know it's solid wood. I'm not going to hurt you. I just don't want you to bolt out of here before I can tell you everything."

Cigarettes. The simplest lie, and she had fallen for it. But when Maxson reappeared behind the desk she was opening a package of cigarettes. She lighted one, turned, and went to the window. Parting the blinds with her thumb and forefinger she looked out into the night. Then, with a voice hollowed by sadness, she said, "You were right about the rain. It's starting."

21

FAY WATCHED HER STAND AT THE WINDOW AND SMOKE the entire cigarette without saying a word. Finished with it, she ground it into the ashtray, then dropped the butt into the wastebasket. With a tissue she wiped the ashtray clean and replaced it inside the drawer.

"A nasty habit," she said, "but not an excessive one." She returned to the window. "'Perfect control.' A poor choice of words on my part. And you're a clever woman who works with words every day."

"But," Fay asked tremulously, "why *not* mention Claire's neck? There was no reason not to, since she told the police and the people at the inquest that my mother had done it to her."

"Yes, no reason. I always think before I speak, but I . . . was so elated writing that message to your father, so happy in the certainty you and I would go on together. But all you wanted from me was an 'M.'" There was a long pause during which the only sound was the traffic in the street below. "You have to understand that I actually liked Claire despite the way she indulged your father. But then, she had twice his strength and twice his character. And still has, judging from their visit yesterday. Where did you get the note?"

"My fa—father. He kept it, with two others."

"Two others?"

"From men."

"All these years," Maxson said quietly. "How morbid. And unfortunate for me."

Despite her fear of the crimes Maxson had possibly committed after killing her mother, despite the fear for her own safety now, Fay gave vent to her anger. "Maybe it *is* morbid, but the reason might be that he kept them as punishment for having been such a coward!"

Maxson's profile revealed a smirk. "My, what nobility you assign him now. Soon you'll make him an equal to the incomparable Earl O'Brien."

The mention of Earl's name put a cry in her throat, but she squelched it. Be still, her instinct told her. Just be still.

"Your mother told me he destroyed the tapes. He should have kept *them* for some cheap excitement. I could tell yesterday he still has a taste for it. His eyes were all over me like a pair of fumbling hands."

Fay's stomach rolled over, and she could *not* be still. "That's not true. He hates you."

"It doesn't stop him from wanting me. Because he's never been able to solve me. That's all lust is—wanting to penetrate the mystery, identify and pigeonhole it, and then move on. To the next mystery. Well, he's never been able to identify me. It wasn't just anger and damaged pride that made him bar me from his and your mother's apartment. It was also his weak temptation."

"Why would he want you when he knew you were my mother's lover!"

A grimace moved across her mouth. "'Lover.' I despise

that word. I wanted your mother as a companion. We *were* companions. We could have had a beautiful life together. With you."

"Then your brother—did sleep with her?"

"Yes."

"And you believe I'm . . . ?"

"My niece? Not at all. It was your mother's last dirty trick."

"So you killed her for it."

"She wanted to die, Fay. She was already doing the job slowly, with her drinking. And her men—playing them off against both your father and me."

Her curiosity outdistancing her dread, Fay asked, "It wasn't the first time for you, was it? That's what you told Claire; that's how you threatened her." When Maxson failed to answer, Fay ventured, "You might as well tell me, now that you're going to get rid of me."

"Get rid of you?" She swung her head around. "That's the last thing I would ever do."

Maxson returned her attention to the window blinds. "My father was an English professor and my mother a high school French teacher. Every summer he would drag her off to Europe where he could hole himself up in some library stacks. Finances didn't permit my brother and me to go along, so we were 'parked' with relatives. I was sent to western Pennsylvania, my brother to Kentucky. I knew my mother disliked this arrangement and would have preferred to stay home. But every year she capitulated. I finally found out why. When I couldn't sleep at night I would sit at the top of the stairs and listen to them talk in the living room. One such night in early June she was pleading with him to let her stay home just this one summer so that, for a change, my brother and I could be with our friends. His answer was 'Damn it, Glenda, I need my sex, and if you don't go I'll just have to find someone else to take care of it.' 'Need my sex,' like 'I need my coffee' or 'I need my socks washed.'

And so, the next morning the yearly announcement was made with the usual instructions to mind our manners and budget our spending money. As always, we celebrated my birthday two weeks early, the day before they left. That summer I turned fifteen." She had her arms crossed, and Fay watched the fingernails of one hand dig into the purple sleeve on the other arm. "Off they went, but my mother didn't come back. She was hit by a car in London as she was on her way to return some books my father had borrowed from a library. He had the funeral there and had her buried there, in a cemetery that she supposedly once told him was 'charming.' So my brother and I didn't even have a grave to visit. Ten months later my father married a twenty-four-year-old graduate student who readily became an even more willing servant than my mother had been. It was back to the books; he never had his nose out of one, except to eat a meal or go to bed. Or to take his usual walk before dinner. And every time he went for that walk I would wish he'd never come back. Then I figured out a way to make sure he wouldn't."

There was a pause, and although Fay knew that horror was forthcoming, she was, for a moment, swamped in sadness.

"We lived five miles from town and the university he taught at, because he liked the privacy. We owned close to ten acres with long-abandoned railroad tracks and trestle. His daily walk was always down the center of the tracks, over the trestle and back. So *I* started taking walks on the tracks, earlier than he did but gradually pushing up the time until we would regularly meet as I was returning and he was starting out. Of course, it finally occurred to him to ask me to walk along, and within a few weeks it became an accepted ritual. I had gone over my plan a million times, I had the exact spot picked out, but I had to wait until we were deeper into autumn when it would be dark by five-thirty. He had always hated and feared trespassers and hunters; in fact he'd called the sheriff so many times that they would purposely make him wait an hour or so before sending a car around. One Tuesday night in late October when we reached that spot on the trestle I stopped and said I saw a flashlight in the distance. When he said he couldn't see anything I climbed up onto the guardrail, holding my hand on the slanted girder, and told him I could see it plainly and that it wasn't a flashlight at all but someone building a fire. I got down and he got up. The rest was simple. It was a seventy-foot drop to the rocks below."

Fay began to moan, and Maxson waited until she was silent again.

"Running home, I threw myself on the ground a few times to make sure I was scratched and tattered. By the time I got to the house I was crying. But the tears were for my mother, my brother, and myself."

Fay's voice came out as tiny as a timid child's: "No one ever questioned? Not your brother? Not your father's wife?"

Maxson shook her head. "My brother's dead now. Heart attack. And Louise remarried, but we still exchange birthday and Christmas cards."

Now the terror, so long delayed by this accounting of the past, began to creep along Fay's skin. "Joe and Sam and Earl," she said in a half whisper. *"Why?"*

Maxson moved to the desk and sat down behind it. "Until a year ago I had everything except a life. A successful practice, a good apartment, a beautiful house in the country, a luxurious car. And all those cultural extras—subscriptions to the ballet, the opera, concert series. But no life until the night of Marsha's party, when you came through the door. You were wearing a black boat-neck sweater, a brown skirt, and your hair was pulled back and gathered by a gold clip. It was like . . ." She turned her eyes on Fay. "Do you remember last Friday when we talked about Vermeer?"

Fay nodded.

"I mentioned that perfect light he could create, the kind

you rarely get a glimpse of in everyday life. *You* were that perfect light, and have been ever since. Even now," she added softly. "Even now that I've lost you." She rested her hands in her lap, one on top of the other, and looked down at them. "That first session was agony for me, I had to maintain such control, strike just the right chord to make sure you'd come back. And during the first six weeks when you were so distant and reticent my heart would jump whenever the phone rang because I thought it might be you, calling to cancel, to say you had decided not to continue. Then, what I hoped would happen *began* to happen. The click, the rapport. You were drawn to me, and I could feel it getting stronger and stronger, and so more than ever I had to guard myself. I've never had to use such restraint. The times I've wanted to ask you out for coffee or a drink, the times I've imagined you sitting next to me at a concert or a play."

It took Fay's breath away: this woman was speaking the same hopes she herself had had.

"I had to tell myself to go slowly, to let it grow until we reached the point where the therapy could be put aside and the friendship, the companionship, could begin."

"But how could you expect . . . You know I'm not a lesbian."

Maxson lifted her eyes from her hands and looked at her head-on. "I'm not interested in sex, Fay. I know that makes me an oddity in a world that's *obsessed* with it. The most I would ever want is to kiss your cheek good night and good morning, hold your hand walking on the beach, brush your hair for you. Companionship, the only love that's true enough to last, that passes the test of time. Women are capable of it. With very few and rare exceptions, men are not. It's not in their nature. Look at them in restaurants, listen to them at parties, eavesdrop on a private conversation between two supposed friends. Do you ever hear a tone of natural affection—I don't mean they have to express it in words. I'm talking about an emotional manner. But how sweet their voices can be when they want to undress a woman."

"That's not all men," said Fay, and then to herself: That's not Earl.

"It's most. Your father, for example. Look at the childhood he gave you, just because you might not be the product of *his* penis. But the four times he was in bed with me—a rhapsody of words. You'd have thought there was an orchestra playing in his throat. Would you care to hear what he said?"

"No." She turned her head away.

"I thought not."

There was a pause. Then Fay spoke, "Why Joe, Sam, and Earl?"

"Because, Fay, I was tired of waiting, tired of the ache. When Kevin turned on you and sent you that note, you decided to drop your alias and start seeing Joe, Sam, and Andrew in public, and I—"

"You encouraged it!"

"And how would it have appeared if I hadn't?"

Although roped firmly to the chair, she felt as if she were going to fall out of it. "You wanted to make it look—look like Kevin was responsible?"

"Hardly. I was sure he would have alibis. By the time I got to Andrew I knew you would finally be ready for my full support. Outside this office. Our companionship could begin."

"Why me?" she said miserably.

"So many reasons, Fay. First, you're my equal—no, you're more than my equal, and now in ways I never expected. Like catching that slip about Claire's wound and hanging on to it. Smart, clever. I'm forced to respect it even though . . ."

She stood and walked to the patient's couch, ran her fingertips over the area where Fay's head had rested during their sessions. "Second, there was the excellent chance I could make you available to me. You were using sex as a narcotic, and it didn't take me long to realize what it was you were looking for. Quite simply, a home. And I wanted to make it *my* home. Your mother had beauty, and charm, once upon a time, and a rare magnetism—but you surpass her in all of them. In the end she proved to be weak and lazy—which you are not. Do you have any idea how many years I've looked for an equal, a complement?

"The life you and I could have had together! Travel. Intelligent conversation. Laughter. I felt your attraction to me. It was as palpable as anything you can touch in this room. After Andrew, our life together could have begun. But then, enter Earl O'Brien, the monkey wrench supplied by your father." She sat down in the chair behind the couch. "'An exceptional man in so many ways'—so you told me Friday night."

She leaned her head back and closed her eyes.

Fay remained speechless, afraid that any words would be the wrong ones.

After a moment Maxson continued. "When I first got to your apartment Friday night, I was so happy. Ecstatic. Naturally, I knew you had lied to me about Sam during our session that morning, saying you had spoken to him when in fact he was already dead. That night your call was a summons to tell me the truth. While I was listening to your story about Mr. O'Brien and his suspicions I kept thinking, 'There will be other nights that we will sit here together. This is just the first time.' Then, as I was leaving, you said, 'I've never met anyone quite like him.' There was a light in your eyes, a softness in your voice, and I realized there was new trouble coming. Yes, I made those calls on Saturday night. Since all the suspicion was pointed at your father, the opportunity was like a gift. O'Brien would be out of *my* way and your father would be out of *your* way. Like in your dreams. You'd have convicted him of killing O'Brien, and of course the others, even if a jury didn't. My only fear was that Mr. O'Brien would not show up or else arrive unalone. If that car hadn't rounded the corner, if he hadn't gone rolling all over the pavement, if my aim had been better. If. Then he would be in the morgue instead of Lenox Hill."

"How do you know where he is?"

"Yesterday, your father said there was an 'attempted' third murder. Last night I telephoned hospitals until I got the right one. I had expected him to be in St. Vincent's, since it's closest to where he was—injured. But I understand his wanting to be at Lenox. It's so convenient to your apartment."

"That's not why!" Fay said wildly. "He was taken there because his doctor is an affiliate."

"The lady doth protest too much. And thereby shows the depth of her concern."

Fay now thought of what Earl had said about a leather punk. "You hired someone to shoot him?"

"I hired nobody. I'm not a coward. I was in disguise, to blend with the sexual scenery of the place. There's nothing to connect me with the incident. I was at my country house for the weekend, and no one would know I had driven into town—to meet Earl O'Brien. And I'm well covered at the times of the other two occurrences. But none of that matters now," she said wearily. "I don't care about the police. I'm too . . . broken. And far too tired to pick up the pieces."

I don't care about the police told Fay to say nothing, and yet she spoke. "How can you possibly feel what you claim to feel for me, and be able to do what you did to them? Joe and Sam, through the *heart*!"

"Through the chest. Their only 'hearts' are what's between their legs." Maxson got up and walked past Fay's chair to the closet. After unlocking the file cabinet, she opened the top drawer, which contained two knives and a gun. She chose a knife; the gun would be used later.

Fay sat rigid, listening but unable to define the activity behind her.

Maxson dropped the knife into her purse and said, "I'm going out for a while."

Before Fay could plead against what she realized was coming, a scarf was being tied around her mouth.

"An extra safety measure. The soundproofing has worked with hysterical patients, but you might have exceptional lung power." She stooped and gave the rope's double knot an extra tightening tug.

And then Fay felt the hand on her hair. Despite her terror, her revulsion, the small part of her that remained rational even now could not deny that the stroking was maternal.

"You're going to live a long life," Maxson said softly. "You've had fears and you've had depression, but you've never known real despair. After tonight, you will. You'll know it as I've always known it. That will be our bond."

There was the hint of a kiss at the crown of her head.

"I won't be long."

The last sound was the closing of the door.

"Evening, Dr. Maxson," said the doorman. "I didn't see your patient come down."

"No, she's rendering services to *me* tonight. She's also my accountant. I'm going out for a while."

Pulling on her gloves, she walked to the taxi whose passengers were just leaving it. She told the driver, "Lenox Hill Hospital."

Claire had just lighted a cigarette and was lighting Sheila's when, over the flame and through the window, she saw it. "There's Maxine, getting into that taxi!"

"But Fay—" Sheila began.

"Claire, you and Sheila get Beckhorn over there and go up to the office. I'm going to follow her."

"But if she's harmed Fay—"

"Then it's done. But I don't think she has. Not *yet*. Now go!"

As the two women crossed the street, approaching Les Beckhorn, Sheila's concern for Fay coexisted briefly with puzzlement over Curt's insistence upon pursuing that woman.

Broken, thought Maxson, broken indeed. So exhausted. With Blakis and Telias there had been great energy, adrenaline. Now, weariness. She wanted to close her eyes, but no, she must gear up for the task. The knife would be silent. Just one thrust. Then she would return to the office to use the gun. She would stand before Fay and shoot herself.

Seeing the taxi ahead continue a steady course up Park Avenue South bolstered Colby's belief that Maxine had not yet hurt Fay. But what had *Fay* said to send Maxine rushing out into the rainy night and toward O'Brien? Had Maxine confessed? And to how much?

The taxi ran a red light at Twenty-eighth Street, and Colby urged his driver to do the same. But too late: a line of cross-traffic passed in front of them, creeping, windshield wipers blinking away the rain. In panic Colby looked out the side window at the public phone on the corner. Its receiver was hanging down, turning in the wind, a clear indication that it was out of order.

The limousine bullied its way onward, shifting from lane to lane, moving like a shark among a school of lesser fish. Colby looked for Maxine's taxi, identifiable by the crescent-shaped dent on one side of the trunk. It couldn't have gained that much distance, could it?

As they crossed Seventy-fourth Street he looked left, to the west: a block and a half away was Fay's apartment. With Maxine's taxi still nowhere in sight, he reconsidered. Had she turned off Park at some point and gone up Madison? Was Fay's apartment her destination? Was there something in it she needed, something incriminating? He remembered her at Rosemary's inquest, her easy acting hiding her chilling self-assuredness. If she were the killer of Blakis and Telias, she most certainly had left no evidence. He himself had seen and heard smugness and caution yesterday afternoon in her office, revealing nothing self-condemning about Rosemary's death, as if she suspected him and Claire of having concealed recorders in their clothing. Would she really chance doing anything to O'Brien in a place where she would be seen, possibly caught? *What had gone on between her and Fay up in that office?*

Before he could consider any further, the driver was stopping at the corner of Seventy-seventh Street; because it was one-way he could not turn and deliver Colby in front of the hospital's lobby.

Seizing his umbrella and opening the door, Colby said, "Drive around the block and wait out front."

Both women at the information desk were on telephones, so he leaned over the chest-high ledge and rasped at one, "Please please, this is urgent! Earl O'Brien's room number."

She scowled and held up one finger, but he persisted until she told the party on the line to hold. Fuming, she consulted a list, then barked out the number.

"In the last few minutes has anyone else asked for the same number? A woman."

"No."

He cast his eyes at the one on the other telephone, and the angered informant reaffirmed, "No one has asked."

The relief he felt as he headed for the elevators was based upon the new likelihood that Maxine had gone to Fay's apartment, for whatever reason. But if that were the case, *had* she harmed Fay first? No, he reassured himself, not in her own office.

He stepped into a waiting elevator at almost the same

moment that another one opened its door on the seventh floor to let Maxson out.

Downstairs, she had had a small stroke of good fortune. As she came through the lobby's revolving door she saw the women at the information desk talking on the telephones. Waiting for one of them to be free would not ordinarily have bothered her, but her weariness had increased significantly during the taxi ride, increased as the loss of Fay touched new depths within her. On her way toward the information desk she passed a security guard and a nurse in conversation and she heard the nurse say, "Yeah, that O'Brien's a card. He had me in stitches this afternoon—pardon the pun." Then, when asked for the room number, the nurse gave it to Maxson.

She paused at the seventh-floor nurse's station and asked the location of the room. "Straight ahead, last one on the left."

Starting forward, she reviewed her strategy if O'Brien was in a semi-private. She would introduce herself as Fay's analyst, say she had important news about Fay, and pull the curtain between the beds. Afterward she would have to be quick, perhaps take the stairs instead of an elevator. She could not leave the knife in him as she had with Blakis, for she might need it to slash her way out of the building. The taxi driver was waiting for her with the twenty-dollar bill she had given him and the promise of two more at the end of the round trip.

The door was closed. She opened it and was greeted by near darkness. The light was off, but the glow from a Park Avenue street lamp shone at the window and defined the slant of the rain. It was a very large single-pane window at the bottom of which was a vent, now opened outward a few inches and letting in both the sound and the wet-concrete scents of the downpour.

Made to order: a private room, and O'Brien asleep, snoring. She waited a few seconds for her eyes to adjust, then approached the bed.

Early Sunday morning she had got only a glimpse of his face, and now she wanted a fuller look. She leaned over.

So this was the "exceptional" man. Certainly not in looks, though he was handsome enough if you liked the type. His "character," his "decency": of course, Fay meant these. To a woman, a man could exhibit character and decency; but just how long they lasted depended on how long his sexual desire lasted. When desire diminished or evaporated, so did the other two.

He was lying on his side. A tactical problem. Could she manage a full and accurate thrust from such an angle? Difficult and perhaps impossible. Then it occurred to her; the throat. Early Sunday morning she might have accomplished the task had she not locked herself into the ritual—aiming for the heart. She could simply have shot him in the back of the head as his hand moved for his pocket after she uttered his name.

Yes, the throat.

Her eyes now adjusted to the semidarkness, she opened her purse and gripped the knife.

Colby approached the room. The bird that seemed to be fluttering around in his chest might have been optimism or apprehension, or a creature maddened by both. The palms of his hands felt oiled; a rivulet of sweat trickled down behind one ear. And although he was walking away from the nurse's station, the voices there refused to recede, remaining as clear as if his hearing had stayed behind and would not follow him.

He gripped the handle of the closed door and pushed.

She saw the intrusion of the hallway light spread across the floor and climb the opposite wall, but as she swiveled her head to look at the door something collided with her ear.

Seeing the glint of the knife as it came out of her purse, he had moved swiftly to strike her with his umbrella. She staggered slightly, away from the bed, and he aimed another blow at her. Her hand caught and clutched the other end of it, and with new, incredible strength she reeled him toward her when he refused to let go. The knife sliced through the air. The blade crossed his throat but cut deeper than the one that had crossed Claire's twenty-five years ago. He felt and, worse somehow, *heard* the splitting of tissues and the snapping of tendons. At once, his mouth and lungs began to fill with blood.

She lashed out again, but struck his upraised hand. That hand grasped her wrist and his head came forward; he sank his bloodied teeth into her knuckles until the weapon dropped to the floor.

Choking, gurgling, his lungs begging for air, he might have collapsed now had he not been bolstered by an energizing self-disgust. Last night his dream of her had betrayed him: in it she had invited him to bed with her, and he had accepted with full knowledge of all her crimes.

She stooped to secure the knife but could not locate it. She heard O'Brien's undisturbed snoring as Colby's fingers closed around her hair and yanked her upward. His hands clamped her neck like a vise, spun her body around, and began steering her backward. Her fingers rose to dig at his face, to find his eyes, but his head kept swaying from side to side, and she couldn't reach her desired targets. The smell of the blood—heavy and almost sweet—propelled her into nausea. And the gurgling from his throat, obscenely like the gurgling of lust, worked to cripple her knees. As he moved her like a mannequin she knew he wanted to back her into the hallway, away from O'Brien—into the hallway, where the nurses would see his wound and run for help.

But he didn't make the necessary turn out of the door.

He kicked it shut, nearly shut, for there was no click although the entire slab of hallway light disappeared.

No, not the door. The window next to it! He was backing toward the window. If only the sound and smell of his blood would go away. . . .

Awkwardly but forcefully, he slammed her against the pane. He could not cry out; he was too full of blood. He would die; he knew that. He *was* dying. But she would die also, *the way he wanted her to*.

O'Brien emerged disoriented from his deep sleep. He had heard a noise, like a limb cracking, and that, with the sound of the rain, put him back in his childhood bedroom in Bay Ridge, the maple tree outside framed by his window.

But the window he opened his eyes on framed two blurred figures, grunting and snarling and coughing. A second "cracking" told him it was the glass. One figure was using the other to smash the window. His right arm slid away from the bed and his forefinger groped, found the button that alerted the nurses' station.

Turning her head to one side, Maxson reached up again to claw at Colby's face. She would have given anything for the power to seal the wound she had inflicted. His blood had gushed onto her face and hair, and a few drops struck her lip, which his hold on her would not let her wipe clean.

He managed to get both knees onto the ledge, straddling her. When her head and shoulders finally broke the barrier, sending large and irregular shards sailing downward with the rain, she knew what he wanted. So be it. She would miss out on killing O'Brien, be denied killing herself in front of Fay. She would have to settle for a lesser reward. So be it. She would die playing him, once again, for the weak fool he was. He had bled on her, bled on her lips. He would pay. Quickly, her mind grasped the possibility that because he was already in a hospital the doctors might be able to save him with one of their occasional miracles.

And so her struggle slackened to the *pretense* of a struggle—but he would only think she was weakening. She allowed him to work her out of the window frame up to her hips; one remaining finger of windowpane glided alongside her skirt without cutting it. She felt him release her neck, knowing he was going to dump her over by pushing against her thighs or buttocks. But she was at the point of leverage where she could throw herself out backward with no help from him. Enough leverage to do that and more.

She reached out and gripped his perfectly knotted tie just as the door opened and the nurse screamed, "Oh, Jesus Christ!"

O'Brien, helpless, lay rigid and watched, trying to determine who the two figures were.

When the nurse stepped back into the hallway yelling, "Security, security!" Colby felt himself being pulled forward by his scarlet-soaked tie until he saw Maxine's clenched teeth. Then she bucked her hips and the two of them disappeared out the window.

All the way down, she held fast to the tie. But Colby closed his eyes against her—blotted her out with the faces of Sheila, Fay, Claire—as they made their descent to join Rosemary.

22

Earl O'Brien drummed one set of fingers on the steering wheel, the other against the vinyl seat of the parked car. He glanced at the closed and empty ashtray, which, if he were still a smoker, would have contained five or six butts after this half-hour wait. After the removal of the bullet from his lung, the doctor had sternly advised him to kick the habit. To squelch the desire for a cigarette and the feeling of deprivation, he recalled his good fortune in being alive. And recalling who was responsible for his being alive he shifted his gaze from the ashtray to the windshield and looked out at Fay kneeling at her father's grave, next to the flowers she had brought with her. For minutes at a time her eyes would close, and he wondered if she was praying. Once during the long ride out here from the city, she had cried, noiselessly and with her face turned away from him.

This was his first time with her here, but she had come twice on her own since the funeral a month ago. He was, of course, still in the hospital the day of the funeral, but

Fay provided a full report on the crowd that showed up for it. Dowd & Dunay Publishers closed their doors for the morning so the entire staff could attend; several of Colby's authors traveled to New York—one, a well-stoned Brent Matheny, all the way from Morocco; the television reporters were not so abundant as had been expected, and the evening news programs showed why—they had to divide ranks because Olivia Maxson's funeral had begun a half hour before Colby's and was held on the West Side. At six o'clock O'Brien had watched a piece of film footage, the variety of which is manna to both the interviewing reporter and the viewers: one of Dr. Maxson's patients stood on the sidewalk outside the funeral home, looked tearfully into the camera, but said angrily into the microphone, "She was a wonderful woman and a great analyst. I will never believe the charges against her no matter *what* evidence they've trumped up." Other glowing testaments to Maxson's character and abilities followed, offered by shocked and tight-faced professional colleagues.

The police, however, remained satisfied with their findings: Fay bound and gagged when they broke open the office door; the knife and gun in the filing cabinet, the gun being the same caliber used on Sam Telias and Earl; the bloodied knife, retrieved from under O'Brien's bed, that had opened Colby's throat; the "Bad Girl" notes O'Brien surrendered from his apartment; and the two pieces of paper Maxson had left on her desk when she walked out of the office for the last time. . . .

O'Brien watched Fay rise, stroke the headstone, and then approach the car. Her oval face seemed longer now, in grief, and in dim angled lighting it appeared gaunt; during the dinners they had shared in the past month she had only picked at her food.

She got in and closed the door.

"All right?" he asked.

"Umm-hmm," she answered, but without looking at him.

They drove for more than twenty miles with only the sound of the engine filling their ears. He did not even dare glance over at her. But then, there was so much he dared not do—declare the true expanse of his feeling for her, even on the two occasions that their sleeping in the same bed had culminated in sex. He could not lay bare his hopes for marriage, ask how she felt about having a baby. It was too soon, too soon.

"Mind if I say something?" he asked at last.

"No. In fact, I wish you would."

"I don't want to sound like—"

"You don't have to qualify it," she said softly.

"Just this. You can't talk to the dead, and sometimes you've got to fight like hell to keep *them* from talking to you. Not to avoid grief and depression—those feelings have to be gone through. What I mean is you can't let them determine how the rest of your life will be."

"I know . . . I know."

There was silence again until it began to rain; all at once, heavy drops spattered against the windshield. He switched on the wipers and said lightly, "Well, here we are—orphans of the storm."

"Yes. But we're not the *only* ones."

He reached across, found her hand, and squeezed it. "Keep remembering that."

The drive took more than an hour from the cemetery in Hunterdon County, New Jersey. There was the long-ago purchased plot next to Rosemary Colby's grave in Connecticut, but Fay and Claire decided that that was the last place Curt should be buried, and Sheila gratefully accepted the suggestion of Hunterdon, where she knew her husband had wanted to buy a weekend house. "He was *your* husband," Claire had told Sheila, and Fay added silently to herself that the Hunterdon area was where her father had innocently been driving around, looking for peace, the day Sam was murdered.

Fay used a speeding, passing car as an excuse to look left—at Earl. He could not know, she thought, to what extent he had been her mainstay these past weeks. And still was. Often her crying was inspired not by grief or anger but by his kindness, his generosity, his fine intuition, which told him when to be silent, when to speak, when to joke. The first time they made love he had known intuitively that she wanted it frenzied, almost rough, to jolt her out of a numbing all-day depression; the second time, he realized she needed to linger, wanting to savor and be savored.

Afterward he had propped himself up on his elbow and grinned. "I've never made love to a woman who makes more money than I do." She answered, "Do you think you can pass as my gigolo?" "Yes, to those who still believe the world is flat." At moments like these she would wonder if Maxson might have been different had she met a man like Earl soon enough in her youth. But no, Maxson had created the mold of her character the night she lured her father onto the guardrail of the train trestle, and she had willingly cast her actions from that mold for the rest of her life. Fay had more than an occasional flash of pity for the woman—pity that Maxson would resent—but at the same time she realized there would be no pity in her at all if the knife had found Earl.

Earl was her mainstay, and she was Claire's and Sheila's. Even now, after a month, she was still astonished at the quality of Sheila's grief: hiding in her room for days at a time; drifting off into distraction in the middle of conversation; disinterested in her evening bourbon and soda, the single glass of which was rarely finished. As in all marriages, Fay supposed there had been something between her father and Sheila that remained unseen by others. That something was reflected in Sheila's sorrow. And in Curt Colby's will.

Each of the three women was left equal amounts of money and stocks; the penthouse apartment went to Sheila outright and without stipulation that Claire be allowed to retain her quarters there. Fay was surprised and said so; Sheila in turn was surprised at Fay. "Your father didn't have to include that. It was understood between us that Claire would live here as long as she wanted. And if it's ever sold, she and I split the money."

Her father had always seemed to her to be one of the world's least trusting people, but he trusted Sheila, who was indeed trustworthy. He had been a poor parent—perhaps worse than poor—and a man with no truly close friends, but he had established some kind of bond with his fourth wife.

He had had the fear and the intelligence, the concern and the courage, to hire a car and wait across the street that night, the wise suspicion to follow Maxson to the hospital. He had saved Earl's life.

Fay's ruminations made his complexity grow daily, and she supposed this was inevitable—that there is no reflection and summing up like the kind that follows death, especially sudden death.

The rain had stopped by the time they reached the George Washington Bridge. In the steel-gray late-afternoon light many of the skyscrapers gleamed, and their striving vertical lines aided the illusion of a city meticulously maintained and perfectly ordered. Riding across the bridge, Fay welcomed that illusion even though it would be gone in a minute.

A chilly wind was blowing when they got out of the car on Park Avenue, and they briskly walked the necessary two blocks.

"Good evening, Miss Colby, Mr. O'Brien."

"Hello, Donald."

In the elevator O'Brien said, "I need a shave."

"You look fine to me. And," she added, "you'll look fine

to *them*." This assurance was necessary because he still felt awkward with Claire and Sheila—he was alive because Colby was dead. The feeling would have to be taken care of by time and familiarity.

Fay thought beyond the evening ahead, to tomorrow. She was meeting Marsha for brunch and a play. She was trying with Marsha, trying harder to answer her invitations to intimacy. Last week over lunch Fay had stopped in the middle of a statement about her father and said, "I'm doing all the talking." With a knowing nod Marsha answered, "It's about time."

When they got off the elevator, no one was waiting for them with the door open. Sheila had insisted Fay have a key, telling Donald it was no longer necessary to announce Miss Colby.

As she turned her key in the lock, O'Brien let out a long sigh. "I know I'd be a lot calmer if I could just *hold* a cigarette in my hand."

"*Fold* your hands instead."

He did, with a comic gesture of childlike obedience.

"Very good. Now keep them that way and thank God you're alive."

She kissed the corner of his grin, then opened the door to the apartment, where her remaining family awaited the comfort of her arrival.

Original tales of family intrigue, murder and suspense

CRAIG JONES